RECLAIMED

HOSTAGE RESCUE TEAM SERIES

KAYLEA CROSS

RECLAIMED

Copyright © 2016
by Kaylea Cross

* * * * *

Cover Art & Formatting by
Sweet 'N Spicy Designs

* * * * *

ISBN: 978-1534809512

Dedication

This one goes out to all my readers who have fallen in love with this cast of characters as much as I have. I truly appreciate all your support and enthusiasm, not just for this series, but for my work in general. You guys rock my socks!

Author's Note

Dear readers,

As the saying goes, all good things must come to an end. It's hard to believe I've reached the last book in the HRT series, and I'll be sad to write The End in this one. But never fear, I guarantee these guys will make appearances in future stories!

In the meantime, get ready for an emotional roller coaster ride as you read Adam and Summer's story. Without a doubt, this one is a true nail biter and several of the scenes had me in tears. This couple has been through so much. They've loved and lost, they've been broken.

But through everything, they have continued to love each other. My favorite thing about them is that they've continued to fight for each other and for their marriage in spite of all the pain they've suffered.

I hope their story touches your heart as much as it did mine.

Happy reading!

Kaylea Cross

Chapter One

Sometimes love isn't enough.

The painful words Summer had said to him kept tumbling through Special Agent Adam Blackwell's head as he rode the elevator of the Jordanian government building to the twelfth floor. He'd just left his teammates a few floors down, waiting for another meeting to break up, because he had a few minutes and wanted to pull off this surprise.

He hadn't wanted to believe Summer's prophetic words at first, but now he recognized that they were true. Love wasn't always enough to make a marriage work. Because sometimes, other things got in the way.

He'd been blind and selfish, had almost lost Summer because of it. Thank God he'd finally woken up and realized all that before it was too late.

At least…he hoped it wasn't too late.

The elevator slowed. A soft ding sounded and the doors slid open. He strode down the hallway, his pulse accelerating and something like butterflies swirling around in his stomach.

Nerves and the buzz of anticipation. All because he was about to come face to face with his wife for the first time in nearly a month and he wasn't sure what her reaction would be when he surprised her by showing up here.

She'd said those fateful words to him a little over a year ago now, though the unraveling of their marriage had begun after a certain event a year before that. They'd been trying to find their way back to each other ever since.

The meeting room doors were still closed, two guards posted outside, one at either end. They nodded at him. He nodded in return and leaned back against the wall across from the room, his hands braced behind him as he waited.

The door handle turned. Voices floated out of the room as it opened. He stood there unmoving, scanning people's faces as they exited. Intelligence officials from various agencies within the U.S., along with their Jordanian counterparts. All part of a massive, multi-national summit to address the ongoing security situation in the region.

He caught a glimpse of red hair in the group of people waiting to exit and something stilled inside him. Everything else faded away as a man stepped aside and Summer suddenly appeared in the doorway. She paused a moment when she saw him, her pale green eyes lighting up with surprise and delight.

Relief spilled through him, and the happy smile that spread across her face almost took his breath away. It had been so damn long since she'd looked at him like that.

"Hey," he said with a grin, glad he'd made the effort in finding her during his short break.

She crossed toward him, smile in place, a formfitting charcoal gray skirt suit hugging her petite frame and black high heels accentuating every muscle in her sexy legs. Her scent reached out to tease him as she drew close, a mix of vanilla and musk that hit him with a thousand bittersweet memories.

Stopping in front of him, her laptop bag in one hand, she reached up and tucked a lock of shiny auburn hair behind her ear, the end of it trailing over her Defense Intelligence Agency ID badge clipped to the lapel of her jacket. "Fancy meeting you in Amman," she teased, giving him an appreciative look that made his heart pound. While they were here they were both on assignment and couldn't stay together, even if they'd wanted to.

"Yeah, imagine that." He wanted to touch her so damn bad but held back. Things were still shaky between them, he didn't want to mess up the progress they'd been making through counseling and all the rest of it. Slow, tentative progress, but he'd take whatever he could get on that front.

Then the residual tension between them reared its ugly head once more, and her smile faded. "Were you guys here for meetings this morning?"

"Yeah. I had a few minutes so I thought I'd run up and surprise you before we headed out." The HRT was here acting as the personal security force for the director and a few other top officials of the FBI.

Her lips curved into a soft smile that told him he'd made the right decision in surprising her. "That was nice of you. So, what do you think of Amman?"

"It's different than most places I've been to over here." And by here he meant the Middle East and parts of South Asia he'd frequented back in his SF days while he'd served in the Army. "Way more liberal."

She seemed amused by that. "It's one of my favorite cities on earth."

Yeah, he knew that. She traveled here at least a couple times a year, for work.

Something to her right caught her attention. She glanced down the hall, acknowledged someone with a nod and held up a finger to indicate she'd be there in a minute and turned back to him.

Her eyes searched his and he took the time to drink her in, every freckle dotting the skin across her cheeks and nose. She'd always hated them but at that moment he would have given just about anything to be able to kiss each and every one of them.

"Maybe if you get some downtime in the next few days, I could show you around. I've got a few favorite restaurants I think you'd love."

The offer took him a little by surprise, since she was here on assignment and she'd be in full-on work mode, but he nodded. "That sounds great." And even though it might be pathetic on some levels, he was just thrilled that she actually wanted to go on another date with him. "Tonight?"

"I'll have to check with my boss, but if not tonight, then tomorrow. Would that work?"

"Sure, whenever. It's a date."

"Good." The hint of a dimple appeared in her left cheek. He wanted to kiss that too. Kiss her all over until she melted the way she used to, before...

He noticed the man at the end of the hall was still waiting for her, watching them. Adam indicated for her to head down the hall. He fell in step beside her as they walked toward the elevator. Her boss and the other man were both waiting for her there.

When they reached them a slight awkwardness took hold as they both stared at him in surprise and Adam wondered how much they knew about his and Summer's marital problems. Probably more than he would like, but he didn't fault her for telling them.

"Jim, you remember my husband Adam?" Summer asked.

"Sure I do." The man held out a hand.

Adam shook her boss's hand, then did the same with the other man, whose name was Mark.

"So, Adam, you and your team here for the summit?" Jim asked.

"Yes."

"Do we have anything important scheduled for tonight?" Summer asked Jim. "I was hoping to show Adam around town a bit if I could sneak away for a few hours."

"Well he won't find a better tour guide than you," her boss joked as he pulled out his phone. He checked something and shook his head. "Just a dinner with some locals. Mark and I will handle it. You take the night off. You deserve it."

Summer gave him a grateful smile. "Thanks."

Adam was thankful too. Their last date had been nearly a month ago and it had been one of the best nights of his life. He couldn't remember the last time they'd had that much fun together, and he knew she'd enjoyed herself too.

The only downside was that they'd both returned home to their separate places with a raging case of sexual frustration. But the counselor had warned them not to rush back into having sex, so he'd put on the brakes that night and held firm, his only consolation that they were both suffering equally. In spite of all the emotional damage she was struggling to overcome, she still wanted him. That had to mean something.

The elevator reached the underground parking garage. Summer hung back with him as Jim and Mark strode to the line of shiny black SUVs idling there, and climbed into the back of the second one.

"So," she asked softly when no one else was within earshot. "Are you glad to be back with the team?"

"Definitely. Especially now with the bonus of getting a date with you out of the deal." He'd requested a leave of absence from the HRT a couple months ago, so he could give saving their marriage a real shot. Getting time off was a problem though, given how busy the team had been, and they'd temporarily lost one of their teammates, Vance, to an injury back in September. So he and Summer hadn't had as much of an opportunity to focus on each other as he'd hoped.

He was supposed to be off right now but his commander had asked him to join this protection detail, and Vance was finally back. DeLuca had wanted all of Blue Team for this one and the truth was, Adam missed the guys as well as the action when he took time away.

"Good. So can you pick me up at my hotel at six?"

"Absolutely."

So many emotions played out across her face as she gazed up at him. Affection. Sadness. Hope. "I'm really glad you're here."

His heart thudded harder. "Me too." She was so damn beautiful standing there, and he was so proud of her. She was an amazing woman, had worked hard to get where she was. He needed to make sure he reminded her of that going forward, make sure she understood what she meant to him. God knew he hadn't done a very good job of that in the past.

She glanced over at the waiting SUVs, regret on her face. "Well, I guess I'd better get going…"

"Yeah." They still had a long way to go before she'd be ready to move back home with him and live as husband and wife again, but at least he knew he was steadily gaining ground with her. For the first time in forever, he believed they might make it through this mess after all.

"Take care of yourself," he murmured, hating to let her go. The distance between them felt wrong on every level, and it drove him insane. Unable to stop himself, he reached out and cupped the side of her face with one hand, letting his fingers coast over the softness of her cheek.

She stilled, surprise filling her eyes at the intimate touch, but she didn't pull away, just kept staring up at him with that mix of hope and uncertainty that made his heart pound.

"I still love you, you know," he told her. As little as two months ago he would never have said it aloud because it made him feel too vulnerable, but over the past few weeks he'd realized that if he wanted her back, he had to lay it all out there and risk it all. If it all blew up in his face, well, at least he'd given it his best shot and gone down fighting.

At his words the uncertainty in her eyes disappeared and a tremulous smile curved her mouth. "I still love you too."

But sometimes love isn't enough.

The thought echoed in his head and he immediately banished it. He was done with the whole sullen, nursing his wounded pride routine. The only thing that mattered was *them*. She was his and he was hers, period. He took his marriage vows seriously and he'd be damned if he was going to walk away from what they'd built together over the last decade. He wouldn't let her leave here without another reminder.

Adam rubbed his thumb across her chin. "We're gonna make it, Summer. If we keep fighting for each other, then we'll make it."

She opened her mouth to respond but her boss suddenly called out from the SUV. "Summer! We've gotta go."

"Be right there," she called back, then looked up at Adam once more, her expression apologetic. "More meetings across town." She hitched the strap of her laptop bag up higher on her shoulder. "So I'll see you tonight at six?"

"Wouldn't miss it for anything."

He expected her to walk away then. With her boss looking on and knowing how career-minded she was, he thought she'd just nod and head to the vehicle.

Instead she reached up and cradled the side of his face in her palm, mirroring what he'd done a minute ago. "I'm really looking forward to spending time together tonight. I've missed you."

Her words hit him deep but the mix of longing, hunger and need on her face had him biting back a groan. Lust and triumph surged through him, went to his head like a shot of hundred-proof whiskey. He loved knowing she'd missed him, as well as the physical part of their marriage. It had been months since they'd last had sex and he was fucking starved for it.

Starved for the taste and feel of her, even if he knew it was too soon for that. Sex had been an integral—and mutually enjoyable—part of their relationship before, but it wasn't going to solve their problems.

"Missed you too." He turned his head to press his lips to the inside of her palm. Her fingers contracted slightly against his skin and her pupils expanded.

God, just that subtle reaction from her and he was already getting hard. Feeling completely possessive and territorial, there was no way he could let her go without staking some kind of claim.

Sliding his hand down to cup her jaw, he bent and covered her mouth with his. A long, firm press of lips that told everyone watching who she belonged to. She was his and he wasn't letting her go.

When he pulled back a moment later and let his hand drop she blinked up at him as though coming out of a daze, her eyes heavy-lidded with desire. Her cheeks turned a pretty shade of pink. "See you tonight."

Adam watched her walk away, let his gaze slide down to admire the way her ass moved with each confident stride. The moment she shut the door behind her the vehicles began to roll forward.

"Blackwell, you ready to roll?" Tuck's voice came through his earpiece.

He reached up to tap it. "Yeah, I'll be there in a minute." It felt like he was walking on air as he strode across to the other side of the underground garage where three more black SUVs were all lined up and ready to go.

His six teammates and commander waited beside the vehicles, all dressed in khaki pants and button down shirts. They might be dressed as civilians, except they were anything but. Each of them had two weapons tucked away in custom-fitted holsters beneath their shirts, and their rifles and other gear were stowed in the vehicles.

Tuck, the team leader, looked over at him and raised his dark blond eyebrows. "You look happy," he commented, his Alabama drawl mirroring his laid-back personality.

He shrugged. "I am happy." Though he didn't say much to the guys and he kind of kept to himself mostly, they were still like his brothers. He'd told Cruzie a little bit about the situation, and of course both DeLuca and Tuck were aware of what was going on, but none of them knew the details. He was just really private about his personal life, always had been.

Schroder, the team medic, grinned at him and scratched at his reddish beard. "So from the look on your face, I'm guessing it went well?"

He couldn't help but grin. And he couldn't help it if it looked a little smug. He was damn pleased with himself. "Yep. Taking her out on a date tonight."

"A date?" Cruzie piped up, his light brown eyes gleaming with interest as he pushed his way around Vance's big frame to get closer to Adam. "That's huge, man. Awesome."

For him it was. "Yeah." He cleared his throat and looked at DeLuca, uncomfortable with the attention placed squarely on him. "So, where to? Still back to the hotel?"

His commander nodded, his eyes shaded by the brim of his Chargers cap. "Lunch meeting, afternoon meeting, then a team briefing. They'll be down in two minutes," he said, looking toward the elevators.

Adam waited with Schroder while the others piled into the vehicles. DeLuca and Tuck with Bauer in the lead SUV, Vance and Cruzie in the third. Evers was already behind the wheel of the second.

Right on cue the elevator doors opened and the director stepped out with two of his staff. After the men climbed into the back of the SUV, Adam shut the door and hurried around to ride shotgun beside Evers, or "Farmboy" as they sometimes called him.

DeLuca's voice came through their earpieces. "Let's go."

The convoy pulled out of the garage under heavy security at the building's perimeters and picked up speed as they headed for the nearest freeway onramp. Adam remained silent in the front passenger seat while the director and his aides talked business in the back. He kept watch out the window and used the mirrors, on alert for any sign of a threat.

The ride itself was uneventful, and when their hotel came into view fifteen minutes later, he let himself relax slightly. Security had the place locked down tighter than Fort Knox.

But as they neared the entrance, the radio on his hip chirped. Static rippled across the frequency, then came the distorted sound of shouting, followed by the unmistakable pop-pop-pop of automatic gunfire.

Summer's convoy.

Adam's heart rate jacked up. He grabbed for the radio as all conversation in the vehicle ceased.

"What the hell's that?" the director demanded.

Adam keyed the radio, his whole body rigid. "This is voodoo six. Do you read me?" Evers shot him a sideways glance as he pulled into the underground parking, heading toward the elevators where more security waited.

Tense seconds passed when nothing came back but the sounds of more panic and chaos on the other end. Then a man's voice, urgent, filled with tension. "…ambush. Too many of them, we need immediate backup—"

The roar of an explosion cut off whatever else he was going to say. Then there was nothing but silence. Adam's chest felt like it was full of concrete. He couldn't breathe.

Summer. Summer was under attack and he wasn't there to defend her. It was all he could think about.

"Blackwell, get the director inside, now," DeLuca commanded. "We're heading there as backup immediately. *Move*."

Ahead of them, Tuck jerked his SUV to a stop in front of the elevators. Adam was out of the vehicle in an instant, ripping open the rear door and bodily hauling the director out. Ahead of him Tuck and the others were climbing out of the SUV.

He locked gazes with DeLuca, who nodded at him, face grim. "I know. We're going."

But not fast enough. It would never be fast enough.

Oh, God, please, he begged silently, fighting to hold it together. She had to be okay.

Adam didn't say anything, his heart in his throat. Feeling numb, he hustled the director inside and handed him over to another security team, then ran back out and jumped into his SUV. Tuck shot away with a squeal of tires and Evers followed suit, with Schroder driving the vehicle behind them.

"How long?" he demanded of Evers.

"Ten minutes, tops."

They didn't have that long.

He could already hear DeLuca on the radio, trying to reach someone from the other security team. Adam put his phone to his ear, the ringing overly loud in his head as he waited for Summer to answer.

Pick up, Summer. Come on, please pick up.

There was no answer. "God dammit, *no*," he moaned, squeezing his eyes shut.

"I can't get through," DeLuca reported to everyone. "Keep trying different channels on the radios, find out what the hell's going on."

Summer was being attacked and there wasn't a damn thing he could do to save her. It killed him.

Adam sucked in a shaky breath and dragged both hands through his hair, unable to fight the terror streaking through him. She couldn't be gone. She just couldn't.

"We're gonna get her, man," Evers said beside him, expression deadly serious as he sped to keep up with Tuck's vehicle.

Adam didn't answer. He wasn't aware of anything going on around them, his thoughts trapped in what had just happened to Summer's convoy. It took eight agonizing minutes to reach the site of the attack. The moment they crested a rise on the highway, they saw the smoke rising off to the right.

"Fuck," he snapped out, gaze riveted to the carnage in front of them. It looked bad. At least one of the vehicles was on fire. He picked his rifle up off the floorboard, fingers squeezing tight. *Hang on, Summer, I'm coming.*

First responders were already converging on the scene, police holding back the crowds of curious onlookers that were coming out onto the sidewalks to watch the spectacle. At the perimeter Tuck's vehicle slowed only enough for him to flash his ID, then sped for the wrecked convoy.

All three of its vehicles sat abandoned in the middle of the residential street, one of them nothing more than a pile of melted, twisted metal.

Adam swallowed, forced himself to keep breathing. Scanning the scene, he couldn't see anyone moving. *She has to be there.*

Evers plunged to a stop behind Tuck's vehicle. The entire team burst out of their vehicles, automatically converging on the scene. Adam raced up to the lead vehicle, weapon to his shoulder.

Two charred bodies lay smoldering on the asphalt next to the SUV, as if they'd been trying to flee when whatever explosive round had been fired hit the vehicle. RPG? Whatever had exploded, it solidified that this had been a well-planned, coordinated attack.

His stomach rolled as he stared at the bodies, his brain unable to process that one of them might be Summer.

No, she was in the second vehicle. Hurry.

He rushed for it, his heart slamming against his ribcage. Evers was already there, checking inside the vehicle. He backed out of the rear seat, looked over his shoulder at Adam and shook his head. "Empty."

Adam spun around, searching the area. Four more people lay either wounded or dead beside the last vehicle. All men. No sign of Summer.

"God*damn* it," he snapped, the frustration eating at him like acid.

He was vaguely aware of Schroder kneeling down beside someone at the third vehicle, couldn't bring himself to care about the suffering going on around him. Where the hell was she?

"Blackwell."

He whirled around at the sound of Bauer's urgent voice. The huge former SEAL was crouched down next to one of the victims at the third SUV while Schroder worked on him, trying to stem the bleeding from multiple gunshots in his torso. A security team member.

Adam rushed over, got to one knee. Without thinking he gripped the back of the man's neck and stared into his eyes, desperate for information. "Summer. Where is she? Did you see her?"

The guy grimaced, both hands covered in blood as he pressed them to his belly. He managed a shaky nod. "T-took her."

Panic roared through him. He squeezed harder, gave him a shake. "*Who* took her? *Where*?"

"D-dunno," the man managed, face contorting in pain. "It…happened t-too fast."

Fuck! Adam released him and surged to his feet, refusing to accept that she'd been taken.

Tuck and DeLuca jogged over, faces grim. "She's not here?"

Adam shook his head, his jaw so tight he could barely speak. "Attackers took her," he managed to choke out, feeling sick. Panic gripped him, constricting the muscles in his throat.

Gone. She's gone and I have to find her, have to get her back. He turned in a circle, desperately searching around for a clue, something that might show him where she'd gone.

"Two others from the second vehicle are missing as well," DeLuca said, his green gaze locked with Adam's. "Her boss and coworker. They took all three of them."

Adam's heart plummeted to his boots at the news. Three DIA employees in one attack. Whoever had done this had pulled it off in broad daylight in the middle of a residential area. Fucking ballsy.

He swallowed back the bile rushing up his throat, wanting to scream in denial.

But this was unfortunately all too fucking real.

The stench of burning metal and flesh invading his nostrils as he stood there, ice spreading through his veins and a crushing sense of helplessness squeezing around his chest.

Whoever they were, the attackers were long gone, taking Summer and their other high value targets with them.

Chapter Two

Nine years ago

The National Museum of American History was as busy as Adam had expected on a Saturday morning.

He wandered slowly through the military collection, pausing at a display case housing an exhibit of uniforms from the Vietnam era, including one from a POW held at the Hanoi Hilton. This entire section was dedicated to preserving what American men and women in uniform had fought for since the country's inception.

He studied the display, remembered seeing his grandfather wearing a green uniform just like it in pictures, thinking about how things in the military had changed over time and yet how they hadn't changed much at all.

War was a constant state with the human race, and he was part of that story.

He finished reading a plaque next to an artifact at the bottom of the case, then straightened and turned around without looking—and slammed right into someone.

He heard a female squeak of alarm at the same time he saw the young woman tip back. He automatically shot his hands out to grab her shoulders as she stumbled sideways. Her book and purse clattered to the floor as she latched onto his forearm to steady herself. "I'm so sorry," he murmured.

She released his arm and looked up at him with gorgeous light green eyes, flashed him a smile that made him go completely still. She was striking, her long red hair up in a sassy ponytail and a group of freckles marching across her nose and cheeks. "My fault. I forgot to shoulder check."

Her quick humor made him grin. Realizing he was staring like a moron, he tore his gaze from her face and bent to pick up her things. A notebook and pen, her purse. Straightening, he handed them to her. Even in her little wedge heels the top of her head only came up to his nose.

"Thanks," she murmured, hugging the book to her chest, hiding the pert outline of her breasts beneath the top of her deep blue summer dress. That was a shame.

Having nearly knocked her down, he felt the need to prove he wasn't an ass. "You doing some research?" He gestured at the notebook, wanting to draw the conversation out a little because he wasn't ready to see her walk away yet.

"Yes. For a final paper." She held out a hand. "I'm Summer, by the way."

"Adam." They shook. Her hand felt so delicate in his. Soft and smooth and feminine. He cocked his head to the side and released her, already intrigued. She looked a few years younger than him. "What are you studying?"

"Political science and foreign relations, with some history mixed in there. I'm graduating next month." She eyed him with those big eyes. "What about you, are you here for research too?"

"No. Just in town for a language course and thought I'd come take a look."

"Oh, what language?"

"Pashto."

She studied him a moment. "Are you in the military?"

"Army."

She nodded, still assessing him with that sharp green gaze that told him she was picking up far more than the average person would. "My grandfather served in the Army."

"Mine too. Vietnam era?"

Another smile. "Yes. That's what my paper's on. He died a few years back so I can't call him up and ask him the things I want to know. But he sent letters to my grandmother and she kept all of them with his medals. I kind of feel like a history detective, tracking down answers to fill in the holes," she added, tucking a bright lock of hair that had escaped her ponytail behind her ear. "So, what do you do in the Army?"

"Whatever my commanding officer tells me to," he answered in a teasing tone.

She laughed softly. "Not gonna tell me? Well that tells me quite a bit, actually."

Yep, she was a quick one all right. Charmed, he shoved his hands into his pockets and studied her a moment. "Hmmm. I might be willing to tell you more if you sat down and had a coffee with me."

She blinked then gave him an impressed look and nodded. "Okay, that's not bad. Not the worst pick-up line I've heard, either. But how do you feel about helping me figure out the last clues to this mystery first? As a soldier, I could use your opinion and insight on a few things to steer me in the right direction. If you're willing. I want to get it right."

A slow smile curved his mouth. If he was willing? He was alone here, had the entire afternoon to himself and getting to spend more time with her was the best thing that had happened to him in over nine months. "That sounds good to me."

While she explained what she was working on he followed her through the rest of the exhibit, already fascinated at the way her mind worked. It was clear that her interest in this topic was genuine, and wasn't all because this was her final paper and she simply wanted a good grade. No, this was personal and she was determined to get to the bottom of the mystery she was trying to solve.

At one display they stopped to check something and she talked about the South Vietnamese soldier who'd saved her grandfather's life over there. In addition to finding out what she needed to know for her final paper, she was on a mission to find out who he was. Her passion was contagious and within ten minutes he found himself caught up in the story.

As she finished explaining she trailed off and paused a moment to look at him, a slight frown creasing her forehead. "Am I boring you, by the way?" Her expression turned rueful. "I didn't come here today with the intent of basically hijacking someone in the middle of the Smithsonian."

He smothered a laugh. "No, not at all. I'm already hooked."

A relieved smile was all the reward he needed. "Well, I've probably taken up too much of your time already. You still want to grab that coffee?"

Hell yes. "That sounds good."

They made their way out of the exhibit and down the street to a coffee shop. At a table for two in the corner, she sipped her iced drink and gazed speculatively at him. "So. Are you going to tell me about you now? I mean, you know where I'm going to school, what my major is, and more about my extended family than you probably ever wanted to know, yet I know next to nothing about you."

"I'm from Kansas, born and raised there. My parents are still back there, and so are my three younger brothers."

Her eyes widened. "Four boys? Wow."

"Yeah. We kept our mom and dad busy." He took a sip of his coffee, savoring the taste of the hot, strong drink. Light-years better than what he'd had during his recent deployment.

"I'll bet you did. And are your brothers in the military too?"

"One is." His baby brother, Jamie. "The others are in the family construction business."

She leaned forward to fold her arms on the table, her full attention focused on him. He liked the way she did that, and the way she seemed genuinely interested in him. "And why did you want to serve your country that way?"

"I always wanted to, ever since I can remember. I grew up listening to war stories my granddad told us about, and I guess they always stuck with me."

"Have you been sent overseas?"

"A few times, yeah. Just got back a few days ago, actually."

"Welcome home. And I'm betting you're in…something infantry-related. But not a regular unit." She paused a beat. "Rangers maybe?"

He hid a grin. "Used to be."

She narrowed her eyes thoughtfully. "You can't tell me, or you don't want to?"

He shrugged, loving the back-and-forth banter. It had been a long time since a woman had snared his attention and intrigued him like this. "I might tell you," he said, cocking his head a little. "If you let me take you out to dinner sometime while I'm in town."

A reluctant smile tugged at her mouth, her eyes filled with humor. "Damn you, that's my weak spot. You just met me two hours ago and you already know I can't turn down the chance to solve a mystery."

That's what he'd been counting on.

She sat back in her seat, arms crossed, and nodded. "Okay. Dinner it is." She held out a hand, wiggled her fingers. "Give me your phone."

The demand surprised him for a moment but he dug it out anyway, accessed his contacts and handed it over, amazed at how much he was looking forward to the prospect of seeing her again. He hadn't been on a first date in a long damn time, since well before his previous tour in Afghanistan. And that relationship hadn't withstood the time and distance of a nine-month combat deployment, as so many didn't.

"This way if you don't call or email, at least I'll know it's not because you 'lost my number' or some other lame excuse guys usually use," she said as she input her information.

Was she serious? "I can't imagine any guy being dumb enough to turn down the opportunity to go out with you," he said with a frown.

"Trust me, I know all the excuses by now." Handing his phone back, she gave him a long, level look. "When do you think this dinner is going to happen, by the way? A week from now? A month? I'm just asking because I've got this paper due and a couple exams next week, so—"

"How about tomorrow night?"

She blinked, as though he'd taken her completely by surprise. He got the sense that it was a good thing, that guys had tended to either let her down or play her in the past. Their loss. His gain, because he didn't pull immature shit like that. "Okay. That works." She eyed him with a hint of teasing suspicion. "Just as long as you don't plan to keep being so evasive over dinner."

She had no idea how good he was at being evasive when he wanted to. He had the best SERE training in the world to thank in part for that. There were certain things about his job that he could never tell her though, due to security clearance issues and operational security. But he didn't have a problem telling her the basics if she really wanted to know. "I'll think about it," he answered, wanting to keep her interested.

Amusement glinting in her pretty eyes, she shook her head at him. "Man, you're good."

You bet I am, sweetheart. She wasn't the only one hooked though, because she'd made one hell of an impression. He definitely wanted to see her again, learn more about her. Find out what made her laugh. What those full, rosy lips tasted like.

One step at a time.

He was only going to be in town for another month or so, before he went back to Kunar Province. It wasn't fair to start anything serious, but a few dates couldn't hurt. Besides, he could already tell this girl was different from anyone he'd ever dated before.

And more importantly, something told him that after meeting Summer, his life would never be the same again.

Chapter Three

Present day

Summer thought she couldn't be any more scared than she already was, but when the truck she was in slowed, she found out differently.

Fear swelled in her chest until it felt like her heart might explode. The initial shock of the attack and kidnapping was gone, leaving nothing but the chill of fear in its wake. As a female captive she faced torture, rape, or worse.

Doors slammed and she heard footsteps approaching the back. Metal creaked, and she caught a breath of cool air through the black hood they'd plunged over her head when they'd taken her.

Terse voices speaking Arabic were close by, but a dialect she wasn't fluent in. She caught the gist of what they were saying though.

Hurry up and put her in the truck. We don't have much time.

Another truck? Where were these bastards taking her?

Strong hands grasped her bound feet and pulled. With her hands tied behind her, her arms were useless.

She twisted and kicked out, her bare feet hitting nothing but air. Ignoring her efforts, the man unceremoniously hauled her out of the back and tossed her over his shoulder. The top of his shoulder blade dug into her belly. She automatically arched away but he swatted the back of her head hard enough to stun her and continued walking.

He dumped her into the back of what she assumed was the truck she'd heard about, threw a heavy blanket over top of her and covered it with something crinkly and musty smelling.

An engine roared to life and the vehicle lurched away. After a minute the relatively smooth surface of the road gave way to something rougher. The tires bounced along the new terrain, jostling her with the jerky motion. The back of her head struck the metal bed she was lying on, making her curse and anger began to replace the fear.

No way was she just going to lie here and let them take her.

She tried to sit up but the man must have tied the tarp down over the bed because she didn't have enough room to do it. After a minute she managed to struggle to her knees, her head bent forward at an awkward angle because of the tarp, but then something hard slammed into the middle of her back.

She cried out and sucked in a sharp breath, dropping to the bed of the truck once more. Pain radiated out from where she'd been hit and it took a minute for her to get her breath back. She was scraped and bruised from the ambush, but otherwise okay.

God, I can't believe this is really happening.

One minute she'd been in the back of the SUV talking about the upcoming meeting with Jim and Mark. The next, bullets had hit the armored vehicle. Their security team had done what they could to get them out of there, but then the lead SUV had been blown up. In the confusion, the gunmen had attacked.

Somehow her security team had been caught unawares and then overwhelmed. One of them had dragged her out and tried to run her to safety but he'd been shot down within moments of exiting the vehicle. She'd grabbed for his weapon, intending to shoot whoever was firing at them but two men had swarmed her, yanking a hood over her and rendering her helpless before she could lift the weapon.

That was the last thing she'd seen. Even now she had no idea whether anyone else had survived.

The truck continued to bounce and lurch up the rough dirt road, and soon the engine took on a high-pitched whine, the driver shifting down to a lower gear as they climbed up into the hills. They'd driven for a while now, they had to be close to the border, and from the terrain she would guess they were somewhere to the north. From the swaying, back-and-forth movement, she knew they were taking a steep mountain road, probably heading for the Syrian border.

More dread coiled within her. She knew if they got across into Syria, the chances of her being rescued were minimal.

Sore from the blow to her back and afraid to move, she wasn't sure how long she lay braced against the truck bed but eventually the vehicle slowed and made a left-hand turn. A minute after that it stopped and the engine shut off.

Every muscle in her body went rigid as she waited to see what would happen next.

Her heart rate kicked up as the truck's door slammed. Someone yanked the tarp and blanket off her, but she was still blind because of the dark hood. She could hear another vehicle coming nearer, wondered if she would be put into that one and driven across the border, but her captor hauled her out and threw her over his shoulder.

"Put her in here," a man ordered. "Hurry."

Whoever was carrying her grunted as he slid her off him and dropped her to the ground. Her butt hit the hard dirt with enough force to jar her entire spine and make her teeth clack together but she didn't dare make a sound.

Metal squealed to her right, the sound raking over her raw senses like sharp fingernails. A lock clanged into place.

Trapped. She was trapped inside something, had no idea where she was or what would happen to her.

Though she could guess, and her imagination kept calling up numerous atrocities that she'd reported about in her files. Every last one of them sent a shiver down her spine.

Muffled male voices reached her and she strained to hear what they were saying. Another door close by squeaked open, somewhere across from her.

One voice became crystal clear, a man speaking English. "Put me down, asshole! Put me—" The angry words ended with a low *oomph*, as though the wind had been knocked out of him. But she recognized that voice.

She scrambled to her knees, faced the direction of the voice and called out, "Jim?"

"Summer?"

"Yes!" She swallowed back the urge to cry. Crying wasn't going to help and she refused to let these assholes know how afraid she was. "Are you all right?" It was probably awful of her but she was so relieved to know she wasn't in this alone.

"I'm...okay. I—" Another grunt, this one filled with pain. Inside the hood, she winced in sympathy. Then his voice came again, growing frantic. "No, leave her alone! Don't you touch her!"

Ice slid through her veins as his meaning sank in. Someone was coming for her, probably to punish her for talking.

Shit, shit, shit...

She scuttled back against the rear of whatever room or cell she was in, until her spine pressed hard against what felt like a rock wall. Hard footsteps stalked toward her, making her pulse spike. They stopped directly in front of her, then something hard and heavy pelted her square in the chest, making her gasp and suck back a cry.

A rock, she realized. It felt like someone had just kicked her in the ribs.

"*Quiet*," a stern voice snapped.

Summer didn't dare move, didn't dare make a sound as she waited for something else to strike her.

But the man walked away.

Squeezing her eyes shut, she pulled in deep, shaky breaths through her nose and fought to get hold of herself. Her body was trembling. She had to stay calm, couldn't let the fear take hold. Even though that seemed impossible right now.

Alone in the prison she couldn't see, she curled into herself and leaned her head against the rough rock wall. Jim was silent and she didn't dare call out to him again. Mentally and emotionally exhausted, she searched for an escape from this hell...

And thought of Adam.

He would likely already know she was missing. He'd be frantic, probably searching for her right now, along with the other IC people gathered for the summit. She knew he would do everything in his power to find her and get her out of here, that the FBI and other agencies represented here would assist.

They'd find her and Jim, it was only a matter of time. And considering they both worked for the DIA and had been abducted in an attack during the middle of an international security summit, that made them high profile. The brazen daylight attack would hit the mainstream media within hours, if it hadn't already. There'd be a major effort made to rescue them in the coming days.

Summer drew on her inner strength and tried not to think about what her captors had planned for them. She had to hold onto the knowledge that powerful people were searching for her, had to remember there was still hope and not give up throughout whatever happened from now on.

She might be a civilian but she was smart, and she wasn't helpless. Adam had taught her so many things over the years. Things she'd never dreamed she might need to put into practice. Now she was thankful for each one of them.

Right now, the unknown was her adversary. The disorientation. Isolation. Anticipation of pain and torture.

Fear.

Fear was by far her worst enemy. Her captors would use it against her, use it to break her if she allowed it. She could not afford that. She had to be strong, no matter how scared she was.

Reminding herself of that, she took several more calming breaths until the worst of the rigidity bled out of her muscles. Again she thought of Adam, called an image of him to mind and held it like a lifeline. She could see him so clearly, on that one particular morning that seemed so far away now, when he'd been sleeping in bed beside her.

She'd woken before him and stared in awe at the man revealed to her gaze by the glow of the sunray peeking through their master bedroom window. He'd been stretched out on his stomach, one arm tucked beneath his head, the sheets draped around his lower back, revealing each dip and swell of muscle, the planes of his face, the dark sweep of his eyelashes against his cheekbones.

Then, as though he felt her stare, he woke.

The moment his pale blue eyes opened, he focused on her and smiled. A slow, sleepy smile so full of male satisfaction that her heart had stuttered, then rolled over in her chest. He'd looked so happy, so content to be lying next to her. And she hadn't appreciated that as much as she should have at the time.

Because a few weeks after that, everything had changed in an instant.

Forcing that dark thought away, she focused on the image of that smile he'd given her, a moment before he'd turned over and rolled her beneath his big body, careful to keep his weight off her belly.

Summer bit her lip. She knew better than most people how short and fragile life was, but her current situation brought that into sharp and sudden focus.

Of all the regrets she had, her biggest was that she hadn't been able to let go of the past sooner. She'd let that hold her back for far too long, had allowed it to nearly destroy her and her marriage.

She leaned against the wall and curled into herself as the cold began to seep into her, exhausted but too afraid to sleep. Adam was a good man and deserved to be happy. She was glad she'd told him she loved him today. At least he'd be certain of her feelings for him if they never got to see each other again.

The thought made her want to cry. She bit her lip, fought to hold her emotions back. No matter what happened, she would always love him.

****

Tarek stalked away from the female prisoner's cell, filled with a heady combination of adrenaline and triumph. It seemed too good to be true. The plan had worked even better than he'd hoped and he now had three important Defense Intelligence Agency captives to use. He still couldn't believe how easily they'd done it, and with far fewer casualties than he'd anticipated.

He motioned to Akram, his most trusted soldier, standing over by the first male captive just as two more of his men brought in the other male prisoner and put him in another makeshift cell. "Bring me their things."

Moving fast, he hurried across the narrow alley and through the door of the small house they'd commandeered from a villager, went straight to the table holding all his maps and other papers. Radio in hand, he checked in with more of his men, who were keeping watch from the top of the hill above the village. "Report."

"We're still clear," came the response. "No traffic or movement at all on the road up here."

Good. That meant they still had some time yet to play with.

He turned as Akram hustled inside carrying a briefcase and some ID tags and set them on the table before him. His beard had begun to fill in during the last few months, another sign that he was maturing. At only twenty-two, Akram had lived a hard life and seen so many of his friends and family suffer or be killed. As they all had. It only galvanized them in their righteous fight.

Tarek eyed the first badge, eager to learn more about his prisoners and what he stood to gain from them. Jim Barnes, the name read. He was middle-aged, had to be around fifty. Probably the one in charge of the other two, and the way the woman had called out to him seemed to confirm that. Tarek would use that to his advantage.

The second man was Mark Grimes. Early thirties maybe. Glasses. He looked like a computer guy, but Tarek could be wrong.

He turned his attention to the woman's badge last, and his heart began to beat faster as he stared at her picture. Summer Blackwell. Pretty name for an attractive woman in her late twenties or early thirties, but he couldn't get past the fact that she was an American infidel.

And oh, did he have special plans for her. A rush of excitement flooded him at the thought.

"It belongs to her," Akram said excitedly as he opened the briefcase. "There's a laptop. It's still working."

"Perfect." He took it and eyed the home screen. Of course it was password protected. He wasn't good with computers and such and to his knowledge none of his men were either, but no matter. He'd get it out of her easily enough. "What's in the paperwork?"

Akram handed him several files. "Maps, files on different people." He frowned as he read them. "Mostly members in the Army of True Believers, looks like from Jordan and Syria. One from Algeria."

"Let me see." He took the file Akram was holding, perused it. His English wasn't perfect but he could read and speak it well enough to get by.

The file contained information on the fighter's vital statistics and service record in the Syrian Army. Tarek didn't recognize him, but a lot of his fellow Syrian brothers-in-arms had deserted at the start of this war to fight with the side that should rightfully rule the country.

Theirs.

There were maps as well, and information on suspected movements, unit strengths and positions. He didn't understand enough of it to get the whole picture, but it was clear anyway. "I'll read it later." He pushed it aside along with the laptop, already planning what he would do with the information the woman named Summer would give him.

Torture, either of her or a fellow prisoner if that's what it took, was an extremely strong motivator, he'd learned.

"What do we do now?" Akram asked.

"We wait."

"Wait?" he asked, looking troubled by the prospect. Everyone knew they were on a tight timeline. With three American intelligence employees in their grasp, they were now hunted men.

Tarek knew he had to be more careful than ever. "The prisoners need time for the full effect to set in. The longer they're isolated and afraid, the easier it will be to get what we want from them."

Akram nodded, his expression brightening at the words. "You want me to get the trucks prepared then, so we're ready to move?"

"Yes." When he gave the word they'd head to the final stop close to the border. The Jordanians would be out hunting them in force after this. He had to time their crossing carefully, after he'd disposed of the captives.

The captives' final stop.

"All right." Appearing relieved at having something to do, Akram left to do his bidding.

Alone, Tarek perused the contents of more files from the briefcase, his resolve hardening with each fact he read. These captives were the enemy.

They'd come here to Jordan, a traitorous so-called Islamic nation that instead supported America in this conflict, to eradicate him and all others like him. To kill anyone who dared to follow the true path of Islam in the fight for the birth of their fledgling nation.

One that would eventually take over the world and crush America, God willing.

As for him, he now finally had the chance to get even. To make a name for himself.

Soon he would leave his mark in a spectacular way and become a rising star within the ATB, a marked man who his enemy loathed and feared in equal measure.

He set the documents aside and gripped the edge of the table. He'd waited for this opportunity for so long. All the risks, all the worry of exposure or betrayal by someone he trusted was worth it now.

The three captives currently locked in their cells didn't know it yet, but they represented his chance to avenge his dead family.

A life for a life, he thought with savage satisfaction, staring at the three badges in front of him. And he would make their deaths as excruciating as possible.

Chapter Four

Nine years ago

Summer couldn't believe how nervous she was as she waited for Adam to come pick her up. She'd been on plenty of first dates and none of them had given her butterflies like this one.

Something about the man drew her to him, made her want to learn all about him. He'd called her bright and early that morning to confirm, something she found adorable, and said he'd pick her up at six.

Going on the assumption that a military man would be punctual, she was on the couch by the front door ready to go at quarter to. When her buzzer rang at five minutes to, she jumped up to answer it.

"Hey, it's Adam," he said in that deliciously deep voice of his.

Yep, punctual. A good sign that he was dependable. She liked that in a man. "Hey, I'll be right down."

On her way out she paused in front of the mirror in the entryway to check her appearance. She'd left her hair down today, using a curling iron to make the ends into soft waves that fell around her shoulders.

The bright green gingham, sleeveless dress was one of her favorites, a 50s style number she'd picked up at a favorite retro boutique in Alexandria. The circle skirt flared out around her hips, the crinoline beneath it making it swish with every step. It was pretty and feminine and made her want to twirl around like a little girl, just to see it move.

She adjusted the wrap around her shoulders as she stepped outside. Adam was waiting for her by the building's front door. His ice-blue eyes widened when he saw her, an appreciative gleam in them as he took her in from head to toe. And everywhere his gaze touched, it left a trail of heat in its wake.

"Wow, look at you." He paused, gestured down at the blue button-down shirt and khakis he wore. "I guess I should have dressed up more."

"No, you look great." Hot, actually. Hot was the word, so tall and dark and handsome with all those muscles stretching the fabric of his shirt like that. "I just hardly ever get to wear dresses like this and I love them, so I thought what the heck."

Maybe it was too much for a first date, but she'd been so excited to have an excuse to put it on. She loved how feminine it made her feel, and she'd wanted to make sure he noticed and remembered her.

"Well, you look beautiful. And it suits you."

Her cheeks warmed at the compliment. "Thanks," she murmured, tucking a lock of hair behind her right ear.

She expected him to turn away and lead her to his car but instead he reached an arm around her to set a hand on her waist and walked beside her. The gallant, almost possessive move sent a secret thrill through her. His big hand was solid against the curve of her waist, the heat of it seeping through the cotton fabric and into her skin.

A strong, capable hand. Protective and caring.

For just a moment she let herself indulge in imagining what it would feel like stroking over her naked skin. Not that she planned to let things go that far tonight, even if he was interested. Still, the fantasy was nice.

"So I was thinking of trying a steak place I've heard about in town," he said, glancing at her as they headed for the black truck parked at the curb. She noticed how watchful he was, as if he was scanning for potential threats. No doubt something that had kept him alive overseas. "That okay with you?"

She nodded. "Sounds great, because I'm starving."

He chuckled and opened the passenger door for her, even handed her the seatbelt. They taught nice manners down in Kansas. "Not something a guy hears too often on a first date."

She gave him a coy smile. "Well I'm not your average girl."

"Oh, I'm well aware of that already." He came around the hood, slid behind the wheel and started the engine. "So, did you get to the bottom of your family mystery yet?"

"Nearly. I'm just waiting to hear back from a contact I was given over in Vietnam. He's going to check records for me there and let me know if he can find the name and service record of my grandfather's guardian angel. I'm really excited."

He gave her a warm smile. "Good. It's a neat story."

"I think so too."

After he parked he dug in his pocket for something, pulled out a piece of paper and held it out to her. "Got something for you."

"What's this?" she asked as she took it.

"I reached out to a contact of mine to see if he could help. He served in Vietnam and is pretty hooked into the veteran community. I told him about your grandfather's story and he said he'd look into it if you give him the details."

His thoughtfulness floored her. "Thank you." It seemed like an inadequate thing to say in light of how much his gesture meant to her.

He shrugged. "No problem."

Even more curious about him, she wondered how long he'd been overseas and how long it had been since he'd been out with a woman. And she had a gut feeling he wasn't just regular Army.

His confidence, the way he moved, the way his gaze remained vigilant with all the people around them the entire time they'd been in the museum, and later at the café. Those were clear indicators to her that he'd seen combat, and she was betting not in a conventional unit.

Inside the restaurant the host seated them at a private table near the back. She stole glances at him as they perused the menu, studying his face. Wide forehead, dark eyebrows, strong cheekbones and a nose that was straight other than the small bump near the bridge that told her it might have been broken at one point.

And when those ice-blue eyes flashed up to meet hers, she felt a ribbon of heat unfurl in the pit of her belly. His slow smile made her pulse skip.

"See anything you like?" he asked, a teasing note in his voice.

"I do." And one of them wasn't on the menu.

After they ordered she stacked her forearms on the table and tilted her head as she looked at him. "So now that we're at dinner, are you going to tell me what you do in the Army?"

One side of his mouth kicked up. "It's been bugging the hell out of you since yesterday, hasn't it?"

"*Yes*," she confessed, not feeling the least bit embarrassed by it. "But I have a feeling you knew it would."

Those broad shoulders she wanted to put her hands on lifted in a slight shrug. "Well, I wanted to make sure you were interested enough to come back for more."

Oh, she was more than interested. She couldn't remember ever being this attracted to anyone. His plan to keep her guessing was working, and then some. "And here I am."

He reached for a piece of bread from the basket between them, his eyes on hers. Pale, startling blue, with a darker blue ring around the outside of the irises. Gorgeous, especially with the contrast of his dark eyelashes and brows. "You really want to know?"

"I really do."

He huffed out a laugh. "I'm Special Forces."

I knew it. She grinned in triumph. "Aha! A Green Beret, huh?" He'd work closely with the local population wherever he was sent, train their soldiers. She knew that much.

He nodded. "For almost four years now."

"How old are you?" she asked, curious. It was hard to imagine this laid-back guy doing such a dangerous job but he definitely had an intense edge to him.

"Twenty-six. You?"

"Twenty-three." She waved a hand and continued. "I took some time off after high school to travel the world, then I couldn't figure out what my major should be. But eventually I got it ironed out."

"And what do you want to do after you graduate?"

That was easy. She'd decided that in her junior year of high school. "I'm going to apply to intelligence agencies. NSA, CIA and DIA. I want to focus on the Middle East. I spent a few months over there after high school and loved certain parts of it."

The only things she'd hated were the way women were treated in some places—like shit—and the poverty she'd encountered in some areas she'd visited during that leg of her trip. "My Arabic is pretty rough but I'm taking a language course for it and plan to keep at it while I work." That would increase her chances of getting hired there.

"What was your favorite city over there?"

She thought about that for a second. "Alexandria and Amman. Have you been to either of those?"

"No, just Iraq, Afghanistan, Qatar. Kuwait. Djibouti."

"Djibouti." She made a face and he laughed. "Are you going back over there after your course is done?"

"Yeah, next month."

"And if you're learning Pashto, then you're going to Afghanistan."

His eyes crinkled at the corners when he smiled. "Right. Damn, you're smart."

She was glad he noticed, and more so, that he seemed to like it. A lot of guys she'd gone on dates with hadn't wanted to know anything about her academic career or aspirations. Maybe they were intimidated, she wasn't sure. But she already got the feeling that nothing intimidated Adam. That was sexy as hell to her.

After dinner it was such a nice night out that they decided to walk around to look at all the shops and restaurants in this little pocket of the city. The March breeze was chilly though and when he saw her tug her shawl tighter around herself, he stepped in close and wrapped an arm around her shoulders. The feel of his strong arm around her sent tingles racing over her skin like sparks.

"That better?" he murmured, and she nodded. "We can go back to my truck if you're too cold."

"No, this is perfect." She loved the solid weight of his arm around her. And he was just so easy to talk to, she didn't want the date to end.

At her place later he walked her to the front door, put

his hands in his pockets. "I had a good time."

"Me too." Best time she'd had in a long damn time. He was smart, focused and had an easy smile. A combination that left her more than a little breathless.

As he stared down at her, his face illuminated by the overhead light at the building's entrance, his relaxed expression turned serious. "Like I told you, I've only got a few more weeks left here before I go back overseas. I want to be up front with you about that."

"I appreciate that. But if you're worried I won't want to go out with you again just because you're leaving soon, you're wrong. Unless you don't want to go out with me again," she added hastily.

"No, I do," he said just as quickly. "I'd love to go out again. I really like you."

She smiled at him, warmth rushing through her. "I really like you too." A gust of wind kicked up, blowing her hair around her shoulders and tugging the end of her wrap free.

Adam caught it deftly in one fist. His intense expression as he held her gaze sent a shiver of excitement through her as he carefully wound the fabric around her shoulders, his fingers brushing against the bare skin of her upper arms.

But he didn't stop there. Sliding his hands to her back, he gently drew her toward him. The breath stalled in her throat as she gazed up at him, pulse thumping in anticipation.

One big hand smoothed up to her nape, his long fingers spearing into her hair as he cradled the back of her head. She placed her hands on his chest, desire pooling low and thick inside her at the feel of those powerful, steely muscles beneath her palms. Everything about him was so unexpected. And exciting. The thought of unbuttoning his shirt and stroking all that raw strength with her fingertips made her heart pound.

His ice-blue gaze dipped down to her mouth. Her belly pulled tight as she tilted her head back, let her eyes drift close. His lips brushed against hers. Twice. Three times. Soft and warm.

And then they closed over hers completely and he kissed her until she melted against him.

His hand remained rock steady at the back of her head, holding her still, the other splayed across her back. That mixture of dominance and tenderness turned her inside out.

She could feel herself melting in his embrace, a little moan slipping from her throat as his tongue slid into her mouth to caress hers. God, the man could kiss. He took his time, exploring, tasting. Teasing. Making her crazy.

When he pulled back a few minutes later she was gripping those broad shoulders, fingers digging into his muscles. And all she could think about was what it would feel like to sink them into his naked back while he used that wicked mouth on other parts of her body.

As though he knew what she was thinking, with another easy smile he leaned in and pressed a gentle kiss to her tingling lips. "You taste just as sweet as I thought you would," he whispered, his fingers dragging against her scalp in a drugging caress as they left her hair.

She had to force herself to release his shoulders, drew the wrap tighter around herself to hide the way her nipples were beaded tight against the bodice of her dress. Her mind was blank, completely wiped clean from a single kiss. That had never happened to her before.

"How busy are you going to be with studying the rest of this week?" he asked.

"Not so busy that I wouldn't make time for you." Yeah, her voice definitely sounded a little breathless, but it was a miracle she could formulate a sentence right now.

His eyes warmed as he smiled. "Good, then I'll call you." The hand splayed across her back rubbed gently before withdrawing, and she immediately regretted the loss of his touch. "Thanks for the date. Have a good night."

She almost asked him to come upstairs, something she never did on a first date. But there was something about him that made her want to throw caution aside, and it wasn't just that he came with an expiration date. In just a few short hours together, this man had already begun to work his way under her skin.

And the truth was, she liked the feel of him there too much to stop whatever was forming between them.

Chapter Five

Present day

Adam shoved open the door and stumbled into his hotel room, barely aware of moving.

Ten hours. Ten fucking hours since Summer had been taken and not a single trace of her. He'd spent that entire time searching in the vicinity where she'd been kidnapped at gunpoint, kicking down doors with his teammates and following leads that had gone nowhere.

The Jordanians were working on the situation with them but so far they'd found nothing of use. By now she could be across the border in Syria for all he knew.

He sank down on the edge of his bed and dragged his hands through his hair, feeling so many things at once he couldn't feel anything at all. And this downtime was killing him because it gave him too much time to think, for his imagination to conjure up all kinds of twisted, sadistic things the captors might be doing to Summer at that very moment.

The door closed quietly behind him and Bauer and Tuck came to stand in front of him, both of them looking hesitant. They were probably afraid to leave him alone right now. "Do you need anything?" Tuck asked softly.

Yeah, I need to find and rescue my wife from those motherfuckers.

The Army of True Believers. That's who had taken her, although the actual person or persons behind it were still a mystery. The group had claimed responsibility for the attack and kidnappings in an official statement released a few hours ago.

Adam knew all about them—Summer was an expert on their organization, it was why she was here in the first place—and had dreaded the possibility. Now that it had been confirmed, he was even more frantic about her safety.

The ATB were murderous radicals taking over Syria and Iraq, spreading like a cancer across the region, terrorizing civilians and launching terror attacks around the globe. They were ruthless, without mercy, known for torturing and killing their captives in spectacular fashion, and for selling women and girls into a life of sexual slavery.

Just thinking of Summer in their hands made his blood run cold.

He shook his head, blew out an unsteady breath as he answered Tuck. "No."

Bauer shot their team leader a worried look before focusing back on Adam, his bright blue gaze intense, his huge frame practically vibrating with unease. "You're probably not hungry now but I'm gonna go grab you something anyway, in case you feel like eating later."

Adam shook his head sharply. "No, don't bother." If he tried to force anything down his throat right now he'd just puke it up, and he didn't see that improving no matter how hungry he got.

Thankfully neither of them bothered arguing or trying to reason with him. He didn't want to talk, didn't want company right now, not even if the guys had good intentions. He just wanted the right to lose his shit in private. But maybe DeLuca had ordered them to watch him.

Tuck lowered himself into the armchair nearby and leaned forward, forearms resting on his knees. His dark brown eyes held Adam's, unwavering. "We've got the best in the business looking for her. The director's personally overseeing it. They're all working on it right now, checking satellites and whatever HUMINT they can gather. They'll be working on it 24/7 until they get a location. Then we'll go get her back. Every one of us is ready to go out there and do whatever it takes to rescue her."

Adam made himself nod, but he wasn't really listening. He was too caught up in his own emotional chaos, trying to figure out where she might be.

As a high value captive, there had to be some higher purpose for the ATB taking her. They'd want to use her for leverage, exploit the situation to their advantage. Money, prisoner exchanges, media attention.

Surely if they'd wanted her dead they just would have killed her during the ambush. And they'd taken two others as well.

Except he didn't feel reassured by that logic at all. He knew what those barbaric assholes were capable of.

"We're here for you, okay?" Tuck said, his Alabama drawl soft in the quiet room. "Just want you to know that. If you need something, you name it and we'll make sure it happens."

"Thanks," he forced out, not wanting to be a dick. He appreciated his teammates' concern, but the fact was, nothing they or anyone else could do would make him feel better until Summer was back safe and sound.

When neither Bauer nor Tuck said anything else, just sat there watching him with identical worried expressions, Adam sighed and scrubbed his hands over his face. He hadn't planned on talking to anyone, and he knew they'd leave if he told them to but if they were staying, so be it.

"We were supposed to go out on a date earlier," he said, his voice rough. "I told her I'd pick her up at six at her hotel." Instead she was now a hostage, somewhere he couldn't find her, afraid, maybe hurt. It sliced at his heart like a razor blade.

A heavy silence spread in the wake of his words, Bauer shifting uncomfortably in his seat. As the grimmest member of the team, this was likely way out of his comfort zone. It said a lot about his character that he was staying. "Yeah, you mentioned that earlier."

Nobody said anything for a long, awkward minute and Adam's thoughts turned to the past. "Things were getting better between us over the past couple months," he said finally. "And then today she…told me she still loved me." He choked up at that, pressed a fist against his lips to hold back the sob trapped in his throat. He couldn't decide if he even wanted to tell them all this, or if he wanted them gone.

"Glad to hear that, man," Tuck murmured.

Adam nodded, staring at the beige carpet at his feet. He swallowed. "All this time, that's what I'd been dying to hear. I knew if she still loved me, we could get through anything. And a few minutes after she told me, she was gone."

Fuck. He jammed his fingertips against his closed eyelids, fought back the tears burning the backs of his eyes.

"We're gonna get her back," Tuck said quietly, his voice full of steel. "There's no way we're not getting her back."

He looked up, met Tuck's deep brown stare as anger

ignited. *And what if we don't?*

He bit the words back, along with the urge to shout them. Snapping at his team leader wasn't going to improve the situation and Tuck was just trying to help. It was clear they were both worried about him.

Adam looked back down at the floor. He wasn't really that close with any of them, yet they all had his back.

That was the part he'd missed most about being with the team—that unshakable bond and camaraderie that came with knowing every last guy on the team would take a bullet for any of them. And they'd all been through their own private hells too, when the women they loved were in peril.

Tuck and Celida hadn't been officially together when she'd been attacked, but everyone had known he'd had strong feelings for her. And Bauer, hell, Zoe had gone through it twice.

Adam shook his head. "How did you guys handle it when they were taken? Zoe and Celida."

Bauer and Tuck looked at each other for a moment before facing him. "It was tough," Bauer answered, his blue eyes somber. "Toughest thing I've ever gone through. So I know how you're feeling, I get it. And like Tuck said, remember we've all got your back through this."

Adam knew all that. He cleared his throat, thought of something to say to fill the pause. He'd been careful not to let anyone know the extent of the deterioration of his marriage or the reasons behind it, but fuck it. These were his brothers and he knew they wouldn't judge him.

"We'd been having problems for about two years now." Bauer and his wife were expecting a baby in a few months so this topic of conversation probably wasn't all that welcome, but he didn't know what the hell else to talk about and he'd held everything in for so long.

He drew in a deep breath. "We lost a baby." It was

such a relief to say it aloud.

A shocked silence filled the room. He didn't look at the others.

"Well, three of them, to be honest. We'd been trying to get pregnant for over a year and nothing happened. Eventually we had to resort to IVF. We lost the first one pretty early on. But the second one was…" He pressed his lips together, fought the sudden constriction in his throat. "It was tough." He risked a look up, saw Bauer staring at him with the kind of sudden awareness only another expectant father could have.

"Shit, man, I never knew. I'm sorry."

"Me too," Tuck added.

Adam nodded. "Thanks. I just didn't want to talk about it with anyone back then." Which, as it turned out, was the main reason things had gone from bad to worse between him and Summer. "We were at that training thing in San Diego when it happened. I flew home as soon as I got the news but the truth is, I…wasn't there for her afterward. Not like I should have been." He'd been upset too, of course, but now he recognized not in the same way she'd been.

When he thought of his lack of communication and impatience with her in the aftermath, he wanted to go back in time and deliver a throat punch to himself.

It still crushed him, shamed him to know he hadn't been there for her in her darkest hour. Not in the way she'd needed him to be. He hadn't understood that until a few months ago, until she'd moved out and been ready to sign the separation papers she'd had drawn up.

He didn't blame her for wanting out. And even though he didn't know what she'd been through on that horrible day, he could guess well enough. He'd tortured himself with it ever since.

You don't know what it was like. You weren't there. *You were* never *there.*

The memory of Summer's emotional accusation reverberated in his skull, wrapped around his ribcage like a python and squeezed.

He blew out an unsteady breath. "I swore to her I'd never let her down like that again. I promised I'd always be there for her after that." And now, when she needed him more than ever and was facing the unthinkable at the hands of those animals, he wasn't there.

He. Wasn't. There.

He shook his head, refusing to accept it. "I've gotta find her. I can't lose her or I'll—" His throat closed up.

Tuck got up and came over to lay a hand on his shoulder, his big hand gripping tight. "We'll find her. And we'll bring her home safe and sound."

On the verge of losing it, Adam dropped his face into his hands and sent out a silent prayer. A vow he'd die trying to uphold.

I wasn't there for you before. And it's true that I don't know what you went through back then. But I love you and I'm not giving up. So wherever you are right now, Summer, please hold on. I won't stop searching until I find you.

****

Eight years ago

The past week had crawled by for Summer with agonizing sluggishness, but she'd been looking forward to this for days and now it was finally time.

She checked her reflection in the bathroom mirror one last time before heading out into her bedroom where she had her laptop waiting on the bed. That familiar sense of excitement and anticipation built as she logged onto her Skype account and waited cross-legged atop her quilt.

Adam had told her he'd call between seven and eight

her time tonight, unless he got called out for a mission or briefing. The last two times they'd tried to schedule this he hadn't been able to make it. Not seeing or talking to him was slowly driving her insane.

She worried about him and his buddies. Normally she stopped watching the news in an effort to avoid seeing the terrible things happening in the area Adam was stationed, but that didn't help much because she got more than ample information about what was going on in southern Afghanistan at work. Sometimes ignorance really was bliss.

Her pulse jumped when the call came in. She answered it, and a moment later Adam's face appeared on the screen. Her cheeks ached from the wide smile that stretched her mouth. He smiled back, the adoration and pleasure on his face making her heart roll over in her chest. "Hey, doll."

She loved it when he called her that. "Hey, handsome. How are you?" God, he looked good. Tired, but good. She missed him so much it hurt.

"Great. Sorry I couldn't do this sooner. We've been busy."

She waved the apology away. "It's okay. Just glad to see you safe and sound."

"Yep, all's good here. How are things there?"

"Good. I've been working long hours." Taking on extra projects and helping her boss with a few things outside of her normal work load. Mostly in an effort to distract herself and make the time go faster. Right now she was analyzing intelligence reports on an up-and-coming faction in Lebanon. "I'm counting down the days until you get back."

"Me too. Nineteen more and I'll be there."

She couldn't wait. "You get any sleep today?" It didn't look like it to her and they routinely went without sleep for two days at a time when they were out on patrol or a mission.

"Yeah, just woke up."

He couldn't talk about the missions he and his A-Team were running, but he knew she was more aware than most of what was happening in his area. He'd tell her more when he got home, all except the classified stuff. She had a security clearance but it was far lower than his. Still, she liked that he shared certain things with her and didn't try to shelter her from what had happened.

They talked about her work for a while, and the whole time she was scoping out the situation on the other end. There didn't seem to be anyone else in the room with him. "Where is everyone?" Normally at their forward operating base barracks he bunked with four other guys.

"I sent them out for a while."

"Did you?" she said suggestively. "Why, were you planning on talking dirty to me?"

He cracked a grin, gave a mock frown. "I would never do such a thing."

Oh yeah, he would. And hearing the sexy things he told her in that deep voice sent a shiver through her now.

Placing the laptop down before her on the bed, she flipped her hair over one shoulder, exposing the front of her. "I bought something for you today."

"Did you?" He was eyeing her cleavage now, pushed up and revealed to maximum effect in the plunging V neckline of the purple halter-top blouse she'd chosen. And what she had on underneath it.

"Mmmm. Wanna see?"

He cocked a dark eyebrow. "That a trick question?"

Smirking, she reached up behind her neck and plucked the button closure of the top apart. Watching his face, she held onto the ends of both straps for a moment, then slowly lowered them.

Adam let out a low groan and leaned closer when he saw the black lace push-up bra she'd bought. It had little crystal skulls on the center of each cup and a little pink bow nestled between them. "Holy shit."

Laughing softly, she shook her hair back and thrust her chest upward, shoving her amped-up cleavage at the camera. "Just wanted to give you a preview of what to expect when you get home. I've been busy beefing up my lingerie wardrobe."

"Take it off." The low command, coupled with that hungry, focused expression, made warmth spread deep in her abdomen.

Instead she teased him by drawing a finger alongside one of the cups, tracing the edge of the fabric as it cupped her breast, following it down to pause at the little pink bow. "But it's so pretty," she protested. She loved teasing him like this. Loved that he still wanted her so much, even after all this time together.

"Do it," he coaxed, his ice-blue eyes hot on her skin.

Hiding a smile, she reached back and unhooked the fastening between her shoulder blades. She drew the left strap down her shoulder and upper arm, slowly, letting it dangle at the bend of her elbow. Then the right one. He wasn't moving at all, his full attention riveted to her still-covered breasts.

Her nipples were already hard points against the fabric, tendrils of pleasure and heat cascading out from there to between her thighs. Watching his expression, she lowered her arms and let the bra drop into her lap.

His answering groan rumbled through her laptop. "Oh God…"

Oh yeah, she loved that look on his face. The one that said if he'd been in front of her right now, she'd be flat on her back with his mouth on her in less than a second.

Feeling sexy as hell, Summer lifted her arms and gathered her hair up behind her, striking her best pinup pose. Adam's stare looked like it might burn through the monitor as he took it all in.

"I bought a little something to go with the bra," she added coyly, shaking her shoulders slightly, holding back a laugh at the way his eyes followed the bounce of her breasts. She wasn't well-endowed but the way Adam looked at her made her feel like the most beautiful and desirable woman on earth. "Wanna see? I thought I'd—"

Her words cut off abruptly when a face suddenly appeared over Adam's shoulder. She had only an instant to recognize Trevor and his goofy grin. "Hey, Sum—oh, shit."

Horrified, Summer squeaked in alarm and automatically clapped her hands over her breasts, eyes flying wide.

Trevor's eyes widened too and then he quickly backed out of view.

"Oh my God!" she cried. Adam was glaring at Trevor now, saying something over his shoulder, but she was too busy burning with embarrassment to give a shit what it was. "Oh my *God*!"

Mortified, she scrambled off her bed, well out of camera range, and cowered there in a heap on the woven rug next to the bed. "Adam!" she shrieked in accusation.

A strangled laugh answered. Adam's. Then Trevor's distinctive Tennessee twang came. "Hell, sorry about that. Might wanna put a sock on the door or something next time you guys wanna get your freak on." A door closed somewhere in the background.

Summer closed her eyes. This was horrifying.

"He's gone now," Adam said with a chuckle.

"It's not funny!"

"Come on, it was a little funny."

Outraged, she reached for the first thing she could find on the bed—her bra—and flung it at the laptop screen. It hit with a splat and fell to the keyboard.

Adam's laughter rang in her ears as she sat huddled there, mortified. How the hell was she supposed to show up at the homecoming now and face Trevor? He was a total perv and would absolutely make a comment about how he barely recognized her with her shirt on.

Getting mad all over again, she picked the bra back up and threw it at the laptop screen a second time. "Why the hell didn't you warn me that he walked in?" she demanded, still huddled out of range.

"Because I was too busy drooling at the show you were putting on. I didn't even hear him."

Whatever. The man woke from a dead sleep if someone dropped a pin in the room. There was no way he'd been so distracted that he hadn't heard Trevor open the door. "I'm so embarrassed," she moaned.

"Don't be. Biggest thrill he's gotten since we've been over here, trust me. Maybe even before that." A pause. "Come on, come back up so I can see you."

She glared at the computer, even though Adam couldn't see her. "No."

Another chuckle. "Summer. Get back up here. We're alone."

Shielding her bare breasts with her hands, she got to her knees and craned her neck to poke her head around and check. Adam was there, grinning at her like an idiot. She shot him a glower, put her bra and shirt back on before climbing back up on the bed.

Adam gave her a pout and opened his mouth to protest.

"Nuh-uh, don't even," she told him. So much for her sex-kitten routine. "God, I'm never going to be able to look him in the eye after this."

"I wouldn't worry about that. I can pretty much guarantee he won't be looking at your eyes after this."

Summer groaned and crossed her arms over her chest while Adam's deep chuckle sounded in her ears. It was a good thing she loved him more than life itself.

Chapter Six

Present Day

Exhaustion clouded her brain like a fog.

Huddled in the back of her cell, Summer scrunched her knees tighter to her body in a futile effort to retain warmth. Her weary muscles shuddered with each shiver, her teeth chattering from the cold, and her hands and feet had long since gone numb.

She had no idea how much time had passed since they'd dumped her in here but it must have been hours. Her entire body was stiff, she was hungry, and she had to pee.

But at least she was still alive and unharmed. Mostly.

She was starting to wonder if she'd be forced to just relieve herself there in the dirt, through her clothes, when muted male voices reached her. Concern over her full bladder disappeared instantly, overridden by her body's automatic fight-or-flight response. Her pulse sped up and her mouth went dry.

Whoever it was, the men continued across the space in front of her, some distance away. A moment later their voices became muffled, as though they'd stepped behind some kind of divider. Soon after, another male voice added to the mix. She couldn't hear any of them well enough to overhear what was being said.

Sometime later, just as she was beginning to doze off, a pained cry rang out. She tensed and held her breath, straining to hear, to figure out what was happening. Had to be Jim. Were they hurting him? What were they doing?

Unbidden, a flood of images bombarded her, all the terrible things they might do to her when they came for her. She locked the thoughts away and gave herself a stern talking to.

This was not the time to allow her imagination to run wild. Panicking about what might happen was only going to make the situation worse.

She mentally shook herself, dug down deep for her diminishing reserves of courage. Whatever came, she had to be strong if she was going to survive this.

She'd already overcome so much. She *had* to get through this and find her way back to Adam somehow.

It made her think of his surprising reaction one day after a counseling session a few months ago, back when everything had looked hopeless.

I'm not letting you go, he'd told her fiercely, holding both her shoulders as he stared into her eyes. *Ever. I'll fight for you, no matter how long it takes. I won't ever give up.*

The words had surprised her so much, part of her hadn't believed him at the time. She'd dismissed his vow, telling herself he'd only made it out of some misguided sense of loyalty to her and their marriage.

There was too much hurt on either side. Why would he want an emotionally traumatized wife who couldn't give him a child and couldn't even be intimate with him, when he was the kind of man who could have anyone he wanted?

Logically she knew the child part was more an issue for her than him, but the sex part definitely bothered him. Why would any man put up with that, let alone someone like him?

But now she realized he had fought for her the whole time, at least in his own way. He'd stuck by her, giving her space to find herself again and he'd gone to counseling both alone and with her. He'd hung in there while she struggled and scraped and battled to drag herself out of the bottomless pit she was in and for the longest time hadn't seen a way out of.

In hindsight she recognized that no one could have pulled her out, not even him. She'd had to do it herself. After she'd done it, the hardest part was putting everything behind her, letting it all go. Forgiving him for his mistakes.

More, forgiving herself for hers.

The bulk of the damage had been done by the stillbirth. She'd retreated into herself, falling into an endless depression. Adam had tried to pull her free and she'd just retreated more. Then he'd become frustrated and angry, not understanding why she couldn't "snap out of it" after the first few months had passed.

After that things had slowly improved, for a while. She'd forced herself back into the land of the living.

And then she'd suffered the third miscarriage.

She laid her cheek against her upraised knee and let the memory wash over her. Looking back, she'd made a big mistake in choosing to have their final embryo implanted. It had been way too soon for her emotionally, but she'd been so desperate to have their child and she couldn't bear the thought of leaving that last embryo in the lab. With Adam's support, she'd done it, and the pregnancy had taken.

For a few short weeks.

A little into her second month, she'd miscarried. And it had broken the will she'd struggled so hard to find again.

Logically it didn't make sense. Even now, she couldn't really explain it. Having a heavy period a few weeks after finding out she was pregnant was far less traumatic than what she'd gone through when she'd lost and delivered A.J. the year before.

And yet, for some reason it had extinguished the inner fire she'd managed to regain since the stillbirth, triggering all those terrible memories and sending her spiraling back into her own private hell.

After that she couldn't even look at Adam without reliving it all. She couldn't handle him touching her, let alone intimately. He'd been angry and frustrated by the setback and things had simply fallen apart.

He still waited for you, she reminded herself, still awed by it.

He could have bailed, walked out and served her with separation papers. A lot of men in his position would have. But he hadn't.

Instead he'd waited for her to find her way back to him again. And in doing so, he'd won her back.

It galvanized her. They hadn't gone through all that for nothing. There had to be a reason and she refused to accept that she might die now that they'd finally found their way back to each other. Her husband had fought for her then and he'd be fighting for her today. She knew without a doubt he'd be out there right now, searching for her.

And she also knew he wouldn't give up. Not Adam. Accepting defeat wasn't in his DNA. No matter what happened, he would find her and bring her home, one way or the other.

She just prayed he found her alive.

The thought choked her up so badly she had to bite the inside of her cheek to keep from crying.

More voices brought her head up. Two men, headed her way. She swallowed hard. What did they want? Her heart rattled in her chest as they drew near.

Keys jangled. The cell door squeaked open.

A hand grabbed the hood, ripped it off her. She flinched at the sudden brightness and squinted while her eyes adjusted.

When she managed to pry her eyelids apart the pearly quality of the light told her it was early morning. They'd left her in her cell for the entire night without even so much as a blanket.

She focused on the two men before her, both dressed in black tunics and pants, with black kerchiefs tied around their heads, each of them holding a pistol. One was slightly built and appeared to be in his early twenties, his beard scraggly and thin.

The other was older, harder, and much bigger, his mouth a thin slash in the midst of his heavy, dark beard. And his eyes—

She sucked in a breath as recognition crashed through her, bringing with it a wave of terror.

Tarek Hadad. Known member of the ATB who had risen to considerable power in recent weeks. She'd done a report on him just two weeks ago. He had a reputation for being ruthless, someone you didn't want to cross.

And she was his prisoner.

There was no hatred in his black eyes as he stared down at her. Just a cold, calculating gleam that turned her blood to ice. "Summer Blackwell," he said in heavily accented English. "What do you do for your agency?"

As much as she hated looking at him, hated that he stood towering over her while she sat cuffed and helpless, she refused to break eye contact. She may be helpless but she was no coward. "I'm an analyst."

"What does that mean?" he demanded in a hard voice. "What do you analyze?"

There was nothing wrong with answering that and she didn't want to risk having him torture her merely because he suspected she was holding something back. If she fed him enough information, maybe he'd be satisfied without her actually having to give anything important away. "Information."

"Information," he repeated in an annoyed mutter. "About what?"

She swallowed, fought to stem the shivers rolling through her even though her muscles shuddered periodically. "Terror groups. Logistics. Capabilities. Funding."

At that his gaze sharpened. A flare of pride and satisfaction lit them up, as if a fire had suddenly blazed to life deep inside him. A sneer distorted his mouth. "Terror groups. So you report about what American soldiers and their allies are doing, then?"

She didn't answer that one.

"No, I thought not," he murmured, folding his arms across his chest.

She'd seen pictures of him before but seeing him now up close, she had a whole new respect for his sheer physical power. He wasn't as tall as Adam, but he was almost as broad through the shoulders and chest, his torso heavily muscled, and he had a commanding presence. She could see why his men wouldn't dare cross him. They'd be too afraid to.

Regarding her with that eerie stare, he tilted his head. "You know who I am?"

There was no point in denying it. "Yes."

He gave a satisfied nod. "Good. Then you know what I'm capable of."

Her stomach knotted even tighter. Not wanting to answer that aloud, she simply looked at him.

Those black eyes continued to bore into her, glowing with that strange inner light that made her skin crawl. He was scary as hell. "I have your boss. And your coworker."

Mark? He was here too? Oh no…

"And I have your laptop."

She sucked in a breath at that, hid a wince. Most of what was on her hard drive was encrypted, but not all. If he accessed the data on it he'd see the intel they had on him and the ATB groups in the region. He'd be able to warn his fellow ATB members about upcoming U.S. counterterrorism operations near the Syrian-Jordanian border.

Another smirk. "If you don't give me the password and reveal what I want to know, your friends will suffer for it." He paused a moment. "And so will you."

Oh God… If she gave him the password she'd be putting American and allied lives in danger. But if she didn't…

Her guts churned at the impossible situation she faced.

A cold, cruel smile twisted Tarek's mouth, telling her he saw her fear and was pleased by it. "You're going to be very useful to me in the coming days, Summer."

She hated that he used her name.

Breaking eye contact with her, he nodded at the man beside him and spoke in Arabic, either not realizing or not caring that she might understand. "Take her outside. We'll get started soon."

With that pronouncement he walked away, leaving her in agonized anticipation of what was coming.

****

Adam stifled an irritated sigh and rubbed at his burning eyes before focusing back on the satellite image displayed on the large flat screen mounted on the wall at the end of the room.

A Jordanian intelligence official was detailing the features of a remote village up near the northern border with Syria. The ATB and other militants were known to use the area for infiltrating across the border and back, and some analyst somewhere thought this might be a likely place for them to stash a couple of captives.

Adam was fast moving past being frustrated into angry territory.

They still didn't know where Summer was, or the name of the person behind the attack. It was driving him insane. The longer they sat here on their asses, hoping for something helpful to come in, the higher the chances were that Summer and the others were running out of time.

Nothing they'd tried so far had yielded any results. Both locations they'd scouted before dawn this morning hadn't turned up anything.

Everyone they'd questioned so far claimed to know zip about yesterday's attack or abductions. None of the intelligence sources had panned out. All the satellite and drone footage they'd reviewed so far had been useless.

He shifted restlessly in his seat, the need to get up and do something constructive pricking him with a thousand sharp needles.

The door swung open and the director walked in, heading for the front of the room with purposeful strides. DeLuca was right behind him. "Sorry for the interruption," he began, taking his place in front of the desk. The Jordanian officer stepped aside to give him room. "I've just received confirmation of who was behind the attacks."

Adam's spine jerked taut. He leaned forward, all ears.

The director paused a moment to type something into the laptop sitting on the table, and a man's picture came up on the screen. "Tarek Hadad."

Adam stared at the picture, didn't even realize he was holding his breath until his lungs started to burn. His knuckles ached from the pressure of squeezing his hands into fists.

Now he had a name and a face for his target. That fucker had taken his wife. The need to storm out of the room and hunt the bastard down was so strong it was all he could do to sit still.

A firm hand landed on his shoulder. He glanced back to find Cruzie behind him, his teammate's golden brown eyes intense. "We'll hunt him down, man."

Adam nodded and turned his attention back to the front. He couldn't wait for the chance to get out there and nail that motherfucker.

The director glanced at him briefly, then continued. "He's a mover and shaker within the ATB. Over the past few weeks he's been escalating his operations within Syria, trying to gain favor with the higher-ups. No one's sure when he made it across into Jordan. I've got analysts working on the details now and I'll pass it along to you as I receive it." He paused a moment, signaling something else important was coming.

Adam didn't have to wait long. Out of the corner of his eye, he was aware of DeLuca watching him, but ignored that, too focused on what the director was about to say.

"Another point of interest is that over the past few months, the ATB has been closely affiliated with the Qureshi network, run out of Afghanistan and tribal Pakistan."

At the mention of Qureshi, Adam, his teammates and the director all turned to look at Schroder. The former pararescueman's face was blank with surprise, obviously not expecting this little twist.

"In light of the situation and the tight timeline we're working with, I've already taken the liberty of contacting Taya Kostas," he continued, naming Schroder's girlfriend before nodding at DeLuca. "You all know her, and what happened to her. After reviewing her previous interviews and court transcripts, we feel she may have more relevant information that might be of use to us in this investigation."

Schroder rubbed a hand over his mouth and chin, looking uneasy at the announcement.

A knock came at the door and an aide popped her head in. "I've got Ms. Kostas on the line," she said. When the director motioned her over, she passed him the phone. "It's on speaker."

"Ms. Kostas, this is Director Foster. I'm here with SA Schroder and his team, along with some other intelligence officials. Thank you for your time."

"It's my pleasure," she answered, her soft, calm voice filling the room. "I was told there's something to do with the Qureshi network you wanted to speak to me about."

"That's correct. Before this goes any further, I need to inform you now that everything about this conversation is classified."

"Understood, and my phone is secure."

Adam listened as Foster detailed what was going on, bringing her up to speed on the situation with Summer and the other two hostages. He told her the bare basics only, leaving out the details.

"Summer Blackwell," Taya said. "You mean Adam's wife?"

From across the room Foster met his gaze, a muscle flexing in his jaw. "That's correct."

"Can Adam hear me?"

"Yes."

"Adam, I'm so sorry."

He hated the sorrow in her voice. Sorrow because she thought Summer might already be dead. He refused to accept that.

"Thank you," he made himself say. It was probably hard for Schroder to hear her right now, to have her dragged into this without any warning, and not be able to talk to her in private first. "I'm hoping you can help us." He wasn't sure what information she had, but he knew she'd been held captive for a long time and must have solid insider info, otherwise the director wouldn't have brought her in.

"I'll help in whatever way I can. What is it you want to ask me, Director?"

Adam hung on every word as she answered specific questions about Qureshi's network at the time of her captivity, and their possible ties to the ATB. Most of it he hadn't been aware of, and he knew that's why the director was asking her in front of everyone.

Foster had no doubt been briefed on all this months ago, but he wanted them all to understand what he was getting at. Taya confirmed there had been connections between the two groups while she was held prisoner in Afghanistan.

Near the end of the conversation, Foster crossed his arms and spread his feet apart. "So let's get right down to it. I'm sorry for the bluntness, but I need to ask. In one of your previous interviews you said that during your captivity you came into contact with female hostages either bought from or sold to the ATB."

"Yes. Several that I knew of. I overheard Hassan talking to Qureshi one night about it. The ATB would sell female captives to Qureshi in exchange for heroin or weapons smuggled out of Afghanistan."

Adam leaned forward and steepled his hands over his nose and mouth, his heart slamming hard against his ribs. The thought of Summer being sold as some fighter or warlord's slave turned his stomach inside out. He was terrified for her. After what she'd already endured and all the emotional baggage she'd worked so hard to unload, being raped would surely shatter her.

Foster nodded in confirmation, then asked, "We have access to several prisoners you'll be familiar with. You have firsthand knowledge of these guys and I want you directly on hand because these are high value hostages and we need to find them as soon as possible. I'd like to bring you on board as a contractor, per se. In the interest of convenience and efficiency, would you be willing to fly here and assist us with the investigation in person?"

A surprised pause followed the question. Adam shot a sharp look over at Schroder. Three seats down from Adam, the medic was scowling, his expression full of alarm.

Adam felt bad for him. He didn't blame Schroder for not wanting Taya anywhere near this hemisphere after all she'd gone through, let alone digging all this up again. But if it helped them find Summer…

"Yes, of course," she answered, and Adam wanted to hug her. She was so brave, always standing tall in the face of whatever life dealt her.

Schroder apparently couldn't take it anymore. "Tay, are you sure?" he asked, his voice full of concern.

"Yes, Nathan. I want to help, and if something I know can help get Summer back, then I have to do this. So I'm coming."

"Thank you," Foster told her, and Adam added his silent thanks as well. "How soon can you leave?"

"Almost right away," she answered. "I just need a few hours to clear my schedule and get to the airport."

"We'll arrange a flight for you, then have an agent come to escort you to the airport. Someone will accompany you on the flight here."

"I'll call Celida," Tuck interjected from beside Adam. "She'll take you to the airport."

"I'd appreciate that, thanks," Taya answered.

Foster ended the call and the meeting broke up a few minutes later. Adam stood and immediately turned to Schroder, feeling a little awkward about what had happened.

"Hey," he began, but Schroder shook his head to stop him and held up a hand.

"It's okay, man. Taya's right, and I know she's strong enough to handle this. If she can see something that might help us break this case open, then I want her here too."

"Thank you," he managed, voice rough. He hoped like hell Taya would be able to give them a clue, a detail they were missing that would enable them to get a location on Summer.

Schroder clapped a hand on his shoulder, gripped tight. "We're family. We take care of our own."

Adam nodded, throat too tight to speak. They *were* family. A band of brothers. And he honestly didn't know what he'd do without them right now.

Chapter Seven

Seven years ago

D amn, it was good to be home.

Adam literally felt a weight fall off his shoulders as he walked up the front walkway to Summer's D.C. townhouse. His contract with the Army had been fulfilled and he was finally free to move on to something else. He'd miss the guys he served with but it was definitely time for him to switch gears, both professionally and personally.

He was moving forward with his life, and he wanted Summer at his side for the rest of it.

He'd been back from his final combat deployment for a few days already but had been busy tying up loose ends with paperwork and bank accounts, having his stuff moved up from Fort Bragg here to D.C. He already had an interview lined up for later in the week.

With his background, service record and letters of recommendation, he had a good shot at being accepted into the FBI. He wanted to make their Hostage Rescue

Team one day.

He slid his key into the front lock, looking forward to what the night held. The time change, errands and Summer's erratic work schedule meant they hadn't seen each other much since he'd been back.

She'd been there to meet him at the airport, hair all done up, wearing one of her retro dresses and a blinding smile just for him. She'd lit up the moment she'd seen him, and raced straight for him, then blushed six kinds of red when Trevor had come up to hug her.

That picture of her waiting there to greet him would always be etched into his memory. He'd dropped his ruck and duffel, grabbed her and lifted her off the ground for a kiss filled with all the hunger and need that had built up during his absence. She'd been through the separation of three different combat deployments with him, but this latest reunion was the sweetest because they both knew it was the last.

The moment he stepped into the foyer, the smell of something awesome greeted him. Grilled meat and something sweet. Grinning, he set his backpack down in the foyer and called out jokingly, "Honey, I'm home."

"Back here."

He took off his shoes and headed for the kitchen. "Whatever you're doing in here, it smells amazing."

Summer looked up from behind the center island, where she stood putting the finishing touches on dinner, and smiled. She had on the frilly black-and-white vintage apron she'd bought with him at a market last year. "I made your favorite. Grilled steak Oscar with roasted asparagus and buttered mashed potatoes."

His stomach growled and he almost groaned as his mouth watered. "I haven't eaten anything close to that caliber in over nine months."

She shot him a knowing grin. "I know. That's why I wanted to spoil you a little."

She did spoil him and he loved it. "Need a hand?"

"Yeah, you want to grab the wine?" She turned away to cross to the counter behind her and he stopped dead, his tongue suddenly stuck to the roof of his mouth.

Jesus, she was wearing heels and that apron—

And nothing else.

He stared at the way the open back of the apron perfectly framed the pert little curves of her ass, those fuck-me red heels emphasizing every muscle in her bare legs.

She stopped at the counter to shoot a look at him over her shoulder, raised a red eyebrow. "Adam."

Huh? He dragged his gaze up to her face.

Her lips twitched. "The wine."

Fuck the wine.

He erased the distance between them in three strides and grasped her hips in his hands, pulling her back against him. "I want to bend you over right here and fuck you from behind until you scream my name," he growled against the side of her neck, pausing to give her a little love bite in the sensitive spot he knew made her shiver.

Summer laughed softly and wriggled her ass against the hard line of his erection shoved against his zipper. "Maybe after dinner. I don't want the fillets to get cold." Then she reached up to cup the side of his face in one hand and turn her lips up to his. The kiss was slow and sexy, her tongue teasing his with the promise of what would happen once they finished eating.

With a low hum of appreciation, he let his hands wander over the curve of her hips to her waist, up to cup the round swells of her breasts. "I love this apron." He'd never dreamed an apron could be this sexy.

Another laugh. "I knew you'd change your mind about it eventually." She grabbed the blender from the counter and deftly poured what looked like hollandaise sauce over the steaks nestled on their beds of mashed potatoes, then added some crabmeat and the roasted asparagus on top.

"Oh my God, you're the perfect woman," he murmured, unable to hide his grin. He was so freaking lucky to have such a sexy, intelligent, driven and caring woman in his life. He hoped he made her even half as happy as she did him.

"Just as long as you realize that," she teased, and handed him his plate. "Should we eat by the fire?"

The fire? He nodded, took her plate from her and gestured for her to go first. "Ladies first."

Her lips curved upward. "You just wanna stare at my naked ass."

"Damn right I do."

The view on the way to the living room was nothing short of spectacular. He was staring at her bare ass like a sex-starved maniac, nearly crashed into the coffee table because he just couldn't tear his gaze from the entrancing sight of her sexy cheeks swaying with each step.

When they reached the couch Summer turned to face him and smoothed her apron down the back of her before sitting and crossing one leg over the other with deliberate slowness. The pose itself was unbelievably sexy but with the firelight glowing over her red hair and naked, pale skin, it was all he could do not to throw dinner aside and attack her right then and there.

She accepted her plate with a little smile that told him she knew exactly how insane she was making him and had been hoping for this very reaction. "Adam. The wine."

Right. Wine.

He rushed into the kitchen, poured them both a glass of red from the decanter she had waiting on the counter, and hurried back.

The dinner melted in his mouth, each bite perfection not just because she was a great cook, but because she'd gone to all this effort for him. To make him happy and show how much she cared. That meant way more than the apron and heels did.

Summer took a sip of wine and gave him a slow smile. "I never believed the saying before, but your mom really wasn't kidding when she told me the way to a man's heart is through his stomach."

"That's mostly true in my family," he admitted, his gaze once again sliding over the length of her. From this angle he could just make out the curves of the sides of her breasts. Just enough for a handful, for each mound to fit perfectly in his palms.

Summer set her wine down and re-crossed her legs. Slowly. Giving him just enough time and just enough room to make out the shadowed flesh between her pretty thighs. The sexy, nerve-rich folds he couldn't wait to bury his mouth against while those heels dug into his back.

She set her glass down in her lap and tilted her head a little, her eyes sparkling in the firelight. "This is way too fun."

"So fun," he agreed, taking another bite of steak. He hated to rush through a meal she'd gone to such care in selecting and preparing, but hell. He could barely remember to chew and swallow with her sitting four feet away, mostly naked, teasing him with every breath.

After eating he ordered her to stay put and took the plates into the kitchen. He'd clean up later while she was asleep—tucked into their bed, exhausted from the best sex of her life. But right now he had something more important on his mind.

He needed to claim his woman once and for all. With the combat deployments and their long separations behind them, nothing was holding him back anymore.

She was still curled into the arm of the sofa with her wineglass when he came out, looking like something out of a naughty pin-up calendar.

Adam went onto one knee in front of her, set her

wine on the coffee table and reached one hand out to cradle the side of her face. "You have no idea how beautiful you are," he murmured. "Or how much I love you."

She gave him an assessing look. "Pretty sure I know that last bit, but I wouldn't mind a reminder to refresh my memory." She took hold of his wrist and tugged, trying to bring him to her as she tipped her face up for a kiss.

Adam answered the invitation by fusing their mouths together in a kiss so hot it left them both panting. When he pulled back finally, Summer made a sound of protest and reached for him, one hand lifting to grasp the ties at the back of her neck.

Adam shook his head and grabbed her hand, bringing it to his lips instead. "Not yet." He had something more important to do before he gave them both the release they were dying for.

While she watched him curiously he slipped his right hand into his jeans pocket and pulled out the little velvet box he'd picked up at the jeweler this afternoon.

Summer gasped and sat up straight, one hand going to her chest, right over her heart. Holding her other hand in his, Adam flipped the box open with his fingers to reveal the round diamond ring.

She lifted her eyes to his, and he saw pure joy and love shining back at him. He'd never felt so complete, or so certain of anything in his life. She was it for him.

"You're everything I could ever want and more and I want to spend the rest of our lives together," he told her softly. "Will you marry me?"

Her answering smile was so bright it almost hurt his eyes. "Yes. *Yes*." She pulled her hand free of his grip and flung her arms around his neck.

He hugged her tight, closing his eyes to better savor the moment, letting her sweet scent and the feel of her supple body pressed against his fill his senses. Then he slid the ring onto her finger and pushed her back to recline on the leather sofa, all that pretty red hair spilling over the side of it. He stroked a hand over it, drew his fingertips down her face and throat, feeling more possessive than he ever had in his life.

She was going to be his, forever.

"Stay just like that," he murmured, reaching for the ties at the back of her neck. He undid them, then reached under her to undo the ones at her waist. The apron practically melted away from her skin at his touch, revealing her in all her naked glory.

With a rough sound of need he leaned in to lick the tight pink nipples waiting for his mouth, and took hold of the underside of her knees. "Feet on my shoulders," he commanded in a low voice, already lifting them into position.

He heard her breathless gasp of anticipation, caught the heady scent of her arousal as she opened for him, the muscles in her thighs quivering slightly. His starving gaze raked over the length of her, open and waiting for him, and settled on the glistening folds between her thighs. He couldn't hold back a moment longer.

Mine.

With a raw sound that came from his gut he leaned forward and pressed his mouth there, demonstrating his claim in a way that didn't require words.

Chapter Eight

Present Day

“Another agent will meet us inside by the check-in counter,” Celida said to Taya as she steered into the multi-level parking garage next to the airport's international terminal.

“Okay,” Taya replied, fighting the nerves buzzing around in the pit of her stomach.

She hated airports. Had ever since terrorists had targeted her in one, and coupled with the fact that she was about to get on a plane and fly back to an Islamic country bordering a warzone like the one she'd been taken captive in…well. Little wonder she was dreading every second of this.

But Summer Blackwell was in danger, along with two other American intelligence employees, and their lives were at stake. It didn't matter that Taya and most of the other HRT women had never met her. Summer and Adam were part of the HRT family, period. If Taya could help the investigators crack the case somehow, then she had to go.

"And I know without a doubt Schroder will be waiting for you on the other end with another couple of the guys," Celida added in a dry tone.

Taya smiled. "Yes." It helped to know that Nathan would be there waiting when she stepped off the plane in Amman. Unless of course they got a tip about Summer that they needed to act on in the meantime.

"Make sure you say hi to my husband for me," she added. She and Tuck had just been married last fall.

"I will. I'll give him a hug from you."

The side of Celida's mouth kicked up in the hint of a smile, the action pulling at the thin scar on her right cheek. A scar from a bullet that easily could have killed her. "That sounds weird, but okay. Hug the shit outta my man for me." She pulled into a parking spot and shut off the engine.

As she approached the terminal Taya's pulse began to race. An innate response she couldn't control no matter how hard she tried to calm and center herself with her breathing. Her subconscious refused to let her forget what had happened at the airport the day of the attack, or what she'd gone through the last time she'd set foot in an Islamic country.

Granted, Jordan was a far cry from Afghanistan, where she'd gone to help the Red Cross, but still. This trip was forcing her to face her old fears head on.

She'd traveled a lot over the years but it had been a while and she'd scrambled around like a madwoman prepping for this one, rearranging her schedule as best she could. Nathan always made it look so easy whenever he got called out at a moment's notice.

Celida stayed right next to her the entire time, alert, her pistol tucked into the holster at the small of her back. That helped too, knowing her friend was armed and vigilant.

Not to mention badass. If anyone tried to attack her now, Celida would drop them before they got within a hundred feet of her.

Taya tried not to let her nerves show as they moved around the lines of people waiting to check in for their flights. She had special paperwork and a first class ticket that allowed her to skip the line, courtesy of the FBI.

Celida escorted her right up to the podium where another woman waited, dressed in cargo pants, a fitted, long-sleeved black T-shirt and light jacket. She had jaw-length cocoa brown hair, a light bronze complexion a shade or two darker than Celida's, and watchful sea-green eyes that missed nothing.

"Agent Thatcher?" Celida asked.

The woman nodded. "Agent Morales." Turning her attention to Taya, she offered a polite smile. But there was a definite edge to her. A don't-mess-with-me edge that was impossible to miss. "You must be Taya."

"Yes, hi." She held out her hand.

"I'm Special Agent Maya Thatcher," she said, and shook hands with her. "I'll be escorting you to Amman."

"Great." Because what else was there to say? It's not like she had a choice, and she was glad to have an armed agent with her. No doubt Agent Thatcher knew all about her past, had already been briefed on everything.

Agent Thatcher took the paperwork from Celida, glanced at everything and handed the ticket to the man working the podium. In a minute flat Taya was checked in and her suitcase put on the conveyor belt. "Okay," she said to Taya. "You ready?"

As I'll ever be. "Yes." She faced Celida with a taut smile. "Thanks so much for the ride, I appreciate it."

Celida waved the thanks away. "Anytime. You're in good hands, by the way. Before joining the Bureau, SA Thatcher was an Air Force security forces member."

"Feels like a long time ago now," Agent Thatcher

said with a wry grin.

Celida took a step back as if she was going to leave, but Taya stepped over and wrapped her up in a hug. "You thought you'd get away without a goodbye hug? I don't think so."

Laughing, Celida gave her a quick squeeze in return. "You're as bad as Zoe."

That made her smile, because not only was Bauer's wife Tuck's cousin, she was also Celida's best friend. "I'll take that as a compliment. I love her."

"She's hard not to love," Celida agreed. "Now go on, you guys will be boarding soon."

Taya stayed close to Agent Thatcher as they made their way through security—expedited by more government paperwork—and to their gate for the first leg of the trip. She tended to make friends easily but she was so nervous she was afraid if she opened her mouth she'd just start babbling about nothing and didn't want to annoy her escort.

It wasn't until they were onboard and buckled into their seats that Agent Thatcher relaxed her guard. "First class, huh?" Taya mused with a smile, pulling out her phone to text Nathan.

"Oh yeah, they pulled out all the stops for you."

Just about to push back from the gate, she told him.

Leaning back in the spacious first class seat, the other woman looked at Taya. "I know this isn't easy. Going back over there after everything that happened before."

Taya glanced at her in surprise. The woman had definitely been briefed on Taya's past, but the way she'd said that made it sound like she was talking from experience.

"They picked me to be your escort for a reason," she went on, settling her arms across her middle. "Back when I was in the Air Force I was stationed at Bagram during my last tour. I was out in a remote village one day providing security during a medical outreach program when we were attacked. I was taken prisoner, along with my now husband and the Secretary of Defense."

Shocked, Taya turned fully in her seat to face Maya, her mouth falling open. "That was you?" she asked, incredulous. "I remember seeing that story when it hit the news." The story had been huge and she'd followed it closely, never realizing she'd face a similar fate a few short years later.

The woman nodded. "The man who orchestrated the attack was named Khalid, but he operated under orders from someone named Rahim."

Oh yeah, she knew all about that asshole. "The American who defected and became a warlord in Afghanistan. And set off a dirty nuke outside Langley."

Agent Thatcher inclined her head in acknowledgement. "He had close ties to Qureshi's network," she added, those mysterious sea-green eyes studying Taya.

A chill went up her spine as the connection hit home. "Wow, I…didn't expect this."

"Yeah, I'll bet. Anyway, that's why they sent me. And also, my husband's a PJ."

Now Taya's eyes widened. "Are you serious?" There weren't that many of them out there, active or retired, so it seemed like an incredible coincidence.

She smiled, showing a hint of white teeth. "Yeah. Our guys probably know each other."

"It's a small community, for sure, so I bet they do too." Taya leaned back against the seat with a smile, suddenly feeling a thousand times more relaxed about everything. "Life is so weird sometimes."

"Tell me about it. And since we've got so much in common, you'd better call me Maya. If you call me Agent Thatcher after everything I just told you, I'll be totally insulted."

"Well we can't have that. Maya it is."

"I've watched a lot of your speeches over the past few months, by the way. My favorite was the one you gave to the UN envoy on behalf of Amnesty International. Everything you said was dead on, and you put into words so perfectly what it's like to be a female captive over there. I'm a huge fan."

Her cheeks heated. "Oh, well. Thanks. I feel like it's my duty, you know? To give a voice to all the women who don't have one. And I feel like I owe it to the friends I met during my time over there and…lost. If I can help get Summer and the others back, I'll feel even better."

Maya reached over and gave her knee a reassuring squeeze. "I get it. Totally. It's why I wanted to become an FBI agent. To help stomp out terrorist networks and make the world a better place," she added with a sharp grin that reminded her a little of Celida.

I wish I knew how to make the world a better place. She was doing her best but sometimes it felt like her efforts were in vain.

They lapsed into a comfortable silence as the flight attendants began their safety demonstration. Taya checked her phone for messages but Nathan hadn't responded. Maybe he was in a meeting, or maybe they'd gotten a lead to follow and were out looking for Summer and the others.

Taya could only hope that was the case.

She switched her phone to airplane mode and put it back in her carryon. Maybe once she reached London there would be some good news.

****

Three years ago

She couldn't remember ever being so nervous and

excited at the same time.

Summer fought not to fidget as she sat in the uncomfortable plastic chair in the hospital waiting room and awaited the call from the nurse. The magazine in her lap couldn't hold her interest for more than a few minutes at a time, she was too busy checking the clock on the wall.

Adam's text chimed from her lap. *You in yet?*

Not yet, she responded. *Any time now. I'll text you once I'm ready.*

OK. Love you.

Love you back. She wished he could be here, but at least he was carving out the time.

"Summer?"

She stood and hitched her purse up on her shoulder, butterflies fluttering around in her belly. "Yes."

The nurse smiled at her. "Right this way."

She was shown into a room and given a gown to change into, then stretched out on the table to await the doctor. A few minutes later the female obstetrician came in. Summer dialed Adam, anxious to be connected with him. They'd been trying to get pregnant for so long and just couldn't on their own, and the IVF clinic had warned her that a positive pregnancy test didn't necessarily mean a viable pregnancy.

"You ready?" the doctor asked, gathering the ultrasound device.

"Yes. Adam, you can hear us?" Summer asked.

"Loud and clear," he answered.

It wasn't as good as having him here beside her, holding her hand, but it was better than nothing. He'd been great through everything so far, all the disappointments and setbacks she'd gone through. Having a baby of their own was more important to her than it was to him, but he'd been completely supportive through this journey so far and she loved him to death for it.

"I'm inserting the probe now," the doctor said.

Summer swallowed and tried to relax, but couldn't slow her racing heart. She'd wanted to have a baby so badly and now that she was finally pregnant, she didn't know if she could bear finding out there was no heartbeat.

She watched as the doctor fiddled with some buttons and knobs on the ultrasound machine, kept her fingers tightly laced together atop her stomach. *Please please please*, she begged, holding her breath.

At first there was no sound at all, then some crackling noises, like static.

And finally, just when her heart was about to burst, she heard it. A faint, pulsing whoosh-whoosh sound.

The doctor smiled at her. "Hang on, let me see if I can get a better angle." She manipulated the probe and the sound grew louder.

Summer unclasped her hands and put one over her mouth as tears sprang to her eyes. She let out a watery laugh. "Do you hear that?"

"Is that it? That's the heartbeat?" Adam asked, excitement in his voice.

"That's it," the doctor confirmed. "Congratulations."

Summer closed her eyes and said a silent prayer of thanks as her husband's delighted laugh filled the room, mixing with their baby's heartbeat.

Against all odds, they were going to be parents after all.

****

Present Day

Adam's fingers flexed on his weapon as they neared the target location. He focused on staying calm, took a steadying breath and kept a positive mental tickertape running through his mind.

Summer was still alive, best anyone could tell. And with this so-called "insider source" having leaked this tip to the Jordanians a little over an hour ago, his hopes were running high that she'd be here.

He rode up front while Tuck drove, Cruzie and Vance in the back. The other three guys were in the vehicle behind them with two Jordanian Special Forces guys who knew the area. DeLuca was back at the operations center, monitoring everything and keeping his pulse on anything else that came in regarding the case.

"Nearing target location now," Tuck reported to DeLuca via his earpiece.

"Got it," their commander responded. "Got you guys on GPS and your helmet cam."

They parked a block away and left one of the Jordanians to guard the vehicles for them. There hadn't been much time to prep for this mission but they all knew what to do, and they all knew what was at stake.

Three American lives hung in the balance. It was up to Adam's team to find and rescue them before it was too late.

The industrial area they were in was rundown, some of the buildings either abandoned or on the verge of being derelict. Lowering his NVGs over his eyes, he crept along in the shadows alongside the warehouse behind Tuck, pumped and ready to rock with the rest of the team behind him.

"Still no movement around the perimeter," DeLuca reported. "We're not getting any heat signatures inside but the walls might be thick enough to block the satellite."

When they were positioned by the southwest entrance, the spot they'd chosen previously to enter, Tuck paused, his weapon up and ready. Adam stood poised behind him, all his senses on alert, and waited for the signal.

Bauer's big hand landed on his right shoulder and

squeezed. Adam immediately reached forward and did the same to Tuck, signaling that everyone was in place and ready to go.

The door in front of them had only a padlock on it. Tuck backed up a step and rammed the sole of his boot against it as hard as he could. The rusted metal snapped and the door swung inward.

Adam threw a flashbang inside to the left, while Bauer did the same to the right. The second they exploded, with a loud bang and a flash of blinding white light, the team stormed inside.

Nothing happened. No shots. No shouts, no flurry of movement as people scrambled to get out of sight.

Only silence.

Acute disappointment settled in his gut. He stayed vigilant, on alert as they moved deeper into the building and fanned out. He noted the empty shipping crates they passed, the broken pallets littering the ground.

He continued on until he'd reached the far corner of the area he and Tuck were responsible for checking. "Clear," he muttered in disgust, barely able to get the word out through his grinding teeth.

"Clear," Tuck echoed, his voice ringing with frustration.

Bauer and Evers reported the same in their corner. As did Vance, Cruzie and then Schroder a few moments later.

Fuuuuuuck. Adam lowered his weapon, unsure if he wanted to scream or put his fist through something. Maybe both.

"Whoever was here seemed to have left in a hell of a hurry," Vance reported, his deep bass voice carrying through the stillness with ease. "I got ammo and other supplies dumped all over the ground here."

Adam and Tuck turned and immediately strode to the opposite end of the warehouse. Sure enough, broken and shattered crates lay tossed about, empty, with bits of their contents strewn around in the dust covering the concrete floor.

There was a set of tire tracks leading in from the closest doorway. Looked like whoever had been here had come in, rushed to take whatever they could before they were spotted, and then taken off in a hurry.

Tuck reported everything to DeLuca, but Adam had heard enough. He pushed his NVGs up, took out his earpiece and stalked away, needing a few moments to regroup by himself.

None of his teammates said anything or tried to follow him.

Alone in the darkness outside the warehouse, Adam ran a hand over his face and fought off the crushing wave of fatigue and disappointment trying to drag him under. Either this "inside source" was fucking with them, leading them on a wild goose chase to help buy the captors time to escape the area, or they'd once again missed their opportunity to find Summer and the others.

All Adam knew was, time was running out to save her. And there wasn't a damn thing he could do to stop it.

Chapter Nine

Two years ago

As another contraction hit, Summer dug her fingernails into the sheets and gritted her teeth to keep from crying out. The vicious pain twisted inside her, corkscrewing from her abdomen around her lower back and then held until she couldn't breathe.

Just when she didn't think she could take it a second longer, when she wanted to scream, it eased, slowly fading away into nothing. But they were getting closer together now, and more intense. And she'd never been so terrified in her life.

Another doctor bustled into the private room, the third physician she'd seen since the paramedics had rushed her into the ER twenty minutes ago. She lay on the narrow bed panting, damp tendrils of hair stuck to her sweaty face.

"Can you stop it?" she gasped out, afraid to look down between her legs where the nurse was pressing something. There'd been so much blood. Bright red with dark clots.

"We're trying. And we're going to do everything we can."

She made the mistake of looking as the nurse pulled the pad away from between her thighs. It came away glistening red, soaked with fresh blood.

Summer cried out and pressed a hand to her abdomen. *No.* No, this couldn't be happening. She was only twenty-five weeks along. She'd already miscarried once, and this was their second IVF attempt. She'd thought that after passing her first trimester without any problems she'd be in the clear, but…

Her lower back had been aching early this morning so she'd gotten out of bed and as soon as she'd stood up, the bleeding had started. Alone and afraid to stand up in case it made the bleeding worse, she'd been forced to crawl to her phone on the nightstand and called for an ambulance. But then the contractions had started on the way here and she was scared to death that she might be losing the baby. That it might already be too late.

No, she ordered herself. *No, you need to think positive. Stay strong, the baby needs you.*

Yes. That was her only job now, protecting the baby. She forced in a shuddering breath, let it out slowly. Then another. And another. *It'll be okay. It has to be okay. You need to slow your heart rate, slow the bleeding.*

But then another contraction started. She tensed up and fought her way through it as it built to an agonizing crescendo and held, tried to lay still when all she wanted to do was writhe and somehow escape the pain. It was all happening too fast. Everything was out of her control.

The staff bustled around the room getting more equipment and monitors set up, injecting more medication into her IV to try and stop the premature labor and reduce her pain. But she'd already lost so much blood. How could the baby possibly survive that?

"We've been trying to reach your husband at the number you gave us," one nurse said, taking her hand. Summer grabbed on tight and dug her fingers in as another contraction grew in strength.

"He's on a…training mission," she gasped out, eyes shut tight as the pain swelled. "In L.A." *Oh God, just make it stop.*

When it faded what felt like an eternity later, she was trembling all over. She was in full-on labor at six months pregnant.

A nurse moved out of the way. Summer raised her head and shot a frantic look at the monitor next to the bed. The little blip of the baby's heartbeat was getting weaker.

Tears flooded her eyes as she put a hand to her swollen belly. *No, please. Please hang on.* She bit her lip but a sob escaped anyway, making her shoulders jerk.

The nurse holding her hand made a sympathetic sound and leaned over to wrap an arm around her back, squeezing her. "Isn't there anyone else we can call to be here with you?"

She shook her head, fighting back another sob. Her family was all back in Indiana, and though she had some good friends here, she didn't want any of them in this room with her right now. There was only one person she wanted, and that was impossible.

"I want Adam," she whispered, the tears spilling free at last. He was so far away, back on the West Coast. Even if he got word and hopped a plane in the next few hours, he wouldn't get here until tomorrow.

By then it would be too late.

That awful squeezing sensation started up again deep in her belly. She moaned and curled into a ball, squeezed her eyes shut as the pain radiated outward. Dimly she heard voices rising around her. Urgent. People rushing around.

This time when she opened her eyes and sought the monitor, there was no blip on the screen.

She stared at it blindly for a moment, then sheer terror ripped through her. "No!" she cried. "*No!*" She clutched at her abdomen with desperate hands as the unthinkable hit home.

My baby. My baby is dead.

A doctor stepped into her view, face grim, eyes filled with sympathy. He looked from the monitor to her, and she knew it was true. Her baby was gone. "I'm so sorry," he murmured, taking her hand in his.

Shock and grief collided inside her, crushing her heart and lungs. She couldn't breathe.

Another vicious pain hit her. Around her she could hear the staff moving, could hear their voices, but it still took a few moments for her to absorb what they were saying. What it meant.

She was still going to have to deliver her dead baby.

Time passed in a disorienting blur of pain and unreality. They finally gave her something for the pain, just enough to take the edge off, and promised it wouldn't be long now. The doctor and two nurses stayed with her the entire time, holding her hand, wiping away her tears and sweat, encouraging her and supporting her as best they could.

It wasn't enough.

Adam, I can't do this without you, she thought frantically, feeling like she was about to shatter into a thousand pieces. *I can't go through this without you.*

But she had no choice.

It took another hellish six hours for the dry labor to run its course. Five more agonizing hours of contractions, followed by one hour of pushing.

"Just one more," the doctor said from his position between her open thighs at the end of the table.

A fiery pain burned all around her vaginal opening, like someone held a blowtorch to her tautly stretched flesh. Gritting her teeth, she gathered her remaining strength and pushed with all her might.

Her legs shook in the nurses' grip, every muscle straining. A strangled scream of mingled rage and pain tore free. She barely felt the tears flowing down her temples and dripping into her hair.

The baby popped free and the pain ceased instantly.

She dropped back to the table, exhausted, shaking all over. And God help her, she was too afraid to look. She couldn't bear to see her dead child.

Her stomach twisted. She gagged and turned her head to the side, where a nurse immediately held a stainless steel bowl beneath her. Nothing came up.

When the dry heaves finished, she collapsed back against the clammy pillow. One shaking hand came up to cover her eyes as her face crumpled.

"Do you want to hold him?" the doctor asked quietly.

Him? A little boy?

Fresh tears bubbled up. The physical pain was over but she knew the emotional pain had just begun.

She dropped her hand, her gaze unerringly going to the tiny figure wrapped in the blanket the doctor held. *My baby. My poor baby.*

Sitting up, heedless of the blood or the nurses trying to clean her up, she automatically reached for her son, desperate to hold him.

The doctor placed him in her arms. Instinct had her cradling him tight to her chest, against her heart. Oh, God, he was so tiny. Way too tiny. Fragile.

She bit her lip, feeling like she was crumbling apart inside. *Why?* Why had God done this to her? To her child?

She made herself pull the edge of the blanket back to see his little face. A funny sound shot out of her. A high-pitched cry of grief and denial.

Adam James. A.J. for short. That's what they had chosen for a boy's name.

And he was…God, he was perfect she thought with another spasm of grief. His little nose was perfect, his skin wrinkled and red. All his little fingers and toes were there; he even had little nails forming.

A tear landed on his cheek. She carefully wiped it away, devastated.

Had he suffered? Had he been afraid? He should still be safely tucked inside her, giving her those wonderful little flutters and kicks.

The nursery had been painted, the crib all set up. She'd grown so used to rubbing her belly and talking to him all the time, eagerly anticipating his arrival in the spring and the moment when she finally held him in her arms.

Not the way she was holding him now. Never that. How was she supposed to go on now?

Another nurse came in, stood by her bed with a phone in her hand. "I've got your husband on the line," she said softly. "Do you want to talk to him?"

She stared at the nurse. *Adam? He knew?* The thought of hearing his voice right now was more than she could bear.

Summer curled tighter around her baby and shook her head as the heartbroken sobs she'd been holding back finally broke free. She didn't want to talk to Adam. Didn't want to talk to anyone.

She couldn't bear this. Didn't know how to deal with this searing pain, this horrible emptiness.

The nurse was murmuring to someone in the background, but the words didn't register, or the fact that it might be Adam on the other end of the phone.

"He's heading to the airport right now," the nurse told her a few moments later. "He said he'll be on the first flight back. He said to tell you he's sorry and that he loves you, and he'll be here as soon as he can."

Summer turned away, curling onto her side with her dead son held tight in her arms. Not caring about anything right now, she didn't answer. She was too lost, too devastated to even comprehend this loss or how she was going to survive it.

All she could do was cradle A.J. to her breast and grieve, alone. It was her fault. Her body hadn't been able to sustain or protect him, yet she'd selfishly gone ahead with the IVF treatments anyway. And he'd paid the ultimate price for it.

Summer bit her lip hard enough to draw blood, welcoming the pain. God, when she thought of this precious little being tucked inside her just a little while ago, relying on her to protect and take care of him…

A hot knife of pain sliced through her. She broke. Felt herself split apart.

Harsh, ugly sobs racked her. She couldn't stop, was inconsolable. Her son. She couldn't let him go. They would come and take him from her soon. How was she supposed to let him go?

She cradled him and vented her grief, her guilt. I'm so sorry, little A.J., please forgive me. So very sorry…

Chapter Ten

Present day

When the pilot announced they'd be landing in Amman in a few minutes, Taya stood up to stretch her stiff back briefly before buckling back into her seatbelt. The injuries she'd sustained in Afghanistan normally didn't bother her much anymore, but sitting in one position for too long made her lower and upper back ache.

It felt like forever since she'd left D.C. She and Maya had spent the first half of the flight to London chatting about their experiences overseas. Maya was surprisingly open about it, but then, so was she.

By the time they'd reached London, they'd forged an intimate bond. There'd been no response from Nathan yet, so she knew he was likely out on the hunt somewhere. For Summer's sake, Taya hoped they found the hostages before she got there.

This second leg of the journey to Amman had seemed to take forever, probably because Taya was both dreading being there but looking forward to seeing Nathan.

When the plane parked at the gate, Maya turned to her and arched a dark eyebrow. "Ready?"

She nodded, checked her phone and found a message from Nathan, sent a few hours ago.

Sorry, we were busy for a while. I'll be at the airport when you arrive. Can't wait to see you!

"Nathan's here," she said, unable to keep the smile from her face. "Let's do this."

Anticipation swirled inside her. It had only been six days since she'd last seen Nathan but she'd missed him like crazy, and seeing him would go a long way to dispel her lingering fears about being here and dredging up all the ugly memories she'd been working so hard to move past.

Maya went up the jet bridge first. Taya followed close behind her, her heart beating faster as they made their way toward the waiting area at the gate. As soon as they turned the corner she spotted Nathan, standing right next to the podium with Tuck.

Everything else faded into the background as she drank him in: tall, his dark auburn hair raked back from his forehead and the start of a reddish beard covering his face.

A big smile split his face and he started toward her. Grinning like a lunatic, she rushed for him and flew straight into his arms.

"Hey, sweetheart," he said, hugging her tight. The feel of his embrace lifted the weight of dread she'd been carrying around from the moment she'd agreed to come here. Then he kissed her and she couldn't think at all until he pulled back.

"Hi," she breathed back, tucking her face into the curve of his neck. God, he smelled good.

He kissed the top of her head and leaned back to look at her, his hazel eyes warm as he cupped the side of her face in one big hand. "Flights were okay?"

"Great. And Agent Thatcher was great company," she said, looking over at Maya, who stood watching them by the entrance to the jet bridge. She couldn't believe how much they had in common. "Her husband's a PJ, so I thought you might know him."

His gaze sharpened with interest as he eyed the female agent. "That right?"

Maya nodded. "Jackson Thatcher."

Nathan's eyebrows shot up in surprise. "No way! I know him, he was a few months ahead of me in the pipeline. Is he still in?"

"Yep, he's stationed at Bagram right now. I'll tell him we met."

"Please do." He shook Maya's hand. "Thanks for escorting my girl over here."

"It was my pleasure." Maya turned to her, her eyes full of understanding. "I meant what I said. You ever want to talk about anything, just give me a call."

"I will." Taya looked over at Tuck, who was waiting patiently by the podium, scanning the crowd of people milling about, always vigilant. She felt safer already with the two of them here. "Hey, big guy. This is from your wife." She walked over and hugged him.

He chuckled against the top of her head and returned the embrace. "Thanks for that."

"Welcome." She took a deep breath, let it out slowly. "Okay. Now get me to that meeting." She was anxious to get started.

Nathan took her carryon bag and laced his fingers through hers. "Everybody's waiting to get down to business."

"Understandable. I just hope I can help. Any new developments while I was on my way over here?"

"Unfortunately no," he said. "Blackwell's going out of his mind."

"I can imagine," she murmured, feeling awful for him, but more for Summer.

At the hotel Maya left them to go to her own room and Taya went with Nathan up to the eighth floor. "Tuck's rooming with Blackwell now, so you can stay with me," he said as they stepped off the elevator. "It's not usual procedure and I may get called out at a moment's notice, but I thought it would be easier on you this way."

She nudged his hip. "And it had nothing whatsoever to do with you wanting me in your bed at night," she teased.

A grin quirked his lips. "Well, not gonna lie, it's a definite perk…"

She took five minutes to freshen up. When she came out of the bathroom he was waiting for her by the door. "They're waiting downstairs," he said, and framed her face in his hands. "You sure you're up to this?" he asked, searching her eyes.

The concern in his eyes warmed her to her toes. "I'm sure. But thanks for caring." She lifted up and kissed him. "Let's do this."

She walked past him out into the hall, and came to an abrupt halt when she saw Adam sitting there against the wall. He rose at once, his piercing blue gaze locked on her.

His haggard appearance shocked her. She'd never seen him like this, all disheveled and drawn.

He looked exhausted, his expression pinched with strain and he had dark circles beneath his eyes. "Adam, hi," she said softly, hating that he was hurting like this. Nathan stepped up behind her, put a comforting hand on her waist.

"Hi." Adam stuffed his hands in his pockets and she wanted to hug him but stayed put. "I just wanted to come by before the briefing to personally thank you for coming here. I know it couldn't have been easy. I really appreciate it."

She shook her head, overcome with the need to reassure him, make it all okay. But the only way she could do that is if they found Summer in time. The demons Taya faced here were only psychological and emotional—mere memories of what she'd endured. The ones Summer faced were far more immediate and dangerous.

Maybe even lethal. They *had* to find her, soon.

"Don't thank me for that." Taya had no evidence to base it on, but her gut feeling was that Summer's captor didn't plan to sell her or gift her to another fighter. No, she was worried that Summer's fate would be much, much worse if they didn't find and free her before it was too late. "I'm going to do whatever I can to help find Summer," she told him.

Adam nodded, and the grief and worry in his eyes made her heart ache. His fear was warranted though. From the little Celida and Maya had told her about the ATB member who'd kidnapped Summer, Taya knew the odds of finding her alive were small. Because from the sounds of it, Tarek Hadad was even more brutal and sadistic than Qureshi had been.

And that meant they had no time to lose.

****

Two years ago

All the lights were off again and it was barely past suppertime. Adam knew exactly what that meant and his heart sank like a rock.

He sighed and turned off his truck's engine, then sat there in the garage as the engine pinged and cooled. He didn't want to go in there because he knew what he'd find and he was so fucking exhausted right now he didn't know if he had the strength to deal with it.

The miscarriage had hit Summer hard. Really hard.

He understood that she'd needed time to grieve afterward. He even understood why she resented him for not being there when it had happened.

But he barely recognized his wife these days. Sometimes she couldn't get out of bed at all, which was totally unlike her. And sometimes she wound up leaving work early and came home to lock herself in their bedroom.

He rubbed a hand over the back of his neck, telling himself to suck it up. She was hurting, dropping fast into a mental and emotional tailspin he couldn't protect her from. He couldn't go back in time and undo what was done and he wanted to help her. It was just that he didn't know how anymore.

Feeling like he had a two-thousand-pound weight on his shoulders, he headed upstairs to their room. As he suspected, she was in there, the door closed. At least this time she hadn't locked it. It drove him nuts when she shut him out, made him frantic to reach her, do *something* to make it all better. Or at least stop her from pulling out of his reach.

He eased the door open to find her sleeping, curled away from him on her side of the bed. His heart squeezed. He hated seeing her so sad, so lifeless. She'd always been so strong, so vibrant.

Careful not to wake her, he stripped and slid in behind her, carefully curling his body around hers.

He knew the second she woke. She hitched in a breath, and he realized there were tears on her cheeks. *Ah, baby…*

"Come here," he murmured, aching for her. What could he do to make her less sad? What could he say to help her heal again?

He reached for her as she rolled toward him, wrapped her up tight in his arms. She laid there, pliant, not making a sound as her tears dried. Her pain pierced him, made him feel helpless.

Not knowing what to say, he simply held her and stroked her hair, her bare back, letting his fingertips drift over her soft skin. He kissed her forehead, down her nose to her cheeks, kissing the tears away. His lips brushed the corner of her mouth, testing, asking. If she'd just meet him partway…

She went completely rigid in his embrace. Stiff as an iron rod, as though she couldn't bear his touch. A second later she shoved a hand against his chest, physically distancing herself from him, then scurried a foot away and rolled over, giving him her back.

Shutting him out physically as well as emotionally.

The rejection was the equivalent of a sucker punch to the face. A sharp pain lanced through his chest, momentarily making his heart and lungs seize.

Adam lay there frozen in the darkness for a few moments, too stunned to move. But when she didn't say anything or make any move to reach out to him, he got the message.

She didn't want him there. Didn't want him fucking *near* her, let alone touching her.

And he couldn't take it.

Rolling from the bed, he dragged his clothes on and left, closing the door behind him.

****

Present Day

Summer woke from a light doze when her stomach rumbled angrily. She was past hungry, famished to the point that she actually felt sick.

Since she'd been locked up here they'd given her nothing but some water and a piece of flatbread. Maybe because they didn't see the point in wasting their precious food supply on a sacrificial lamb who wouldn't be alive much longer.

She swallowed hard at the thought and shifted her shoulders in an attempt to ease the stiffness in the joints. Her wrists and ankles were raw from where the plastic flex cuffs had rubbed away the skin in some spots.

Two of her captors had released her bindings only long enough for her to relieve herself, while under guard, in a pit someone had dug behind the building she'd been housed in.

She'd only had a minute each time to take in her surroundings while she did her business before the guards had ordered her out from behind the blanket serving as a kind of privacy screen and put the hood back on her. The small village they were in seemed to be perched on a hilltop. She'd seen five small dwellings in her vicinity but nothing else to help orient her.

With the guards keeping close tabs on her, there had been no further opportunity to look for or try to communicate with Jim or Mark. She didn't even know whether they were both okay.

Rapid footsteps approached and her growling stomach shrank into a hard ball beneath her ribs.

It was time. Hadad must have finally finished whatever meetings he'd been in. He had sent for her and he'd be expecting her to unlock her laptop for him.

The cell door squealed open. A rough hand seized her upper arm and hauled her to her feet. She stumbled, her balance hampered by the plastic ties around her ankles.

Her guard cut them loose then he began towing her out of the cell, shoving her head down as they passed beneath the low, narrow opening. She hurried to keep up with his long strides, every part of her wanting to dig in her heels and fight.

But that would not only be useless, it would be stupid. And it might get Jim or Mark hurt or killed.

He dragged her across an open space and into another building.

"Take off the hood," she heard Hadad command in Arabic.

She blinked when it was pulled over her head. Hadad stood behind a desk with her open laptop on it. And Jim and Mark were both seated on the floor next to the wall to her left.

They stared up at her with identical tight expressions. Jim had a split lip and a black eye and Mark looked nearly gray in the light from the single lantern hanging from the wall above them.

Hadad turned her laptop around so that the screen faced her and stood tall, folding his arms across his chest. "Your password."

There was no mistaking why he'd brought her coworkers in here for this. If she didn't comply, he'd beat or maybe kill them right in front of her. And she knew his reputation well enough to realize that he would be ruthless unless he got what he wanted.

She shot a furtive glance at Jim. He knew exactly what kind of sensitive intel she had on her laptop. Not everything, not the Top Security files, but enough that it could help Hadad's network, and hinder U.S. and allied forces' efforts to curtail them. Jim stared back at her, his expression giving away nothing.

If she did this, lives would be put in danger, maybe even Adam's. She thought of how worried he must be right now, waiting for word on whether she was alive or not. He'd be searching for her, planning some kind of rescue op with the other intelligence personnel.

For just a moment, a desperate plan formed in her mind. Without an Internet connection she'd never be able to send a message to anyone.

But if she was fast enough, maybe she could access the most sensitive files and delete them without Hadad noticing. She could make it look like she was accessing something for him, quickly erase a few files without drawing attention to it. They'd still be buried on here somewhere but maybe she could hide them deep enough that they wouldn't be able to find them.

Maybe.

"The password," Hadad growled. "Now."

When she hesitated he signaled to one of the guards, who immediately pulled a wicked-looking blade from his belt and stalked toward Jim.

"No!" she cried, fingers reaching for the keyboard. She told the password to him as she typed it in, waited until her desktop loaded. "There, it's done." She flipped it around for him to see.

"Show me the files on it."

Averting her eyes to hide her intent, she turned it toward her and searched up a folder containing some of the more sensitive intel. Moving fast, she pulled up a less critical one and opened it.

But when she had the opportunity to delete it, she hesitated. Hadad was watching her too closely. If he saw her or suspected what she was doing…she didn't even want to think about the consequences.

He peered at the screen, seemed to be reading the contents of the first document she'd opened. About suspected ATB strength and movement along the Syrian border with Jordan.

Her heart drummed in her ears. She stood there without moving, cold sweat gathering beneath her arms as she waited for his reaction.

His radio beeped. Without taking his eyes from the screen he answered it in Arabic. A man warned him that a reward had been offered for information leading to their location. The Americans and Jordanians were looking for them, might have a drone or two searching right now.

Summer kept her gaze on the floor, listening to every word. She didn't catch all of them, but enough to know the pressure was on. Her heart thudded harder, this time with a renewed burst of hope.

Suddenly Hadad snapped the laptop shut, the sound overly loud in the enclosed space. He stared at her for a long moment, then jerked his chin toward her and the others, his jaw tight. "Get them out of here," he growled to his men.

He was going to move them again.

No! The thought reverberated in her skull. If people were out looking for them and there might be drones in the area, moving again would reduce the chance of being found.

One of the guards grabbed her arms and secured her hands behind her while others seized Mark and Jim. Even though she knew there was no hope of escape, she couldn't just stand there, docile as a lamb while they took them to a new hiding location.

She flung her head back in an attempt to avoid the hood the guard tried to put on her, then lashed out with a foot to kick him in the knee. He hissed in a breath then seized her chin in one hand and squeezed, his bushy black eyebrows knitted together in a fierce frown.

Fuck you, Summer told him silently, glaring right back, and sunk her teeth into his hand. He cursed and jerked his hand away, then backhanded her.

The blow caught her across the face, stunning her. She stumbled backward, crashing into the wall.

"Hurry," Hadad snapped. "Move them *now*."

Two more guards converged on her. She tensed and ducked her head, bracing for the beating she was sure was coming. But they only plunged the hood back over her head, secured her ankles and carried her outside.

She could hear engines already running. Rough ones, as though the trucks were old.

Again her captors flung her into the back of one. She hit the metal bed with a bone-jarring thud, her right hip and shoulder taking the brunt of the impact.

Summer gritted her teeth, a pained groan slipping out as she tried to roll over. Heavy blankets were piled on her, then the tarp was secured on top. Within seconds the truck was moving, taking her out of the village.

She lay pinned in place, despair and hopelessness a crushing weight on her chest.

If they smuggled her across the border and into Syria, chances were she'd never get out alive.

Chapter Eleven

Ten months ago

S ummer didn't bother moving when she heard the sound of Adam unlocking the back door. She lay curled up on her side in their bed—well, her bed now, since he'd moved into the spare room a few weeks ago—in the darkness, and waited.

He didn't call out her name. He knew she was home because he would have seen her car parked in the garage on his way in.

When she heard his footsteps coming up the carpeted stairway, rather than excitement tingling in her gut, there was only a heavy foreboding.

His hushed footfalls came to the door and stopped. The door creaked slightly as he opened it. He didn't come in, just stood there backlit by the sunlight streaming through the windows at the front of the house and stared at her a moment. Well, what he could see of her huddled under the blankets with all the blinds drawn in the room.

"It's two in the afternoon," he said, his tone loaded with a disapproval that made her feel even worse.

She shoved back the annoyance. She knew exactly what time it was. And she didn't want to have this fight again so she didn't bother answering.

Adam expelled a sigh and folded his arms across his chest. "This is the fourth time in two weeks."

The fourth time in two weeks she'd left work in the middle of the day and come home to lie in bed in the dark. Alone. Ever since this latest miscarriage had sent her careening back into the tailspin she'd struggled so hard to pull out of after the stillbirth.

This time she wasn't sure if she'd make it.

She fought the urge to roll her eyes at her husband. Like she needed to be reminded of that? She was more than fucking aware of how much work she'd missed. Her boss was growing increasingly annoyed with it too. His fading support didn't hurt as much as Adam's though.

When she didn't respond she could literally feel the poisonous silence spread between them. Normally the building tension would eventually push her sadness into anger, which was a relief in a way, but lately rather than arguing she'd just begun retreating farther into herself instead.

The release of yelling and fighting felt good in the moment, but it always made things worse in the end and she'd crash even harder. So, better not to say anything at all.

Adam stood there for a full three minutes, staring at her. Waiting for her to say something, or maybe hoping she'd spring out of bed and "get over it already", she wasn't sure. She could feel the weight of his judgment, the heavy pressure of his frustration pressing down on her. And she was already so deep beneath the surface, she was afraid that one day she may never come up for air again.

It was clear he would never understand how badly she was hurting inside. That he didn't get it.

So many times they'd fought about it. She'd tried over and over to explain how badly the stillbirth and latest miscarriage had affected her. But it didn't matter how many times she'd talked to him about it, tried to explain her side of things.

Bottom line: He hadn't been there. He hadn't seen what she'd gone through. He hadn't held little A.J.

None of that was his fault; she knew he'd gotten to her as fast as possible. But she couldn't forgive him for this.

He had no patience for what the counselor had warned them would be a two steps forward, one step back kind of recovery. Maybe because hers was more like a one step forward, one step back cycle of endless suffering.

Just when she felt like she might finally be making progress, it hit her all over again. The guilt and loss.

She wasn't the kind of person to make excuses or curl up in a ball when things got hard. But this had crippled her emotionally. Nothing had worked. Not even the meds she'd finally agreed to try to help balance her brain chemistry.

Some days she functioned at an almost normal level and others were like this, when the crushing sadness hit her like a brick wall and she had to leave work. Sometimes it took two or three days for her to be able to drag herself out of bed and go to the office.

No one understood her pain, and no one could help her. Even though they meant well, she'd stopped taking calls from her family and friends. She was sick of the pep talks, of Adam's tough love speeches.

You have to want to help yourself.

You have to get out of bed and try.

You need to let go of the past.

It didn't matter that she understood the reason behind them. Adam couldn't stand seeing her like this and wanted to fix her. Well, he couldn't *fix* this, and every time he opened his mouth he just pushed her farther away. Yes, she was perfectly aware that adoption was a possibility for them, that plenty of babies and children out there needed a good home.

But she'd wanted so desperately to have her own child.

Still in the doorway, he took a deep breath then let it out in a slow exhalation of air. Obviously trying to make an effort to curb his frustration and not get angry. Still, she braced herself for another lecture.

His SF background made it impossible for him to accept her current condition, or that there was nothing he could do about it. As far as he was concerned, she could conquer anything if she just put her mind to it. He was angry because in his opinion, she'd given into the depression. To her it felt like he didn't even try to understand what she was going through.

Yeah, because I really love being fucking depressed.

But he hadn't gone into early labor and delivered a dead baby. He would never grasp the level of grief she'd experienced.

"So, you just gonna stay here for the rest of the night?" he asked, voice tight.

She didn't answer. There was no point.

The force of his frustration beat at her with invisible hammers. "Fine. You want something to eat?"

She couldn't remember when she'd last eaten. But she was too sad to think of food. Part of her didn't feel like she deserved food anyway. "No thanks."

Was that her voice? All fragile and weak. God, she hated that. Hated being on this awful rollercoaster of anger, grief and numbness. Hated herself for buckling under the weight of this and not being able to pull herself out, for not being able to connect with anyone, even her husband.

Unable to look at him a moment longer and see that disapproving expression on his face, Summer closed her eyes. *Just go away. Go away and leave me the hell alone.*

Another minute ticked past before he spoke again. "Fine. I'm going out." He turned away, shut the door behind him.

Sometimes the sound of his retreating footsteps hurt her more. Made her feel abandoned. Today she felt only an aching emptiness, and that confirmed what she'd suspected for a while now.

This was getting worse. Every part of her felt hollow. Her heart. Her womb. There was just…nothing left.

Even after he walked away, this time there was no spike of pain or loneliness. He didn't slam the door on his way out of the house.

A few moments later she heard the sound of his truck engine firing up, then driving away. And a sense of relief washed over her.

She wanted to be alone in the darkness. It was the only way she could cope with the pain she'd shoved down into the black pit of despair inside her.

****

Present day

Was this what Summer had felt like when she'd lost A.J.? This grinding, acidic boiling in the pit of his stomach, the constant state of helplessness?

Adam dragged his aching body into the back seat of the SUV beside Vance and Cruzie, with Evers and DeLuca up front. They'd just come from another possible target location on the outskirts of Amman. After searching the building and surrounding area thoroughly, they'd found squat and it looked like no one had been inside it for a few days at least.

Evers drove south, back toward the city center. Adam laid his head back against the headrest and closed his eyes. Searching for a happy thought, he called to mind a picture of Summer on their wedding day. They'd had a small wedding, just their immediate family and a few close friends.

She'd looked so beautiful in her strapless white gown, her bright auburn hair pinned up with curls falling down the back of her neck and at her temples. And that brilliant smile she'd given him when she'd started down the aisle of that little chapel had almost stopped his heart. He couldn't believe how lucky he was, that she'd agreed to be his wife.

A wrapper of some sort crinkled in the background, then a deep voice said, "Eat this."

Opening his eyes, he saw a partially unwrapped protein bar held in Vance's dark fist, inches from his nose. He made a face, his stomach rolling in both hunger and distaste.

"Go on," Vance said, waving it a little. "You gotta eat something, man."

"And drink this while you're at it," DeLuca added from up front, reaching back with a bottle of water in his hand.

Adam took them both, muttered a thank you. The first bite took two swallows to get down, and for a minute he was sure it would come right back up. When it didn't, he took another, chewing slowly, and swallowed a mouthful of water after.

From what he knew of the ATB, wherever she was, Summer wasn't being held in good conditions. She was probably starving, cold. Scared. He felt guilty as hell for eating anything while she was going through all that.

"You're no good to her if you starve yourself," Cruz pointed out beside him. "You gotta keep your body fueled up for when we get the green light."

That was true. The guilt lessened slightly.

In the distance, the tall buildings that marked the downtown core came into view as they crested a rise. DeLuca's cell phone went off. He answered, spoke briefly, then handed the phone back to Adam. "It's the director."

"This is Blackwell," he answered.

"I know you're frustrated, and so am I. We were all hoping this latest location you guys checked out would give us something solid."

"It was…disappointing." Understatement of the decade.

"I wanted to update you on our status. Taya's been a big help so far with helping fill in some blanks between Qureshi's network and the ATB. We've got more background intel on Hadad as well."

Adam gripped the phone tighter and waited.

"He's thirty years old, former Syrian Army. Known hardliner who's been looking for a convenient target within Jordan and this summit gave him the perfect chance to act on it. He's an up-and-comer in the organization, looking to make his mark, and he's got quite the reputation for cruelty already. To put it to you straight, he's one evil bastard. His family was killed by a joint Jordanian/U.S. airstrike ten months ago. That's when he defected and pledged his allegiance to the ATB. So for him, this is personal."

Shit. None of that came as much of a shock because Adam had already been fearing the worst about him, but this intel wasn't good news for Summer and the others and it upped the stakes. If this was personal for Hadad, negotiations weren't possible.

"I get it." He rubbed at his eyes, his head spinning. Hadad was a warped, sadistic son of a bitch, and he had Summer. "Any more word on a possible location? Or proof of life?" Something. Anything to give him hope that she was still alive.

"Not yet but we're doing everything we can to get both of those. And if they'd killed the hostages they would have made a statement by now. They're not going to keep quiet about something like that."

"Yeah," he muttered. Hadad and his followers no doubt had something special in mind for their captives. He scrubbed a hand over his sweaty hair.

"Taya helped confirm some of the players we've suspected are linked between the ATB and Qureshi's old network. They've got ties throughout Afghanistan, Pakistan, Iraq and Syria. Most of their funding comes from drug and human trafficking."

Adam grunted to show he was still listening. He knew Taya had been given to one of Qureshi's fighters as a wife. That was so fucked-up. "What do the analysts think? Is Hadad going to want to barter Summer for money?" He couldn't bring himself to say *sell her*.

"They think it's unlikely."

But she *was* likely still alive. He had to hold onto that. "Thanks for the update."

"I'll let you know if we find anything else."

Adam handed the phone back to DeLuca, who was watching him closely. "Anything?" his commander asked.

He repeated what the director had told him. "They think she and the others are still alive."

No one said anything to that. Adam leaned his head back again. Fuck, he was tired. As tired as he could ever remember being, even through SF selection and on his toughest missions in Afghanistan. "I want to go to her hotel," he blurted.

Behind the wheel, Evers glanced at him in the rearview mirror in surprise. "What for?"

He shrugged, fought the urge to snap at him. What did the reasons matter? "I just do."

Evers shot a questioning look at DeLuca, who nodded his consent. "Let's go."

At the front desk it only took a minute after flashing his FBI badge and explaining the situation for the hotel manager to personally escort him to the elevator. Vance came up with him while the others stayed in the lobby.

Adam put the keycard in the lock, waited for the little light to turn green. He cracked the door open and Vance's voice startled him out of his thoughts.

"You want me to wait out here?"

Adam looked back at him, having forgotten he was even there. God, he was definitely losing it. "Yeah, man. Thanks."

"No worries." He stood with his back up against the wall beside the door, as though he planned on guarding it. Which he likely did.

Flipping on the light, Adam shut the door behind him and took a deep breath, something easing inside him. His team was awesome and all the guys had been really supportive so far, but it was a relief to be alone for a while.

He glanced around the empty room. Just an ordinary hotel room, yet as he drew in another deep breath he swore he could detect the faint scent of Summer's perfume in the air.

In the middle of the room the bed was freshly made and there were fresh vacuum marks on the carpet, so housekeeping obviously had been in recently.

Next to the bathroom stood a sink and vanity where some of Summer's toiletries were laid out. He walked over to it and stood there for a moment, looking at each item.

Her toothbrush was sticking up out of the glass she'd placed it in. The little bag holding her makeup and the powder she used to try and diminish her freckles with lay beside her brush and hair straightener. A pair of pearl earrings he'd given her for their first anniversary sat beside a tube of toothpaste.

Staring at all of it, he felt…empty. Like his insides had been hollowed out.

Exhaustion pulled at him, a heavy, seductive weight waiting for the moment to pull him under. Sleep would help him escape this for a little while. Sooner or later he'd have to give into it. But right now he just couldn't.

Gripping the counter, he looked up at his reflection in the mirror. He looked like hell. Eyes bloodshot, dark smudges underneath, lines of strain visible on either side of his mouth through the few days' worth of growth on his face.

He looked grief-stricken, like a man mourning the loss of the woman he loved. Only he refused to acknowledge that Summer might be dead, or that she likely would be soon if they didn't find her.

And suddenly the need to smash something was so strong he could barely control it. His muscles quivered with the strain of holding back, his breathing turning erratic. He gripped the counter tighter to quell the urge to smash his fist into the mirror and break it into a thousand pieces.

Staring into the mirror, he forced himself to breathe until the anger dissipated.

The waiting was killing him. Second by second, minute by minute, the hope he'd been clinging to was slowly fading. And now, standing here with her things laid out in front of him, things she'd touched the morning she'd been taken, he almost couldn't bear it.

With a shaking hand he reached for the bottle of perfume she'd left beside the sink. He pulled off the cap, paused a moment to brace himself, then lifted it to his nose.

The warm, vanilla musk scent slammed into him, so familiar, piercing him like a red-hot blade. Hurriedly he put it down, fought the rise of tears at the back of his throat.

She's still alive, he told himself sternly. *She's not gone yet.*

In the mirror he saw behind him the desk set against the wall on the other side of the room. There were some bottles of water and a few snacks she'd left on it. He turned around and crossed over to it, his gaze landing on the bag of M&Ms sitting there.

His chest constricted. They were her favorite. She could never turn them down and she never saw a movie without them.

He picked up the little brown bag, the colorful candies inside the open end blurring together as tears flooded his eyes. He'd bought an economy-sized bag of them for her when he'd taken her to the drive-in on their last date, and packed them up with thermoses of hot chocolate and sleeping bags and pillows...

That night had been one of the best of his life.

As the memory rushed back, he lowered his head and let the tears fall.

Chapter Twelve

Three months ago

I never imagined it would come to this.

The thought kept hitting Summer over and over again as she entered the house for the final time to grab the last of the moving boxes, and paused to look around their kitchen. It felt surreal to be leaving, and guilt pricked at her conscience. No matter if she knew this was the right decision, on some level she still felt like she was abandoning Adam.

But she knew it was for the best. For both of them.

She had to leave, have her own space. For a while at least, maybe forever.

She couldn't take being here anymore and Adam knew that. Every day she spent here brought back more painful memories, and every time she saw Adam was yet another reminder of what she'd been through and all she'd lost. A big part of her just wanted to make a clean break and start over, for her own sanity. Even if she knew it was selfish in a way, that didn't change the facts.

Adam had made it clear that he didn't want her to go. But if it's what she needed, then he said he understood. That made it even harder to go.

She still loved Adam, would always love him, but she was too angry and hurt and sad to stay. For months now she'd been constantly torn, not knowing how or even if she could ever open herself back up to him again, while at the same time knowing it wasn't fair to keep punishing him over and over by continually pushing him away.

No, this was the right move, for him as well as her.

It had taken her months to come to this decision, after she'd weighed it over endlessly in her own mind and sought counseling advice about it. Even though she was ready to take this next step, the thought of settling into the one-bedroom apartment she'd rented across town was both scary and exhilarating.

She'd needed to make a big change, do something drastic to jerk her out of the mental hole she'd fallen into and couldn't seem to climb back out of. Moving out on her own was the only thing she hadn't tried yet. It had to work, because nothing else had and she didn't know what else to do.

Looking around the bright, tidy kitchen, she felt mostly relief that she was leaving, but there was sadness too. This had been her home for years now. She'd cooked countless meals in here, baked her grandmother's banana bread recipe that Adam loved. They'd painted the place together right after they'd moved in. They'd made love on the rug in front of the fireplace and on the kitchen table.

So many memories were imprinted in these walls. For a long time, it had felt like those walls were closing in on her, squeezing and trapping, the once happy memories slowly crushing her under a weight of resentment and grief.

She blew out a breath. "Time to go," she said to herself, stopping the negative train of thought in her head.

It took constant effort to do it, to snap herself out of the line of thinking that had become as familiar as breathing over the past two years.

Lifting the last box from the center island, she stopped short when she saw the note Adam had left for her beneath it.

I love you.

That was it. Just three words, not even his name beneath them.

The sight of it made instant tears blur her eyes. *Oh, Adam…*

They'd both agreed it was probably better that she move out while he was away for work, so it was less painful. He'd flown out of town on a training mission this morning. But now she realized that leaving was going to hurt no matter when she did it, and whether he was here or not.

This *hurt*. This *sucked*. But it had to be done.

She didn't want to admit their marriage was over, that she'd had preliminary separation papers drawn up. At this point she wasn't even sure what had kept her from going through with the legal separation, to be honest. Some part of her simply refused to accept the idea of losing him forever, she guessed.

Except she couldn't see them ever reconciling after this. Adam saw her leaving as a proverbial line in the sand. Once she stepped over it…

She pushed aside the tiny voice of fear in her head. The one that warned her there was no going back once she left.

Her fingers shook slightly as she picked up the note and slipped it into her pocket. "I still love you too," she murmured into the empty kitchen.

But unfortunately, love wasn't enough. Not for her. Not for him. And she couldn't stand to hurt him anymore by staying.

Better to yank the bandage off in one shot, rather than little by little.

Steeling herself, Summer turned off the light on her way out and locked the door behind her.

****

Present day

Tarek paused in reading the contents of the file he'd opened on the laptop twenty minutes before, a new, deeper rage burning inside him. Because of the translation it had taken him a while to figure out the specifics detailed in the document before him, and now that he had…

He turned his head to aim a lethal glare at the female captive. She was seated against the wall, her knees drawn up, her cheek resting on them. Asleep now, exhausted from the constant questions he'd thrown at her, and because of the sleep deprivation they'd subjected her and the others to.

"Wake up," he snapped.

Her lids flashed open, her eyes blurry with sleep as she focused on him. He saw the moment she was fully aware of where she was. She stiffened slightly, her lips pressing together in a mutinous expression he longed to wipe off her pretty fucking face.

Soon enough, he would.

He jabbed a finger at the screen. "This report. It says there are spies in our network."

She didn't answer, just stared back at him with that defiance burning in her blue eyes that made him want to break her.

"Is it true?" he demanded. "*Answer* me," he barked when she didn't respond right away.

"I only know what it says in the report."

Oh, she knew far more than that. He had no doubt.

The urge to take out his knife and cut the answers out of her was nearly overwhelming. With effort he reined it in, forced himself to pull in a slow, even breath. He would not let this bitch best him. Her little act of defiance was nothing. And she would soon learn the true meaning of pain.

The thought sent a pleasurable shiver rocketing down his spine.

He'd learned enough to know that he had to be careful. Even more careful than he had been. If spies had infiltrated their ranks, he couldn't trust anyone.

He turned off the laptop and shut it with a thud. For all he knew the Americans might be able to trace a signal to it somehow, even though he wasn't connected to the internet. He'd send it with Akram tomorrow, have him deliver it to one of the generals across the border. Tarek would be there in person soon enough.

The woman continued to stare at him, wary, watchful. He thought of his dead fiancée and family. His parents and siblings. All killed when their village had been destroyed by an American and Jordanian airstrike.

Beautiful, innocent and God-fearing people, obliterated in the blink of an eye. Blown into so many pieces that there was no way of identifying the remains except for DNA testing, which there hadn't been any time for.

The bits of flesh and bone Tarek and the other rescue members had been able to find in the smoldering rubble had been hastily buried in a pit on the outskirts of the village. His entire world had been leveled that night. His home, his family, the woman he loved, all taken from him. And the Americans had the nerve to say the ATB were the evil ones?

He narrowed his eyes at the woman, his breathing speeding up as the anger took hold.

It wasn't right that this American bitch, with ties to the very same intelligence agency that helped plan air attacks like the one that had taken everything from him, should live.

"Your country took everything from me," he told her, his voice shaking at the horrors he'd seen that night. He would never forget the smell of burning flesh, the acrid stench of the buildings as they smoldered around him. He'd never get it out of his nose, out of his mind. Vindication made his heart race. "And so I'm going to take everything from you."

A shadow of fear flickered in her eyes, and a rush of triumph roared through him, so powerful it made him dizzy. She probably feared he or the others would rape her.

He wouldn't tell her it was unfounded. That neither he nor any of his men would lower themselves and risk tainting themselves with her infidel flesh.

He stopped and sucked in a deep breath, reminding himself that vengeance was only hours away. "Get her out of my sight," he commanded one of his men.

Tarek didn't look at her as she was yanked to her feet and shoved through the door, on her way back to her cell. His jaw flexed, the urge to throw something almost getting the better of him. Until this war he'd never known that he could hate so completely. That he would be able to take a human life without a single pang from his conscience.

But this rage was all-consuming. It fueled him, kept him going even when all seemed lost. And combined with Allah's will, it gave him the strength to do what must be done.

Summer Blackwell and the others were already living on borrowed time. Tomorrow he would make the video. After that, she would have only hours to live.

He couldn't wait to hear her screams.

Chapter Thirteen

It was two in the morning by the time Nate finally made it up to his hotel room. He'd been looking forward to spending time alone with Taya all day but they'd been working late again. They'd just come back from a recon op at a village up north, but again, no dice.

Everyone was frustrated and Blackwell, quiet and stoic as he was, had to be close to the breaking point. Anyone in his position would be. Hell, Nate remembered too well the sickening horror he'd felt when Taya had been taken at gunpoint when she'd showed up to testify at the Qureshi trial. And that had only lasted for a matter of hours, not days.

He opened the door as quietly as he could, expecting Taya to be fast asleep.

Stepping inside, he was surprised to find a lamp on low in the corner of the room. Both queen size beds were empty.

His gaze flew over to the window and found Taya curled up in the armchair there. She had a book on her lap and coloring books and pencils scattered on the floor around her. Apparently she'd been keeping herself busy after her long day of meetings with Director Foster.

She looked up, gave him a relieved but tired smile. "Hey," she murmured.

He shut the door and crossed the room to her, smiling in turn. "What are you doing up? You've gotta be exhausted from the jet-lag and all." Not to mention the nature of the meetings today. It had to have been hard on her emotionally.

"Couldn't sleep until I knew you were okay." She shook her head as she put the book aside and stood. "Wanted to wait up for you."

Nate drew her into his arms and exhaled a deep sigh. He was so lucky to have her here, to be able to hold her like this. She pressed tight to him, wrapped her arms around his ribs and rested her head on his chest, the familiar scent of her shampoo teasing him.

His gaze slid to the book she'd been holding, and he realized it was her journal. He knew what it contained, understood what her working on it signified.

Hell.

Being here had obviously triggered a lot of shit for her. Shit he wished he could erase from her memory forever, but he couldn't. And God knew, he still had the remainder of his own baggage to deal with. Since they'd gotten together he was handling it a thousand percent better than he had been, but it was still there. This trip had made it worse for her.

He hugged her harder, hating that she was hurting inside, that she'd been dragged into this. "Rough day, huh?"

She nodded, her cheek rubbing against his shirt. "Any luck with you guys?"

"No." This whole situation had triggered the specters from his past as well.

He was lucky that they'd been in briefings and on recon missions most of the day, because it gave him something to focus on. The less time he had to be in his own head, the better. Having Taya here soothed him on the deepest level. She had a way of silencing the constant chatter in his head that he couldn't explain.

She made a sympathetic sound, rubbed a hand over his back as though he was the one in need of comforting. "How's Adam?"

"Shredded." Honestly, Nate didn't know how Blackwell was even hanging in there at this point. The guy had barely slept since Summer had been taken. He was functioning, steady on the job when they were out on recon, but barely himself. Both DeLuca and Tuck were keeping a close eye on him.

"God, I feel horrible for them both."

"Yeah, it sucks." Classic Taya. Worried about others when she'd just been put through an emotional meat-grinder herself. He put a knuckle beneath her chin, tipped it upward so that she met his gaze. "What about you?"

Staring up at him with those pretty gray eyes, she gave a half-shrug. "I'm okay. It was just hard, dredging up all those things. All the memories again."

"I'll bet." Traumatic memories like that and the flashbacks they brought made everything feel fresh and raw, as though it had all just happened rather than years ago.

Taya knew that better than anyone. And yet she hadn't hesitated to come here and help, even knowing what she'd face. Was it any wonder why he loved her so much? "I heard the director said you've been a big help so far."

"I don't feel like I did much. Mostly just identifying people and the connections between them. I saw…two men who were part of Qureshi's inner circle while I was captive. In a way it was therapeutic, I guess, but looking at them in the flesh again even via video call was really hard."

"I'm sorry you had to go through that."

"If it helped the analysts at all, then I don't mind. Just wish I could be more of a help and find out something that would tell them where Summer and the others are being held. From what I found out today about his predilection for torture, Tarek Hadad sounds like he's pure evil."

"I know." Anyone capable of torturing innocents the way he reportedly did meant he was a formidable enemy. Negotiations would never work. The only way to stop him was to kill him.

But Nate didn't want to think about any of that right now. Not with Taya all warm and pliant in his arms.

He lowered himself into the armchair and tugged her down into his lap, cuddling her to him. He didn't want to talk about any of this; he'd rather push it all aside for now and lose himself in her. Because all this shit would be right there waiting for them when they woke up in the morning.

He stroked a hand over the thick, curly mass of her hair and breathed in her fresh, clean scent. Neither one of them said anything, just soaking in the comfort of being close to one another. She was only a few years older than him, but her emotional maturity made her seem wise beyond her years. The result of having survived the hell she'd gone through.

Even after a shitty day like this one, her mere presence still calmed him. She had a way of making the rest of the world disappear just by being in the same room as him.

Glancing down at the journal, he looked at the new lines she'd penned tonight. "You want to talk about it?" he offered, his lips against her hair.

The journal writing helped them both, a lot. He'd first tried it at her suggestion months ago and had been surprised at how therapeutic it was. It had really helped him to mentally file the ugly memories in the past, where they belonged, allowing him to move forward.

She lifted a shoulder. "Not really. Just…seeing those faces and hearing the voices of some of Qureshi's fighters again was hard. It brought back a lot of things I'd rather forget."

He made a low sound and kept stroking her hair, understanding perfectly. The truth was, he'd been struggling somewhat with his PTSD issues again since landing in Amman, and fighting like hell not to let it show. The team had enough to worry about without feeling like they needed to keep an eye on him too.

He wasn't sure what had triggered it. Something about the climate over here maybe, about being back in a place where the Islamic call to prayer rang out across the city, had put him instantly on edge the moment he'd walked out of the airport.

He'd been working hard to slay his personal demons these past months, journaling and seeing a therapist periodically about the mission from hell when he'd lost a close friend back in Afghanistan.

She lifted her head and looked up at him, the pale scars on the left side of her neck and jaw silvery in the lamplight. Looking at them, he was struck by a wave of gratitude. They both went through hell in Afghanistan, Taya more than him.

But if they hadn't, they wouldn't have met and he wouldn't be holding her right now. So even though he sometimes still had nightmares about losing O'Neil, he didn't regret all of it.

She put her head back on his shoulder. When she didn't say anything for a long time, her breathing slow and even, he thought she might be asleep.

But when he glanced down he saw that her eyes were open, staring off into space across the room. Lost in memories he knew she'd never be able to forget.

He could definitely help distract her from them, however, at least right now.

Cupping her jaw in one hand, he brought her gaze to his. "I'm really glad you're here," he told her. And the soft weight of her in his lap was having predictable results. It had only been six days since he'd last seen her, been inside her, but it felt like a lot longer. He craved her with a power he'd never known was possible until the day she'd reappeared in his life.

She gave him a smile full of understanding and rubbed her cheek against his palm, the kittenish move making him want to nuzzle and kiss her all over. "Me too. I just wish we could find her."

"We all do. And we will find her." Every last person involved with the case was aware that the odds of finding Summer were already slim, and getting slimmer with each passing hour. He seriously didn't know what the hell they were going to do if she didn't make it. God, and poor Blackwell would...

He slammed that door in his mind shut before he could finish that thought and focused on Taya. The way she smelled. The way she was nuzzling his chest and how it made his dick throb.

The room was quiet, the air around them suddenly charged with anticipation. Staring into Taya's eyes he felt that deep, unshakable connection between them snap into place. It centered him, helped banish the ghosts swirling around the edges of his consciousness. He wanted to do the same for her.

Tipping her face up, he bent his head and took her lips in a slow, thorough kiss. She melted into him with a little hum that set his blood on fire, her tongue doing a slow, erotic dance with his. He was already hard.

Gripping her hips, he stood and walked her backward to the closest bed, laying her down on it. When he came down on top of her she surprised him by pushing at his shoulder, trying to roll him over.

He moved onto his back, a hot thrill racing through him when she straddled him, then grabbed the hem of her sleep shirt and pulled it over her head. He reached up to cup the full, round globes of her breasts but she caught his wrists and pressed them back against the sheet.

The intensity in her eyes stole his breath, made his heart pound as he allowed her to pin his hands above his head, surrendering to her. His gorgeous little warrior was making it clear without a word that she needed control tonight, and he wanted to lose himself in her. He was more than happy to let her be in charge right now.

He lay back, lifted his torso as she peeled his T-shirt off, his pulse spiking at the appreciative hum she made, her fingertips tracing the lines of his muscles. When she trailed a hand down his abs he raised his hips so she could get him naked, tugging his pants and underwear off. Her hands and mouth wandered over his naked skin, raising goose bumps and drawing every muscle tight.

Her eyes glowed with desire as she sat upright. By the time she straddled his waist, his heart was tripping all over itself and his mouth was dry.

All the static in his brain was on mute. He couldn't think at all as he stared up at the luscious mounds of her breasts, the hard nipples begging to be teased.

Lips curved into a knowing smile, she cupped his head between her hands and leaned down to offer him a taut nipple and he was lost. With a groan he took her into his mouth and sucked, his cock twitching at her gasp of enjoyment.

Her hands were in his hair, fingers rubbing against his scalp with an erotic pressure, then she reached back with one hand and wrapped it around his swollen, straining cock. He groaned deep in his throat, fought to keep his hands where they were and not cup the generous flesh he was pleasuring.

She stroked him with skillful fingers, rubbing her slick, open folds over his lower belly, the wet sound of it driving him wild.

Sitting up, she pushed her hair back from her face, her curls tumbling down her back. Her eyes were like molten silver, hot with need, her cheeks flushed. "I want you inside me."

"Hell yes, ride me."

He curled his hands into fists and stared up at her, mesmerized by her sheer, feminine power. His breathing was erratic as she stood him up and scooted backward to hover over him, the head of his cock just kissing her slick entrance. Watching him, she sunk her teeth into that full lower lip and eased down slightly, inching him inside her.

Tight, slick heat enveloped him, stealing his breath. He squeezed his eyes shut, a shudder rolling through him. And when he opened his eyes to find her stroking her clit while he was buried inside her, he almost lost it. His fingers clenched with the need to take over for her.

"You're so damn beautiful," he rasped out, squeezing his fingers tighter into his palms to keep from reaching for her, seizing her full hips in his hands and taking control.

A slow, appreciative smile curved her mouth and her eyes went heavy-lidded. She rocked forward, the glide and pressure shooting sparks of pleasure up and down his spine. Her hum of enjoyment turned into a soft, liquid moan as she rode him, slow and sweet and sexy, her breasts swaying with each roll of her hips.

"God, you feel so good inside me," she gasped out, eyes squeezed shut, the hitch in her breathing and the strain on her face telling him she was already getting close. "You're just so…hard," she moaned, rocking faster now, fingers swirling gently across the swollen nub between her thighs.

Nate shuddered again, his building release already a warning tingle at the base of his spine. He couldn't speak, could only clench his jaw and hold on while she rode his cock in utter abandonment.

A few strokes later she threw her head back and cried out as she broke. Her inner walls squeezed him in a rhythmic caress, pushing him past the point of no return.

Rearing upward, he grabbed hold of her hips and rolled her beneath him. She was still coming as he pounded into her, fast and hard, over and over…then drove deep one last time and held there while he shattered. He groaned like a dying man and let it roll through him, the pleasure wiping out everything.

When it finally faded he relaxed his grip on her hips and bunched his hands in her hair, raising his head to seal their mouths together in a deep, intimate kiss. Then, gently withdrawing from her warmth, he rolled them onto their sides and tucked her into his body, pulling the covers over them both.

"I love you," he whispered, kissing her forehead.

A sleepy smile curved her mouth and she didn't open her eyes. "Love you too."

She was half-asleep when he came back from cleaning up and washed between her legs with a washcloth.

Knowing how lucky he was to have her here, to have her in his life at all, let alone her heart, he cradled her against him and held her tight.

Chapter Fourteen

Adam jerked awake from a nightmare with his heart hammering and his skin slick with sweat. He sat upright in the bed, the fear still gripping him as he struggled to get his bearings in the darkness.

It took a few moments for his sleep-deprived brain to process everything. The hotel. Tuck was asleep in the other bed.

Scrubbing a hand over his face, he drew a shuddering breath and got out of bed. Fragments of the nightmare kept assaulting him, the images vivid, horrifying.

Summer, staked out on the ground as her captors assaulted and tortured her. Her screaming his name, begging for help while she endured the unthinkable.

The muscles in his jaw tightened, saliva pooling in his mouth. As his stomach lurched he stumbled for the bathroom.

"You okay?" Tuck said groggily from his bed.

Adam didn't answer, too busy holding back the little bit of food he'd forced down before going to bed a couple hours before. He threw the bathroom door shut and flipped the toilet seat up just as his stomach heaved. He dropped to his knees and threw up until his abs burned and his throat felt raw.

Afterward he dropped his head into his hand and sat on the cold tile floor, covered in clammy sweat. He felt broken inside. Lost.

He scrubbed a hand over his damp face, forced his wobbly legs to unfold and push him to his feet. After rinsing out his mouth and brushing his teeth he hit the shower. As the scalding hot water pounded down on his bent head and neck he stood there with his hands planted against the slick fiberglass walls and fought to clear his head.

But all he could think of was Summer.

That night at the drive-in he'd wanted so badly to take her upstairs to her apartment and finish what they'd started. But he hadn't. Back then he'd thought they'd have plenty of time to get around to that; that the buildup and anticipation would pay off for them in the long run.

Now it just seemed like a huge fucking wasted opportunity. Maybe his last, to make love to the woman who meant everything to him.

Aside from the stillbirth, everything that had pulled them apart seemed like bullshit now. He would trade places with her in an instant, give his life for her if it would set her free. Did she know in her heart that he was searching for her? That he wouldn't give up?

He wouldn't leave Jordan without her. He was taking her home, no matter what.

He just prayed it wouldn't be in a body bag.

Tuck was waiting for him when he finally emerged from the bathroom. That deep brown gaze swept over him critically.

"Don't say it," Adam warned. "I'm still fully operational."

Tuck didn't respond for a long moment.

If they were reunited again, Adam vowed then and there that he'd make sure Summer would never doubt his love for her ever again.

A cell went off.

Adam's gaze shot to the nightstand where he'd put his, but realized it was Tuck's ringing. At this hour, the call had to be important.

Tuck leaned over and grabbed it. "Tucker." His eyes met Adam's as he listened. "Yeah, he's right here."

Adam's heart beat faster.

"We gotta get down to the command center. A tip just came from a reliable source about a possible location on the cell, up near the Syrian border."

The news hit him like he'd been mainlining shots of espresso for the past hour. Instantly all the fatigue was gone, his brain clear and alert, his body primed for action. Without waiting for Tuck, Adam grabbed his gear and rushed for the door, yanking his shirt over his head.

He was going to get his wife back.

****

Something big was about to happen. She could feel it. And Hadad was growing restless.

For about the past half hour Summer had watched him rushing back and forth, coming in and out of view as he disappeared out of and back into the building. He was barking orders, overseeing what his men were doing, and she only caught bits and pieces of what he said.

She could see it all clearly because they hadn't put the hood back on her. Something that only made the churning in her stomach worse. If they didn't care if she saw what was going on now, then it had to mean her usefulness to them had come to an end.

Her heart thudded hard against her chest wall and clammy sweat gathered beneath her arms, on her hands.

What were they going to do to her? She'd seen a video of Hadad beheading a prisoner, and crucifying another. Cruel, agonizing and terrifying ways to die.

She tried to keep from imagining all the horrific ways they could torture and kill her, things she'd seen at work but now that her imagination had gotten rolling, it was impossible to cut off that train of thought.

Trying not to draw any attention to herself, she stayed motionless against the back bars of the cell. They'd put her in it a few minutes after Hadad had looked down at her with those chilling black eyes and told her he was going to take everything from her.

They'd cut her hands and feet free, tossed her dirty socks and a beat up pair of old running shoes before slamming the cell door shut and locking it. Huddled there in the dirt, she was pathetically grateful for the extra warmth. For the first time since she'd been taken, her feet weren't numb from cold.

Except she had a terrible suspicion she wouldn't be able to savor that for long.

From her position at the far end of the long, abandoned building they were in, she couldn't see Jim or Mark but she had a clear view of Hadad's men as they moved about, setting up some kind of equipment in the center of the room. She'd heard one of them talking about their location earlier, and she was pretty sure she'd overheard the name of the village they were in.

Northern Shuneh.

She knew the place, located up near the northern border with Syria. A poor, remote area that had come up during her research prior to this trip. The DIA had suspected the ATB might be using it as a staging area for their operations in the region. Now she knew for sure.

Out of the corner of her eye, she spotted movement and turned her head toward it. One of Hadad's men approached her cell, carrying something in his hands.

It was black, about the size of a laptop. But it wasn't her computer. Hadad had given it to his second-in-command earlier, the moment he'd finished with her in that unsettling interrogation. He'd made her wait since then to find out what her fate would be.

She now knew firsthand that the intel reports on him were right. He was a master of psychological warfare. He knew she was afraid, knew it was torture to imagine what might happen and was letting that fear grow while she waited for his next move.

The ATB fighter was nearly to her now. There wasn't any room to move but she shrank back against the unforgiving bars and watched his every move, careful not to make eye contact.

But he didn't unlock the cell and deliver the beating or rape she'd feared.

Instead, he lifted the thin, rectangular-shaped item he held and used more plastic zip ties to secure it around the bars at the front of her cell. Then, without giving her a second glance, he sauntered away.

Summer remained frozen in place, not daring to move yet. When he moved out of her line of vision, she could see others assembling what looked like a large tripod in the center of the building.

A minute later, someone came in holding what looked like a camera. They set it up facing a stage of sorts, where two men were hanging the ATB's infamous black flag as a backdrop.

Just the sight of it sent a wave of nausea rolling through her. Whatever Hadad was planning for them, he was going to film the entire thing. No doubt to make as big a statement as possible in the media and solidify his reputation as one of the most powerful up-and-comers within the ATB.

She watched everything closely, tried frantically to think of a way to save herself. To somehow buy more time in case intelligence officials had found them and were planning to mount some sort of rescue.

But as the minutes ticked by, she couldn't come up with a single idea that might help her and the others. Bartering more time from Hadad by giving him sensitive military information might not appease him, and it would result in innocent people dying. She was in a no-win situation.

There had to be something else. Another way. But being trapped in here with no means of defending herself, there was literally nothing she could do.

In front of her, the men continued to set up their filming area. She shifted slightly, winced as a sharp stone dug into her hip. As she moved off it, an idea hit her. It was desperate and probably ineffective, but right at that moment, having something she could use as a weapon seemed a hell of a lot better than having nothing.

The shadows back here at the end of the building gave her good cover. She observed the men ahead of her carefully, making sure no one was paying any attention to her.

Keeping her movements small, she tucked her legs beneath her and reached down to slide off her left shoe and sock. She held the sock in one hand as she slipped the shoe back on, then tugged the hem of her robe down to hide her bare ankle.

No one was watching her yet.

Feeling around in the dirt behind her, she began to pick up every stone and piece of gravel she could find and put them into the sock. Once it was nearly full she waited until the men's backs were to her before tying a knot securely at the top.

As a weapon it was pathetic, she knew that. Still, it was surprisingly heavy and would pack one hell of a punch if she could get enough leverage to swing it at someone.

Adam had taught her more than a few self-defense tricks over the years. She'd never imagined having to use them in a situation like this but now she was eternally grateful for the tips he'd given her. If someone came to get her, she might be able to use the stones to strike out.

Her mind raced. The bars of her cell were wide enough apart that she could easily slide her arm through them. All she needed was for one of the men to come close enough, be unaware enough, and she could potentially use it as a makeshift club.

From what she'd noticed, each of them carried at least one pistol. If she could swing the stones through the bars with enough force, she might be able to knock one of them out, or at least stun him long enough to take his weapon. After that she'd have only seconds to attempt an escape but she would keep shooting, take out as many of these bastards as she could before they killed her.

She gripped her crude weapon tightly in her right hand, waited a few beats to make sure no one glanced her way. Then, moving fast, she lifted up to reach beneath the hem of her robe and tucked the sock into the back of the waistband of her panties.

By the time she'd straightened the robe her heart was hammering in her ears. No one had looked her way yet but the camera and flag were all set up. They were rigging lights now, bright lights that illuminated that hideous black flag for the upcoming drama about to unfold on the stage.

She didn't dare move again, the weight of the sock pressing against the small of her back a cold comfort. A flurry of movement caught her attention to the right as the men scrambled out of the way to reveal Hadad.

He was heading straight for her, along with his second-in-command. Her pulse ratcheted up when that cold gaze locked on her. The chances of her disabling him or his lackey were small, but taking both of them down? No way.

Frustration and helplessness flooded her, making her want to scream at the unfairness of it all. This might be her only chance to disable one of her captors. She'd only have one shot at it, one chance to take someone down before she lost the element of surprise, and now that the moment had arrived, she couldn't even seize the opportunity. It would be suicide.

Her hands flexed at her sides, itching to grab for the stones, the urge to fight pulsing through her bloodstream. When she thought of what might be coming, of the agony and terror they would surely inflict, part of her was willing to risk pissing them off so they'd shoot her here now as punishment.

A quick death like that was surely a thousand times less painful to whatever heinous plan they had in mind.

But her survival instinct was too strong. It refused to let her give in to the idea.

She wanted to *live*, goddamn it. She wanted to see Adam again, make a life with him again. She'd do anything for that chance, even if it meant selling her soul. As long as the chance at being reunited with him existed, then she would endure anything.

Brave thoughts. They did nothing to quell the surge of terror that lashed through her when Hadad drew nearer.

His cold black eyes stayed locked with hers as he stalked toward her, and she saw the fervor there. The lust for blood and vengeance.

She fought back a shudder as a chill snaked through her, held her breath.

He stopped mere feet from her cell door, stood there staring down at her for a long moment, letting the anticipation and fear swell. She could see how much he loved this. How much he relished toying with her mind.

Her chin came up, her spine snapping taut.

You pathetic fucking bastard, she told him with her eyes, glaring up at him with every ounce of contempt she felt. What she wouldn't give for a five-minute hand-to-hand fight with him.

She'd use every trick Adam had ever taught her, show this piece of shit excuse for a human being that she was the opposite of helpless. She'd smash in that long, straight nose and gouge at those hate-filled eyes.

He was far bigger than her, way stronger, so she knew she'd come out the loser in that altercation. But at least she'd go down swinging and not like the helpless victim he was making her.

"You're going to be the star of my little show," he told her, his accented voice smug with satisfaction. "But first you will make a video statement using the guidelines I give you. If you behave and do as you're told, you will be rewarded. If not…" He let the sentence trail off, the cruel smile he gave her telling her just how much he hoped she disobeyed. "You will be punished."

Gritting her teeth, Summer held that dark, soulless stare, refusing to be the one to look away. If he was going to the trouble of making a video of this, then it likely meant he intended to broadcast it. Clearly he meant it as a taunt to her government.

Officials would see it. They would know she was still alive, and that would ramp up search efforts. Maybe somehow an analyst would be able to figure out where the signal had originated from and locate them from there.

But she already knew that was a long shot and that she and the others couldn't wait that long. She had to somehow figure out a way to tell them where they were, without tipping off Hadad and his men.

Her mind whirled, racing to come up with a plan. If she could somehow convey their location, give some sort of embedded message during her statement, that might be enough to enable authorities to stage a rescue effort.

But *how*? What could she say and how could she say it without giving herself away?

She thought of Adam. As soon as the video went live, it was only a matter of time before he was alerted to it. He knew her better than anyone.

There had to be a way to come up with a secret message he'd understand. She had to think of something, it was her and the others' only chance.

Her heart raced as ideas tumbled through her mind. *Think Summer, think!* She'd been working on a report that mentioned Northern Shuneh, had left it at the hotel.

Yes! Hope and elation exploded inside her. It had to work. She had to figure out how to relay the message.

She had a brief moment's satisfaction when Hadad's smile faded in the face of her silent defiance, but it was quickly replaced by derision. "Stand up," he commanded quietly, the deceptively soft tone somehow ten times scarier than if he'd shouted it.

With no other choice but to obey, she did. Slowly. So as not to disturb her little weapon tucked safely out of sight. There was a slim chance she might be able to use it yet.

"Turn around, hands behind you," he ordered, his voice gruff now, impatient.

They were going to cuff her.

Her heart sank at the realization, then redoubled its rhythm, the blood pulsing in her ears. With both men standing here, she had no chance. And without being able to use her hands, she was pretty much defenseless against them.

It went against every instinct she possessed, but there was no other way. Moving carefully, she turned and backed toward the bars of the cell door.

One of them, probably Hadad, grabbed her hands in a painful grip and twisted her wrists, making her wince and bite back a cry as he secured the plastic cuffs around them.

Tight enough to cut off the blood supply. Already she could feel the veins in her hands swelling, the cuffs trapping the blood there.

A squeal of metal hinges signaled they'd opened the door. Before she could turn her head to see what they were doing Hadad yanked her backward, making her stumble.

Her back hit his chest and she froze, heart seizing as the stone-filled sock dug into his belly. An agonizing second slipped by, then another as she waited for him to strip off the robe and search her.

When he merely shoved her upright and continued to drag her out of the cell, her heart began beating once more.

As he turned her about to face forward with an impatient shove, she finally saw what was attached to the outside of her cell. A digital clock.

It read ten hours, in glowing red digits.

Hadad saw her looking. Holding her gaze, he reached up one hand and with great care, hit the button on the side of the clock.

Instantly the digital numbers began ticking down, counting backwards from nine hours, fifty-nine minutes. Her gaze flashed up to his, understanding slamming into her with a new horror.

She had less than ten hours to live.

An evil smile twisted his mouth. "That's right, Summer Blackwell. Time's running out for you," he said, and jerked her toward the waiting stage.

Chapter Fifteen

One month ago

Adam unrolled the second sleeping bag and paused to shoot a grin at Summer over his shoulder. "Just like old times, huh?"

Her lips curved upward, that little dimple appearing near the corner of her mouth. "Yep. Colder than I remember it being last time, though."

"I'll keep you warm, don't worry."

One of their first dates had been to the drive-in, but that had been in the middle of July. They hadn't needed sleeping bags and knit caps then. This was almost better though.

He'd parked on the same hill they always did, in a farmer's field just off the drive-in property. From here they could still tune into the radio station needed to hear the audio for the movies, but they didn't have to pay anything.

Not to mention the added benefit of privacy.

There were a few other vehicles parked on the hill as

well, but far enough away that they couldn't see them from their view in the back of his truck.

"You didn't by chance happen to bring any M&Ms did you?" she asked, perched on the side of the truck bed in her jeans and down jacket. Her red hair blew around her cheeks in the cold breeze, her cheeks a pretty pink.

"Yes ma'am, I did. And hot chocolate."

"I should have known you'd come prepared," she teased. "Except I might not make it through the second movie because I'll be in a sugar coma."

He chuckled and spread the second sleeping bag out on top of the first, which he'd placed over top of a big piece of foam. "I'm not worried. But if you did, I'd figure out a way to revive you." He'd stacked the pillows against the back of the cab, and parked the truck so that they could see the huge screen down below through the open tailgate.

Things had been going well between them lately. The counselor had suggested they go back to doing things they'd done early on in their relationship, to try and rekindle the spark they'd lost.

He'd come home one night last week to find two loaves of homemade banana bread waiting on the counter, the entire kitchen smelling like heaven. She knew it was his favorite, so she'd baked them before work and dropped them off on her way to the office.

That weekend he'd taken her hiking, to one of their favorite spots up in the hills of West Virginia. Today, he'd planned this. Normally the drive-in was closed for the winter but Christmas was right around the corner and the weather was good so the owner had advertised a Christmas-themed double feature to begin at dusk.

Sitting on the edge of the bed he'd made up for them, he began unlacing his boots and looked over at her. She was watching him, unmoving. A little stiff. He smiled to put her at ease. "You nervous?"

She flashed him a shy smile that hit him square in the

heart and tucked a lock of hair beneath the knit cap she wore. "A little."

"Don't be." He understood why she was nervous though. It had been a couple of months since they'd had sex last, and for various reasons it hadn't been very good for her, despite all his efforts. She'd been too deep in her head, stiff, and hurting inside. He got the impression it had triggered a lot of stuff for her emotionally but she hadn't said anything.

Since then she'd pulled back and they'd barely touched one another, with the exception of a few kisses and hugs over the past couple weeks.

That was all changing tonight if he had anything to say about it.

Hard as it was for him not to jump back into a sexual relationship with her—because he was dying to be intimate with his wife—he'd give her the time she needed.

In all honesty he was actually looking forward to this chance to ignite the fire between them once again. He'd begun to rebuild her trust in him brick by brick. He wouldn't risk ruining everything now by rushing things.

Holding his hand out, palm up, he reached for her. "Come on."

She looked at his hand for a moment, then put her hand in his, curled her fingers around his own. Just that simple touch meant so much to him. An unspoken show of trust that he wouldn't have gotten a few months ago.

He tugged gently until she came down to kneel on top of the sleeping bag. "I won't bite."

Her cheeks turned even pinker and she grinned as she began to undo the laces on her running shoes. "I should warn you that I've been up since four and I worked really late last night. I might not make it far into the movie."

"That's okay." The whole point of tonight was to reestablish the intimate bond they'd lost. As long as he got to hold her for a while, he didn't care if she fell asleep.

The first movie was already starting, the audio coming through the open window at the back of the cab.

He pulled down the top sleeping bag and settled beneath it, his back against the pillows, held it up for her. Summer scooted in next to him and mirrored his position, close enough that their hips and thighs touched. Leaning over her, he tucked the sleeping bag around her and reached under to lace their fingers together.

Turning her head, she gazed up at him in the pale purple light, her gaze soft. "This is really nice. Thanks for inviting me."

"Thanks for coming," he said, giving her hand a squeeze.

Summer shifted closer and leaned against him, then rested her head on his shoulder. That simple gesture shouldn't have affected him so much, but it did. Releasing her hand, he lifted his arm and wrapped it around her shoulders. She rewarded him with a sigh and snuggled closer.

As the opening credits rolled, he reached over and took out the bag of M&Ms, opened it and offered them to her.

She shot him a mock scowl. "You're an enabler," she told him, taking a fistful.

"They're so little, they barely count in terms of calories."

"Easy for you to say, with your muscle mass and the way you guys work out. You can eat five times what I can and never gain an ounce." She popped a few into her mouth and sucked on them. She always ate them that way, sucking off the candy coating first, never crunching them.

Neither of them said anything for a few minutes but he could already tell that something was definitely different between them tonight. The lingering tension that had been present for so long wasn't there. He felt utterly relaxed and at peace as he cuddled with her, and she seemed just as content to be here, pressed up against his side.

About half an hour into the movie, her head became heavier and heavier on his shoulder. He glanced down, found her eyes closed, lips slightly parted.

Adam stared. He'd always taken her for granted. He hadn't meant to, he'd just...gotten lazy and assumed she'd always be there. Now he'd had months to wish he'd been more careful about that, wish that he'd been more supportive and understanding while she'd grieved for the children they'd lost.

He studied the sweep of her lashes, the freckles she loathed, and felt himself falling in love with her all over again. She was so precious to him. Smart and fiery and capable and independent. He loved a thousand little things about her.

Her eyes flew open when her head slipped a notch. She jerked upright, gave him a guilty look. "Did I fall asleep?"

He shook his head, lifted his hand to brush a stray strand of hair back from her cheek. "Just dozed a little." She stilled at the touch, her eyes on his, but didn't pull away. "You warm enough?"

"Yes. Can we lie down though?"

I thought you'd never ask. "Sure." He scooted down and adjusted the pillows so that just his head was propped up.

Rather than stretch out alongside him, however, she chose to sit between his legs and lay back against his chest. She tilted her head back to look at him. "This okay?"

"Yeah," he answered, his voice sounding a bit strangled. In this position her ass was snuggled right up against his groin. That was all it took to make him hard. She didn't seem to mind though, just sighed and settled her arms atop his, which he'd folded over her stomach.

He had no clue what was happening on the screen. All he could focus on was Summer, the feel of her and the warm, sweet scent of her perfume drifting up in the cold breeze.

He bent his head to inhale, his blood pumping hotter when she leaned up to press her temple against his mouth. Kissing her there, he followed the line of her cheekbone to her jaw, let his lips skim the sensitive flesh below her ear.

She shivered, tipped her head to the side to give him better access.

He took it. One hand coming up to cradle her jaw, he rubbed his nose and lips up and down the side of her neck. She made a purring sound and shifted in a purely sensual move that told him she was getting as hot as he was.

Then she surprised him by sitting up and turning around to straddle him, one knee on either side of his hips.

He didn't dare say anything as she stared down at him in the light coming from the screen down the hill, her fingertips tracing the line of his nose, his jaw, his lips. He grasped her hand, held it while he kissed her fingertips, earning a secret smile from her that turned his heart upside down.

"I'm not really into the movie," she confessed in a whisper.

"What movie?"

She laughed and framed his face between her hands, leaned down to kiss the tip of his nose, let her lips brush the edge of his mouth. "You're still so gorgeous. Sometimes I can hardly believe you're real," she murmured. "And I've missed you. Missed this."

A wave of raw emotion hit him. He tightened his arms around her back, pulled her closer with a groan. "Me too."

And then she kissed him. A slow, sensual melding of lips that made arousal burst to life inside him. She teased him for long moments, building the anticipation, and he stayed still, one hand splayed between her shoulder blades as he waited to see what she'd do next.

Her tongue darted out to taste him, following the seam of his lips once, twice, before gently sliding into his mouth. Adam groaned and palmed the back of her head, tugging the knit cap free so he could slide his fingers into the cool, silky fall of her hair.

She tasted like chocolate, her tongue gliding silkily against his, fueling the craving he'd been trying to suppress. His cock was rock hard and aching, trapped behind his fly.

Still kissing him, she slipped her fingers down to grasp the zipper at the top of her jacket and draw it down, shrugging out of it and tossing it aside. A second later she opened his and stretched out atop him, her breasts flush to his chest.

Going with his instinct, he rolled them, reversing their positions. With his hips lodged between her thighs and his forearms braced on either side of her head, he lowered his weight onto her, watching her face. Her lashes fluttered and her head fell back, a low groan of need and enjoyment rising from her throat.

God, he wanted inside her so badly. Would have given anything to peel away the rest of their clothes and sink into her heat. But it was too soon. Much as it killed him, he had to leave them both wanting more.

Summer wound her legs around his thighs and sank her fingers into his shoulders. Even through his shirt he could feel them digging in.

He skimmed a fingertip down the center of her throat, following the V at the front of her sweater to touch the skin there. She stared up at him, waiting. Wanting.

Leaning down to kiss her neck some more, he reached down to ease the bottom of her sweater up. A see-through red lace bra met his hungry gaze, a little jingle bell nestled between the cups.

"It's an early Christmas gift to myself from you," she whispered. "Thanks, by the way."

One side of his mouth quirked up. "You're welcome. Damn, I have good taste."

"Yes you do." She sucked in a breath as he flicked the front clasp open and brushed the cups aside. Her small, firm breasts spilled free, her nipples a deep pink and flushed from either the cold or arousal, or both.

He couldn't wait a moment more to taste them.

Cupping one breast in his hand, he lowered his head and took the taut center into his mouth. Summer groaned and plunged a hand into his hair, holding him close as he sucked her, dragging his tongue repeatedly across the straining flesh. When she was moaning and writhing in his hold, he switched to the other breast to give it the same loving attention.

"God, Adam," she whispered, reaching down to grab his ass and grind her pelvis against his swollen cock. When that wasn't enough she tried to reach beneath him to undo his fly.

He shook his head, reached down to grab her hand, stilling her. "No sex," he reminded her, then leaned in to suck at the spot in the curve of her neck he knew made her crazy.

She made a frustrated sound in the back of her throat, rubbed against his covered cock. "Why not?"

Yes, why not, his cock screamed. Hell, his entire body screamed it. "Because the counselor said so."

"Screw the counselor."

He grinned against her velvety skin, amused by the annoyance in her voice. He loved knowing she wanted him so badly, but sex wasn't going to fix their problems. No matter how much he wished it would. "I'm gonna tell him you said that."

"Good." She rolled her hips against his, tightened her

thighs around his legs. "God, I'm so damn wet and…frustrated."

Her words made every muscle in his body tighten but he ignored the painful throb between his legs and leaned down to suck her nipple again, reveling in her moan, the way she arched and gripped his hair.

Releasing the taut bud, he raised up to take her mouth in a consuming kiss. A reminder of how good they were together, how much he wanted her. That she was his.

Summer twisted beneath him, restless. Adam pulled back to stare down at her, and the sight of her made him bite back a groan. Her lips were wet and swollen, her eyes heavy-lidded, naked breasts rising and falling with her rapid breaths, the deep pink nipples hard.

"Why did we stop making out like this?" he asked, perplexed. It was so fucking hot, turning her on this way. And there was something to be said for leaving them both wanting more, for taking the time to savor each and every sensation, the buildup. When in their relationship had sex become a race to the finish for both of them?

She made a growling sound and wriggled against him, her desperation clear. "Because it's so frustrating," she groaned.

Chuckling, he bent and kissed the bridge of her nose. This was total role reversal, him putting the brakes on. He searched his mind for the reason why he couldn't peel her jeans and panties off her and bury his mouth between her thighs, slide his tongue into her tender core and make her come. "The counselor said it's good for us. Gives us something to look forward to next time."

At that she stiffened. He raised his head to find her glaring up at him. "Are you seriously thinking about leaving me all worked up like this?" She sounded outraged at the very idea.

He hid a grin. "Doctor's orders, sweetheart. Sorry."

"Sorry? I'm literally coming out of my own skin

here. God, you can't do this to me," she whined in protest.

"If it's any consolation, I'm hurting every bit as bad as you are, doll, trust me."

She pouted, gazed up at him with those pale green eyes. "Please?"

He almost laughed, a big part of him wanting to cave. "No can do, sorry."

With a defeated groan she closed her eyes and let her head drop back to the pillows, still breathing hard. "This is torture. I'm never gonna get to sleep after this."

Good. He wanted her to crave him as badly as he did her. "Sure you will. One good orgasm and you'll sleep like a baby."

She opened her mouth to argue but he dipped down to nibble the soft skin at the curve of her neck, making her gasp instead. "After I drop you off tonight, I want you to climb into bed and spread your thighs wide, pretend it's my tongue on your clit and inside you while you finger yourself."

Her eyes sprang open, heavy with desire and challenge as she peered up at him. God, she fired him up. "You gonna think of me when you stroke yourself then?"

"I always do."

She seemed inordinately pleased by that revelation, a little smile playing around the edges of her lips. "Then I guess we're even, if we both have to suffer."

"Guess so." He was so damn hard he hurt, but it was worth it.

Wanting to ease her down from the high gently, he spent a few minutes giving her little kisses, stroking her hair and face until she calmed and her breathing evened out.

He did up her bra, pulled her sweater down and zipped up her jacket. The first movie was almost over already. "Still want to watch the movies?"

She made a face. "Not really." Then her expression

evened out and she gave him a gentle smile. "But I don't want to go home yet, either."

Warmth spread through him, a gentle fire in his veins. "Come here then," he coaxed, and maneuvered them so that he was once again on his back and she was draped half on top of him, her cheek nestled in the curve of his shoulder. "Why don't you sleep for a bit?" he suggested.

In answer she tucked her arm around his ribs and slid her bent leg over his thighs, let out a deep sigh. "This was the best and yet most annoying date I've ever been on," she confided a moment later.

"Tell me about it."

She relaxed fully against him, her breathing growing heavier and heavier as the minutes passed.

Adam stroked her hair with one hand as he held her, enjoying the incredible peace of the moment, and gazed upward. The stars were so clear, sparkling against the black velvet sky. Tucked beneath the sleeping bag with his wife curled against his body, he didn't even feel the chill of the December breeze.

And as she drifted off to sleep in his arms, he'd never been more hopeful for the future. A future of living as husband and wife again.

Chapter Sixteen

Present Day

When Adam burst into the command center with Tuck and the others right behind him, everyone inside was in a flurry of activity. Director Foster glanced up at him from an analyst's desk, his expression grim.

Adam stopped moving, his feet suddenly stuck to the floor. He couldn't move. That look on the director's face was something straight out of his nightmares. It told him the unthinkable had happened.

Then DeLuca appeared out of nowhere, stepping in front of Adam and gripping his shoulders tight. His jade green gaze met Adam's squarely. "She's alive."

Adam closed his eyes and let his head drop forward, his legs damn near buckling underneath him. A ragged groan escaped him.

DeLuca squeezed harder, holding on. "I know, man."

He sucked in a painful breath, raised his head to look at his commander. "How do you know?"

"Captors released a video of her a few minutes ago. We just heard about it while you were on your way over here."

Adam jerked his attention to the large screen at the end of the room. "Let me see her."

"Okay. They're just starting to analyze it now." DeLuca released him and moved out of the way so he could see what was going on. A group of analysts and the director were all gathered around a laptop set up on the long rectangular table.

Adam headed for it without being conscious of moving, his eyes glued to the screen, hungry for the sight of his wife.

The director straightened. "We've watched it through once. She appears to be in good health and she says Jim and Mark are both still alive as well. If the date and time are right, it was made just a little while ago. Right now it looks like the people who recorded this sent the video to another source for broadcasting, to make it harder to track them. The NSA is running diagnostics now, trying to get a lock on a location. Or a signal origin. Anything that might tell us where they are."

"Let me see her," he rasped out, staring at the screen with burning eyes.

The analysts gathered around it looked at the director uncertainly. Foster nodded at them. "Put it on the big screen and turn up the volume."

Adam was aware of his teammates silently gathering around him, standing on either side of him. All their attention was riveted on the screen at the end of the room, all of them revved and waiting for the chance to mount a rescue.

Tuck stood closest to him, so close their shoulders touched. Maybe because his team leader was worried Adam might keel over once he saw the video. Bauer stood on his other side, a huge, solid presence. If Adam did drop, he knew his teammates would catch him before he ever hit the floor.

It was comforting to know, but if Summer didn't survive this then no one would be able to soften that blow.

Steeling himself for what was coming, he braced his feet shoulder-width apart and folded his arms, his hands curling into fists. His stomach was in knots, his pulse erratic as he waited for the video to load on screen.

Finally it began to play. Arabic music and writing appeared against a black background, spewing whatever bullshit propaganda the ATB was using. Then Summer appeared on screen.

He'd thought he'd been prepared for the sight of her, but the truth was nothing could have prepared him for this.

He covered his mouth with one hand, stood there staring through swimming eyes while he felt his heart crack in two. They had her dressed in the robe of a burqa with her hands bound behind her back. Her red hair lay limp around her shoulders, her skin pale, dark circles beneath her eyes. The left side of her face was bruised, her cheek swollen.

Her expression was completely devoid of emotion as she stared into the camera. She looked...broken. As broken as she'd been after the stillbirth and the last miscarriage.

That, more than anything, hit him in the solar plexus with the force of a sledgehammer.

Sweetheart, what have they done to you? he cried silently.

"My name is Summer Blackwell."

The sound of her voice triggered something in him, cracked his defenses apart. He felt the tears gather, didn't fucking care that he was crying in front of everyone. He blinked to clear his vision, afraid to look away for even one moment.

Tell me where you are, he begged her. *Tell me how to help you.*

"I'm an American citizen working for the Defense Intelligence Agency." She gave the time and date—today's date—and announced that she was being held by the ATB in retaliation for war crimes committed by the United States and its allies against the Syrian people.

The entire room was deathly silent as she continued.

She glanced to her left off screen, looking at someone, then back at the camera. And this time that blank mask disappeared for a moment. She swallowed visibly, drew in a deep breath. "Adam, if you're watching this, I want you to know how much I love you. And I'm so sorry for everything I ever did that hurt you."

Jesus, he couldn't fucking take this. He clenched his jaw, fought back the sob trapped in his chest, his shoulders jerking sharply with the effort. He was shattering inside watching this, hearing her talk like she knew she was about to die.

A solid hand landed on his left shoulder. Bauer. The grip locked tight. "Hang in there, man," he murmured.

Adam didn't answer. He couldn't. It took everything he had to hold onto what was left of his rapidly shredding composure.

On screen, Summer continued. "It's funny how at a time like this, all I can think about is us. I've been thinking about our honeymoon, and the picture we took of us at the lake that day."

He knew which one she meant, pictured it instantly.

He'd only been able to squeeze a few days off in between contracting jobs, so instead of the tropical vacation she'd wanted, they'd taken off to the Blue Ridge Mountains together. They'd spent their honeymoon in a snug little cottage he'd rented for them, hiking and canoeing during the day, making love by the wood-burning fireplace at night.

During one of their hikes they'd stopped on top of the slab of rock they'd climbed to and taken a selfie. The shot showed her snuggled into his chest with his arm curled around her, and the spectacular backdrop of the fall foliage of the Shenandoah Valley in the background. She'd had it framed as soon as they'd gotten home from their honeymoon.

She smiled now, an impossibly sad smile that managed to break his heart even more. "You know how much I love that picture of us, I take it everywhere with me when I travel. I always keep it with the things that mean the most to me." She let out a deep sigh, her mouth quirking in the semblance of an ironic grin. "I wish I'd listened to you *in the first place* and stayed home this time. Anyway, whatever happens, just know that I'll always love you. I need you to remember that, remember the good times."

The camera panned out, showing her standing there staring at the camera in silence. And mounted on the wall behind her, a digital clock reading nine hours, fifty-four minutes was counting backwards, the seconds melting away as he watched.

A deadline. The message was clear. If Summer was still in the ATB's possession by the time the clock hit zero, she was dead.

The screen turned blank, and he bit back a cry of protest, feeling like he'd just lost his last connection with her.

In the ensuing silence, everyone in the room turned to look at him.

Fuck. Adam doubled over, covered his eyes with shaking hands and fought to breathe. He felt shell-shocked. Was practically reeling on his feet.

Someone dragged a chair over.

"Sit down." Schroder practically muscled him over and pushed him into it. Adam dropped down, barely aware of his surroundings. The medic was bent on one knee beside him, a big hand splayed over the taut muscles of Adam's back. "Somebody get him some water."

"No," Adam snapped, just wanting everyone to go away and leave him the fuck alone. He felt raw inside and out, like someone had peeled his skin away with a dull knife and left him bleeding out slowly from a thousand separate cuts.

Schroder dropped his hand and stood. Adam closed his eyes and focused on breathing in and out no matter how much it hurt. Every atom in his body was now clinging to the hope that the NSA or whoever could somehow get a location for them to target. Anything that would allow them to reach Summer before the time ran out.

The room remained silent as they played the video again. And again, over and over, analyzing it repeatedly. Looking for some hint, any clue that might help locate the hostages.

Eyes closed, Adam kept listening to Summer's voice as it repeated her personal message to him at the end. Through the fog of pain and despair, something about her words kept calling to him. No, the cadence of her voice. The part where she was talking about the picture, and how she wished she'd listened to him and stayed home.

In the first place.

She's emphasized those words above the others. It sounded strange enough in the sentence and context to catch his attention.

He looked up, gaze pinned to her on the screen. She was smart. Fucking brilliant, actually. And resourceful. He wouldn't put it past her to try and give him a secret message somehow. But what? What was she trying to say?

"Play that bit back again," he ordered suddenly, his urgent voice cutting through the room. People shot him surprised looks but the analyst controlling the video feed did as he said.

Adam stared at her, trying like hell to decipher whether there was any hidden meaning to her words or whether he was just hoping for something that wasn't even there.

"You know how much I love that picture of us, I take it everywhere with me when I travel. I always keep it with the things that mean the most to me." That deep sigh, followed by the wry grin. "I wish I'd listened to you *in the first place* and stayed home this time."

"Stop," he said, shoving to his feet as a chill ripped down his spine.

DeLuca and the director were staring at him. "What?" his commander asked. "What do you see?"

He shook his head. "It's not what I see, it's what she said." Adrenaline poured through him, his heart a staccato drumbeat in his ears. "I think she gave us a clue."

They all stared at him like he'd just lost his mind. And maybe he had, he was sure desperate enough to grasp at any straw available right now. But wasn't it worth checking it out?

"The picture she talked about," he continued. "She literally takes it with her when she travels, including here. I think she was telling me that she's got it in a place where we can find another clue. Listen to how she emphasizes *in the first place*. That's no accident or coincidence. It's another clue. We need to go to her hotel room and find that picture."

DeLuca and the director exchanged dubious looks, but then his commander faced him and nodded. "Okay. It's worth a shot."

Adam was the first one out the door. He literally ran to the SUV he'd ridden there in and jumped behind the wheel.

Evers was two steps behind him, snatched the keys out of his hand. "Nuh uh, brother. You're in no shape to drive right now."

Scowling, Adam just slid over the center console into the front passenger seat. "Fucking hurry up then."

Thankfully the team was loaded and ready to go in just another few seconds. The short drive to the hotel seemed to take forever. Two guys stayed down in the lobby while the others followed Adam up to her room.

He raced up the stairs, refusing to even wait for the elevator. Every second counted. They were up against a deadline and Summer's life hung in the balance.

Inside her room he headed straight for the nightstands on either side of the bed. They were empty except for a Quran and a phone book.

He rushed over to the desk, where Tuck was looking. "Anything?" The half-eaten bag of M&Ms was still there, tormenting him with its bittersweet memories.

"Nope."

Fuck. He had to be right about this. Just had to.

Bauer was over at the closet. "There's a safe in here."

The safe. Of course, why hadn't he goddamn thought of that first?

Adam rushed over, pushed Bauer aside and tried to think of what code she might have used. Taking a wild guess, he punched in her birthday. His. Their anniversary. Her social security number.

Nothing.

He tried her cell number.

No luck.

Tapping his earpiece, he contacted Cruzie, who was down in the lobby with Vance, and kept trying. "Get security up here with someone who can unlock the safe. *Now*."

"You got it."

The wait was agonizing. While the others searched the entire room and came up empty he kept punching in code after code, everything he could think of that might be sentimental to her. Their address. The day they'd gotten engaged. Her favorite numbers.

Nothing worked.

"We're on our way up," Cruzie announced.

Thank God. "*Hurry*."

"You know it."

A minute later they were at the door, practically carrying a middle-aged man who was red-faced and panting, no doubt from trying to keep pace with them up all the stairs.

Adam grabbed him and hauled him over to the safe. "Open it," he commanded, wishing he could just pry the fucking thing open with his bare hands.

Pulling out a master key, the man did as he said. The moment it popped open, Adam hauled him back out of the way and shoved a hand inside it without looking while Vance escorted the man out into the hall.

His fingers touched something cool and smooth. He pulled out the framed picture, a spear of grief hitting him when he saw the familiar shot of them together in the Blue Ridge Mountains.

They looked so happy, so in love. It touched him deeply to know she still took it with her wherever she went.

Inside with it he found her passport, some cash…

And a file folder.

Adrenaline sliced through him. He grabbed the file, flipped it open and quickly perused the contents. Her emphasized message played in his mind. *In the first place.*

The first place mentioned in the file?

He scanned the document, looking for a location.

And found it at the end of the third paragraph.

Northern Shuneh.

Was that it? Was that where she was? He pulled out his phone and immediately reported everything to Foster and DeLuca, still back at the command center. The area mentioned wasn't a big place. "Can you get a satellite or drone in there?"

"You sure this is what she was trying to tell you?" Foster asked.

"Yes. Has to be." He couldn't calm his heart rate. The deadline was just over nine hours away. He wanted eyes in the sky on that location *now*.

"All right. I'll make it happen."

Adam closed his eyes, expelled a hard sigh. "*Thank you.*"

Foster grunted. "Don't thank me yet, it may be another dead end. And there's a weather front moving in, possibly a sand storm. Even if I can get the resources we want, we're looking at a tight window to utilize them."

"I understand." It couldn't be a dead end. He knew it was right. And there had to be enough time to find them.

Summer's life depended on it and this time, he wasn't going to let her down.

Chapter Seventeen

Only two hours in, and the video was already going viral.

Tarek ended his call with an ATB contact who had uploaded and broadcast everything for him, a hacker who had proved himself highly useful over the past few weeks. Even if the intelligence agencies hunting for them managed to find their location, it wouldn't be until after they were gone.

He turned to Akram. "It's working." Even better than he'd anticipated.

The female captive had performed beautifully. She'd delivered the scripted message he'd given her, then added a short personal message to her husband. The end result was perfect. The sight of her bound and helpless, staring into the camera while she gave that sad little speech would tug on heartstrings all over the world.

It would make the global reaction to tomorrow's executions even more spectacular.

The younger man grinned broadly at him. "I know. I just talked to one of our media reps a few minutes ago.

Cable news networks all around the world are picking it up already."

"Good." Now all that was left to do was make the final preparations and stick to the timeline he'd set. "Is everything else ready?"

Akram nodded, but looked away, clearly uneasy. Tarek knew his friend wasn't comfortable with what was coming, but that was because he had no stomach for such things. Akram preferred to work behind the scenes with logistics and personnel, resupply and finances.

Tarek wouldn't hold his lack of bloodlust against him. In truth, he'd been much like Akram before the war started. He'd seen killing as a necessary part of his military service, but only against an armed combatant.

Growing up, his parents had raised him in a loving home, imparting on him a strong sense of right and wrong along with a kinder, gentler interpretation of the Holy Quran and its teachings than he followed now.

All of it had burned to ash the night they'd been killed. In the wake of that tragedy, a new man had risen from the ashes like a metaphorical phoenix. He didn't miss the old him. He was stronger now, wiser, and understood better how the world really worked.

He picked up the small video camera on the table before him, resolved in his course of action. "We'll save the woman for last."

"So all three will be…" Akram trailed off, unable to finish the sentence.

Tarek was growing annoyed by the hesitation. "Yes, all three," he said curtly. "But the woman last. It will have the most impact that way." The most shock value. The entire world would be holding its breath, praying he would spare her.

They were in for a huge disappointment.

When Akram continued to stand there shifting his weight from one foot to the other with a troubled frown on his face, Tarek sighed and set the camera down. "What is it?"

Akram rubbed the back of his neck. "I always thought the plan was to sell her. With her being young and American and considering her position at the intelligence agency, there would be many buyers interested. She would have gone for a fair price and you know we could use the money. Our supplies and ammunition stores are running low."

Only until they got back to Syria, which was in a matter of hours from now. "After this, the money will come pouring in," he told his friend, completely confident in the course he'd set. "Once our supporters around the world see this, and see the power we wield, they'll send us more money than we'll know what to do with."

The ATB would make good use of it, dividing it amongst its groups. And since he'd been the one to plan and orchestrate this whole thing, he'd likely be promoted right away. Maybe even to field commander, a position he'd wanted for a long time.

"She makes me uneasy," Akram murmured at last, glancing toward the door as though he could see her at the far end of the building.

He snorted. "She's a female trapped behind bars with no weapon. How could she possibly make you uneasy?"

Akram paused a moment before answering. "There's something about the look in her eyes. Other female captives we've taken, their spirits are broken after a while. Not her. She's far from broken. And whenever she looks at me I can tell she's thinking about killing me. Just like the ones who fight with the Peshmerga."

Tarek made a scoffing sound. "That's ridiculous. She's an analyst, not a soldier." She probably had next to no weapons or hand-to-hand combat training at all.

"It's not just me," Akram protested. "The others feel the same, that if she could get her hands on a gun, she'd

kill as many of us as she could before we took her out."
He mock shuddered. "None of us want to be killed by a
woman, it would be the ultimate shame for warriors like
us. And you know it would also mean we wouldn't get
into heaven."

Tarek knew of the superstition circulating through the
ranks, but usually it was the uneducated guys who bought
into that crap. Though he personally dismissed the idea as
ridiculous, he couldn't deny that a tiny part of him wasn't
willing to ignore it entirely and risk taking that chance.
Just in case it happened to be true.

"Well she's not getting a weapon, so don't worry. And
she might have been strong up until now but everyone has
a breaking point, believe me. She's going to reach hers in
the morning." Part of him almost felt bad for her in a way,
for the suffering she was going to endure.

Almost.

Akram nodded, his worried expression clearing
slightly. "What else do you need me to do?"

"Take the suits to the other prisoners. I'll deliver the
female's myself."

Taking the neatly folded garment from the table, he
left the room and walked across the open space of the old,
abandoned building. The woman's cell was at the very
back of the building, deep in the shadows.

But the moment he stepped out of the room he could
see the glowing red numbers of the digital clock attached
to the bars. A little under eight hours remained in the
countdown.

He flipped on a floodlight. The beam lit up the cell,
showing her slumped in the corner. It was bright as
daylight now but she didn't awaken, exhaustion finally
having caught up with her.

She'd actually held up surprisingly well under the
harsh conditions thus far. With barely any sleep, little
food or water and their execution imminent, he'd seen

plenty of so-called tough men crack and beg for their lives.

But not this woman. That annoyed him even as he had to grudgingly respect it.

"Wake up," he snapped out.

Her head came up, her eyes opening a fraction. She flinched at the brightness, threw up a hand to shield her eyes. He stepped into the high-powered beam, cutting off the worst of the blinding effect, and strode over to the cell door.

Then he paused and waited for her to look at him.

It didn't take long. She shifted, moving stiffly, and swiveled around to look up at him. Her expression was neutral, giving nothing away, but there was an unmistakable mixture of hatred and resentment in those light green eyes.

Feelings he returned tenfold for her and all her countrymen, but especially for the people involved in and behind the scenes of this war.

Staring down at her, he thought of the picture he carried in his pocket. He kept it with him always. Of Lely and him, a week before she'd been killed.

They'd just gotten engaged. His father had taken the picture after they'd made the announcement following a family dinner. He'd met her at the university, when she was in her first year and he'd been about to graduate as a teacher. Before that day he hadn't believed in love at first sight, but after meeting her, he'd become a convert.

Lely had been such a sweet, caring person. A devoted sister, daughter and friend and he'd loved her so much. He'd have done anything to protect her, make her happy, and had been so looking forward to spending the rest of his life with her.

Then her life had been cut short. Far too short. And that dream, his heart and his world had been blown apart in a matter of seconds.

She'd been just twenty-three years old when she died. For a while afterward he'd wished he'd been with her that night, that he'd been killed alongside her. It hadn't been until weeks later that he'd come to see the reason he'd survived. Out of the smoldering ruins of that dream, a harder, cynical Tarek had been born.

That night had changed him forever. But he knew this was what God wanted for him.

It ate at his soul like acid that this enemy female infidel was alive and healthy before him now, sent here to wage war against him and his brothers by her government when his beloved had been killed by one of their bombs.

"Less than eight hours left," he told her, taking great pleasure in the sudden tension in her posture. "It's too late for anyone to find you now. No one's coming for you."

"When my government finds and kills you, I hope you burn in hell," she fired back.

Her choice of words amused him. "Long after you," he assured her. But Akram was right. This one had more spirit than most. And there was definitely something in her eyes that sent a tiny frisson of unease down his backbone, even if he'd never admit it aloud.

"Tarek!"

He turned at Akram's voice. His friend was rushing toward him, all out of breath. Tarek frowned. "What is it?"

Akram slowed and bent over to catch his breath before answering. "There's a new weather update. The latest front coming in is growing stronger. A sandstorm has already started southwest of us. It's already big but it's getting bigger. It might knock out power and disrupt communications."

The video was key. He needed to film the executions and get across the border as soon as possible. The storm was narrowing their window, but it might also help provide cover for them to escape once the deed was done.

Drones and satellites would have a hard time tracking them through a sandstorm.

Tarek thinned his lips. "How long do we have?"

"Four or five hours. At most."

That put them in a serious time crunch.

Pulse accelerating, he faced the female captive. And smiled. Let her try and stay brave in the face of this. "Make that only four hours left." He tossed the clothing he'd been holding through the bars.

When she saw the orange jumpsuit lying in the dirt her already pale face blanched of all color, telling him she knew what it signified. That she was truly afraid. She would have seen the videos of former captives wearing them during their own executions. And right now she was wondering what form hers would take.

He took out his knife, held it up in the light so that the lethal edge to the blade flashed like silver. Just to scare her even more.

A heady wave of anticipation swelled inside him. Sliding the blade back into its sheath he folded his arms across his chest and stood staring down at her, feeding off her fear. This was for Lely. For his family. "Put that on. We have a tight schedule to keep."

In a matter of hours she and the others would be dead—Americans working for the same war machine that had killed Lely and his family. He would finally have not only revenge, but the respect he'd wanted for so long from the high-ranking members of the ATB. The entire world would loathe and fear him.

Then, once it was done, he and his men would melt back across the border like ghosts and arrive to a heroes' welcome by their ATB brothers, more determined than ever to win this war.

****

Fly, baby, fly.

Stretched out on his stomach on the rocky ground near the crest of the hill, Special Agent Brody Colebrook lay still and kept his movements small as he maneuvered the joystick on the drone's controls. The wind was gusting already, making it hard to get the little guy off the ground.

He gave the drone more lift, maintained the pressure until their little spy finally got into the air and jerked its way into the sky, moving forward toward its target: the long, rectangular-shaped building in the center of the village in front of him.

"Drone deployed," he announced over his comms, alerting the other six guys on his sniper team. Five years he'd been on the HRT sniper team, had been its leader for two of those, and he'd spent a helluva lot longer than that in the military before joining the FBI.

His job was never boring, he'd give it that.

"You should let me do it, I play way more video games than you," Napoli remarked from beside him.

Brody shot his spotter a dirty look. "Not happening. Get your own drone."

Grinning, Napoli ducked his head to check through the laser range finder. "Six hundred yards to target."

Brody watched the screen on the remote control he held, steering the drone into position. It was bumpy as hell up there, but this latest model was state-of-the-art and was able to overcome the turbulence without much problem. "Coming up on target," he said. "Thirty seconds."

On screen the drone's camera gave a bird's-eye view of the village, the night vision optics cutting through the murk without a problem. Soon there would be so much sand in the air that all the optics in the world wouldn't make a difference.

Come on, give me what I need.

Just one piece of solid intel. Some way to determine the hostages they were looking for were in there, so he could relay it to headquarters and pull the trigger on the rescue op.

The drone circled the building. Three American intelligence employees could be in there, one of them Summer Blackwell. Brody always did his job to the best of his ability and would save any hostages no matter who they were, but knowing a teammate's wife was in there gave this mission a whole new level of urgency. For all of them.

Every guy on the team wanted her found and taken out of here alive. He had to get the intel they needed now, before the storm became too much of an issue.

"Any movement outside?" he asked.

"Negative," the others all responded.

He centered the drone over the target building and did a slow pass. The infrared camera picked up several heat signatures, indistinct blobs moving inside the building. "Got possible targets on screen. Moving in for a closer look." He dropped the drone fifty feet, the reduced distance making the orange-ish blobs inside more distinct.

"I've got seven…make that eight tangos moving around inside," he told them, "and three stationary."

"I got movement."

Brody didn't take his eyes off the monitor. "Where?"

"Four o'clock."

"I see him." Someone stepped out of the building, checked around him and hurried alongside the building. "Idiot left the door open," he said to Napoli. Not much, but enough to get a peek inside. The unsuspecting tango was now busy taking a piss against the east-facing wall of the building. "Can you see anything?"

"Negative, the angle's wrong."

Brody seized his chance and shot the drone into a steep dive, hoping the wind would cover the high-pitched whine of its motor from the guy around the corner. He flew it down and angled it until he could get a look inside the open door.

Yup. Seven people moving around, and three seated, unmoving. Each of the three appeared to be inside some kind of structure.

Had to be the hostages.

Bingo. Adrenaline and elation punched through him as he shot the drone back up into the sky. "It's them."

"You sure?" Napoli asked, still staring through the range finder.

"Yeah." Now it was time to pull the trigger and kick some ass.

With one hand holding the remote control he pulled out his radio and contacted DeLuca back at HQ.

"Go ahead, Charlie-Kilo," his commander said, using Brody's operating initials.

"I've got visual confirmation on our three hostages," he replied. "Stand by for coordinates."

Chapter Eighteen

Adam's eyes snapped open when someone touched his shoulder. He lurched upright on the bench he'd been dozing on for what seemed like only seconds, blinked up into Tuck's face.

"What?" he asked, his brain instantly clearing. The whole team had crashed in this office about an hour ago.

"Foster just called us back in. Something about a change in the timeline."

What? Instantly alert, he got up, rubbed a hand over his eyes as he rushed out the door with the others. Up in the command center, the mood was tense.

A familiar sinking sensation formed in his gut.

DeLuca was over at the conference table with Foster, a cup of coffee in hand, his features drawn with fatigue. While they'd all been grabbing whatever sleep they could, their commander had been in here all night—again— without any rest. He straightened and nodded at them. "Everybody gather around."

Adam and the others fanned out in a tight semicircle around DeLuca and Foster. Dread curled in the pit of his stomach. *Don't say she's dead. Don't say it.*

"The sand storm is moving in faster than expected. We just got a call from an informant who says Hadad is planning to move up the executions. He wants to do them before the storm hits and use it as cover to escape across the Syrian border."

Adam sucked in a sharp breath. "Who is it? Do you have a location?"

"It's not confirmed yet but our sniper team is already at a village up north near the Syrian border for some recon." They'd only brought one seven-man sniper team with them for this mission, leaving the other back at Quantico with Blue Team's second assault team. "They'll update me as soon as they're in position at the village. And the informant is…" He looked at Foster.

"Essentially he's a double agent. Though not a very skilled or trustworthy one," the director added. "Still, we can't discount that his intel might be accurate so we're checking it out." He gestured to the team of people working behind him at workstations they'd set up using tables and desks.

"How much time do we have?" Adam asked, every nerve in his body screaming at him to *do* something proactive, to get out there and grab Summer before that clock reached zero.

"Less than four hours."

Adam felt the blood drain from his face. Holy fuck. That was less than half the window they thought they had initially. He swallowed back the fear rising inside him. "Has the sniper team reported in yet?"

"Not yet, but we're expecting a report soon. Here, take a look." DeLuca swept aside some paperwork on the long table and revealed a detailed topographical map.

"Somewhere in here," he continued, indicating a little valley below a tiny village in the Northern Shuneh. "We're trying to get a satellite feed but the visibility's already dropping because of the storm. Sniper team's sending up a recon drone, so hopefully we'll still have eyes on the target location soon."

Adam's entire body was strung taut as he listened to the rest of the intel briefing. In the middle of Foster explaining the layout of the village in question, DeLuca put a hand to his ear and stepped away from the table, expression tight as he listened to whatever someone was saying via his earpiece. Adam watched him closely, saw his lips moving but couldn't get the gist of what he was saying because DeLuca was too far away.

"All right, stand by," DeLuca said as he returned to the group. "Colebrook just reported that he's got visual confirmation via the drone. We'll get a live feed on screen."

Brody Colebrook, their sniper team leader. Adam had known and worked with him ever since he'd first made the HRT. He was one of the best snipers Adam had ever met, and an all-around solid operator. It helped to know someone he trusted had eyes on the target location. If Summer and the others were in there, Colebrook and his team would find out.

Grabbing a nearby laptop, DeLuca typed in some commands, hooked up a few cables and brought the feed up. "One sec and I'll get this on screen." A moment later it popped onto the big flat screen.

The tiny drone's camera showed a small group of what appeared to be dilapidated buildings in the green glow of its night vision optics. Several blurred heat signatures were visible in two of the buildings.

DeLuca tapped his earpiece and spoke to someone, presumably Colebrook. "Can you get a closer look at those heat signatures?"

In answer, seconds later the drone swooped down to a lower altitude and did a slow pass over the longer of the two buildings. Adam counted eleven faint heat signatures inside it, and one outside. The one outside seemed to be positioned next to the front entrance, as if the person was standing guard.

It had to be the right place. A burst of excitement and hope flared in his chest.

He shifted his gaze to DeLuca, who was looking at Foster. "Fits the intel we have," their commander murmured.

Foster nodded, watching the screen closely. "Three of the heat signatures haven't moved since the feed started, and all the others have," he said, pointing to two stationary people positioned on either side of the south end of the building, and one alone at the north end.

Maybe because they're bound and can't move. Adam stared at the screen, every heartbeat ricocheting throughout his chest. Were they the hostages?

DeLuca tapped his earpiece again. "Okay, copy that." He looked up and nodded at the team. "Colebrook confirms the coordinates match the ones we got earlier and he reads a total of eleven heat signatures as well. He's sending four guys in for a closer look now. We should know for sure whether it's the hostages in the next thirty minutes."

Adam started to shake his head. That was too long to do nothing. The intel seemed to justify them heading out to investigate. With the clock ticking down and the weather front closing in they couldn't sit here and wait, they had to set the wheels into motion.

"So are we going?" *Say yes, dammit.* He was going out of his mind waiting.

DeLuca set his palms on the table and shifted his gaze to Foster. "Your call, sir."

Before Adam could interject, the director nodded. "You'll plan the op as if it's a go and organize a Jordanian crew to fly you up there. If Colebrook and his team report back that the hostages are there, I'll green light the mission."

Best fucking news Adam had had in days. An invisible weight lifted from his chest, allowing him to breathe more easily. He couldn't wait to get in there, kick the door down and rescue Summer and the others. He imagined it happening, imagined finding and carrying her out of there, and swallowed hard.

"All right, boys," Tuck drawled, taking center stage at the table. "Let's get to work and be ready for wheels up in thirty minutes."

****

Outside the building, Summer could hear the storm picking up. The wind howled along the sides of the building, shaking the thin roof. She shivered and wrapped her arms around her knees, curling into a ball to retain what body heat she could.

The hideous orange jumpsuit they'd forced her to wear provided no real warmth but she'd had no choice but to put it on. Hadad had literally stood there and watched her do it.

She'd been lucky that her rock-filled sock had remained a secret. He hadn't made her turn around while she stripped down to her blouse and underwear, the hem of her shirt covering her to her upper thighs.

The sleep deprivation had pushed her to the point where she couldn't think clearly. Maybe that was for the best considering the circumstances.

A shudder of revulsion ripped through her when she thought about all the ways they might be intending to kill her and the others. She'd seen enough similar videos to know what was going to happen. It felt like her stomach was full of hot bits of metal, acidic and churning.

She kept thinking about her message in the video. She'd planted it as carefully as she could with only minimal time to prepare her words. Hadad hadn't reacted to her words at all, so she knew he didn't suspect anything.

But maybe she hadn't been obvious enough. Would anyone who had seen the video have been able to figure out she was trying to tell them where they were? Had Adam even seen it yet? He was her only hope because he was the only one who could figure it out.

She dropped her forehead to her upturned knees and closed her eyes.

A door opened somewhere at the opposite end. The wind gusted inside, swirling through the building. It kicked up dust and sand as it carried toward her, coating her in a fine dusting of grit.

Floodlights switched on around the building. She raised her head, squinted through the light, her attention glued to the men who entered.

Hadad was in the lead. He was ordering the others to move things around. Men rushed about, relocating the tripod, shifting the existing lights to different locations.

She resisted the urge to shrink away when one of them stalked toward her. Her right hand slid to her hip, ready to grab her weapon.

Her pitiful, probably useless weapon.

But the man didn't try to enter her cell. Instead he took out a hammer and began prying at something on the right side of it. The plywood or whatever the wall was made of gave way at the corner. He peeled it back, exposing the iron bars and tossed it aside where it hit the ground with a clatter and he moved around to the left side.

After removing that one he did the same to the back. And once he peeled that board away, she finally understood that she wasn't in a cell at all.

She was in a cage.

A sickening wave of dread slammed into her. They'd caged her like an animal in this prop carefully designed for the video shoot and were planning to kill her in her steel prison.

Pausing by the front of the cage, the man stopped to look down at her. He stepped to the side, allowing the blinding beam of light to hit her in the face. She got to her knees, ready to defend herself, turned her face away from the glaring light just as he spat at her and walked away.

Gritting her teeth, she bit back the urge to scream at him as he retreated. Anger replaced the fear, burning deep inside her, fueled by the helplessness, the sense of being confined. These assholes were going to kill her while penned up like an animal? They were weak and gutless, afraid to let her out and fight back.

A sharp beeping noise startled her out of her thoughts. Her head jerked toward the clock on the front of her cage, heart thundering. Another loud beeping came from over near the stage area.

The clocks. They were almost at zero. Less than two minutes left.

No. Oh my God, no…

She tore her gaze away from the clocks in time to see Hadad step out of the glare in the center of the building. She knew it was him, from his build and the swagger in his gait.

He was walking toward her. Carrying something in one hand. Something square-shaped, about the size of—

"Ah, you're awake," he called out to her. "Good."

Every second that passed was its own separate torture, each of his footsteps seeming to echo off the sides of the building. Behind him she could see his men moving around, readying the camera. She could just make out the shape of two other cages on either side of the far end.

Jim and Mark.

Her gaze jerked back to Hadad. He advanced on her at a leisurely pace. What was in his hand?

She was on her feet without even realizing she'd moved. There was no thought, just instinct. Her knees felt weak as she stood there, every cell in her body screaming at her to run, run.

But there was nowhere to go, no way out.

Hadad stopped about ten yards from her cage and set whatever was in his hand on the ground. Straightening, he stood there, his silhouette blocking most of the light. She couldn't make out his expression but she could hear the smugness in his voice as he spoke.

"I've decided to save you for last. That way you'll get to see the whole show first."

So she'd have even more time to be terrified of what was coming.

Rage built, obliterating everything. Without thinking she lunged for the front of the cage, teeth bared, and curled her hands around the iron bars. If he'd have been within range she would have clawed his face off.

"Fuck you," she spat, her chest heaving as the fury rolled through her. It felt so much better than the blank terror that had eclipsed her a minute ago.

His low, evil chuckle sent a chill skittering over her skin. "Your time's up, Summer Blackwell. May your God have mercy on your soul."

Without another word he turned and walked away, moving out of the light so that it blinded her. She threw up a hand to shield her eyes, too late.

"Get the camera started," he called out to his men.

Shaking all over, she gripped the bars and dropped her gaze to the object he'd left on the ground. When she saw what it was, a cry ripped from her chest. Her skin shriveled in horrified revulsion.

A can of gasoline.

They were going to douse her and the others with gas then set them on fire and film them while they burned alive.

Summer's heart lodged halfway up her throat as she watched Hadad position himself next to the camera his men had set up on the tripod. He stood with his feet braced apart and arms folded across his chest, his expression completely impassive while one of his men reached for another can of gasoline and started toward the cage Mark was in.

"No," she cried, her entire body numb, bloodless fingers clamped around the cold iron bars, her mind refusing to accept what was happening right in front of her.

Except it was. And there was nothing she could do to stop it.

Mark scrambled to his feet and pressed back against the rear of his cage, his only option. They'd removed his hood too, and unbound his hands and feet.

So he could see exactly what was coming. So *all* of them could see what was coming.

"Fucking *animals*," she screamed at them, yanking futilely on the bars holding her prisoner.

Mark yelled out something and shielded his face with his arms as the fighter stopped in front of his cage and began splashing the gasoline through the bars. It hit Mark's head and arms, soaked his torso and legs, darkening the orange jumpsuit.

No. No, please, she begged, praying with all her might. This couldn't happen. It was beyond cruel.

Hadad didn't move from his position, watching everything with a closed expression and his arms crossed over his chest. Another man stood behind the camera, capturing every moment on film.

"Don't!" Mark shouted, shaking his head as he cowered in the corner of his cage, eyes wide with a terror she could feel from the other end of the building. "For God's sake, no!"

"Stop!" she yelled, enraged, shaking all over. "Let him go, you fucking *evil* assholes!"

No one even glanced her way at the outburst. And then, before she could utter another word, another fighter stepped up, lit a match and tossed it inside.

The gas ignited with an audible whoosh, completely engulfing Mark in flames.

****

The steady beat of the Blackhawk's rotors pulsed against Adam's ears as they flew through the pre-dawn darkness toward their target. Cold air rushed in the open doors, his NVGs giving him a spotty view through the storm of the hilly terrain below.

Visibility was decreasing fast. They had a short window to work with before the worst of the sandstorm hit. The helo could fly in it but the pilots would have a hell of a time navigating even with the advanced avionics.

Adam wasn't worried about the extraction window. The only one he cared about was the one that was rapidly closing in on the deadline that would mark the end of Summer's life. He was desperate to get to her before that. He'd do fucking anything to save her, wished he could trade places with her.

The Jordanian pilot's voice came through the headset, his English perfect. "Two minutes to LZ."

To maximize the element of surprise, they had to insert about a mile from the village, and hump it in on foot. Not ideal but the last thing they wanted to do was risk the hostages' lives by alerting the captors to their presence and the Blackhawk's powerful twin engines weren't exactly quiet. And this way the noise of the wind would help disguise their arrival as well.

The guys all checked their gear one last time and settled back to wait the final seconds. They flew over the landing zone once, to ensure it was clear of enemy fighters, even though the sniper team on the ground had already reported the area was safe.

Circling back, the pilots lowered into a hover. When Colebrook's voice came through their comms announcing the perimeter was secure, Tuck led the way off the helo.

Adam jumped out after Vance and raced for the ridge that ran along the top of the valley below the village they needed to get to. Sand and grit scoured his face but his goggles protected his eyes. He had a clear view of his team as they rushed across the LZ and met up with Colebrook and his spotter.

The dark-haired agent waited near the ridge, close to where his spotter lay prone on the rocky ground, his gaze trained through his binos at the village above. "Three guards keep circling the perimeter," Colebrook told them. "Except for one guy, nobody else has come in or out of any of the buildings since we've been here. There's another group of fighters lower down in the valley," he added, pointing his thumb behind them. "They haven't moved yet but we're keeping an eye on them."

Adam glanced at his watch. They had less than two minutes to infiltrate the village and storm the main building to free the hostages before the deadline hit. There was no way that was going to happen. He was strung tight, every muscle in his body locked, frantic to get moving.

"We need you guys to provide overwatch while we get in position," Tuck told Colebrook. "On my signal, take out the guards. Then we'll handle the breach."

"You got it," the sniper team leader replied instantly, then got on comms and informed his guys of what was going to happen. Colebrook looked back at Tuck a few moments later and nodded once, his hazel eyes intense. "We're ready. Go get 'em."

Tuck waved them forward. "Let's haul ass."

Adam swung into line behind Vance's big frame as the assault team headed up the ridge. The climb was steep, their boots slipping as they clambered up over loose rock and dirt while the wind gusted around them. They stayed off the footpaths worn into the hill, where the enemy would be watching. At the top, they paused as Tuck and Cruzie took stock.

"Forty yards to the target building," Tuck murmured over the comm. "Stand by." He waited a few seconds, then signaled Colebrook.

The sniper teams fired, taking out the exterior guards.

"Guards down," Tuck confirmed a moment later. "*Go.*"

Adam pushed his body up and over the edge of the ridge and shoved to his feet, taking off at a dead run behind Vance.

They were seconds away from the front of the building when he heard it. The sound of bloodcurdling screams coming from inside.

Even though he'd never heard her make that sound before, Adam knew it was Summer. The hair on the back of his arms stood up and his stomach plummeted.

Oh my God, we're too late. Too fucking late.

Chapter Nineteen

T he horrifying spectacle playing out before her was already permanently seared into Summer's brain.

She screamed over and over at the top of her lungs, the sound shrill and filled with all the revulsion and shock she felt, unable to stop. Her skin crawled, chill after chill racing over her body. She kept waiting to wake up and discover this was nothing but a horrible, vivid nightmare.

But this was no dream. And even though she wanted to look away, she couldn't. She was paralyzed, unable to move, unable to even close her eyes to block out the hideous sight.

Mark was on fire in front of her. His agonized, panicked screams were filled with such raw terror that bile rushed up her throat, her heart so full of grief it felt like it might explode.

He was rolling around on the ground in his cage, twisting back and forth in the dirt in an effort to smother the flames. Instead, the gas soaked into the ground ignited while Mark's executioners stood around enjoying the show.

There was no escape for him, no matter which way he rolled. No reprieve from the unbearable agony he suffered as the flames blistered his skin and bit deep, stripping away the flesh from his bones.

She caught a glimpse of his face through the flickering flames as he struggled to his feet, his arms flailing, and wished she'd turned away. His face was already blackened, unrecognizable as human.

She was crying now. Deep, racking sobs that shook her entire body. She could feel the wetness of tears tracking down her cheeks, her chest and shoulders jerking with the force of her sobs. All to no avail.

These men had no mercy. No compassion.

As the seconds passed Mark's screams grew quieter, then stopped altogether. A few seconds after that, he ceased struggling.

He fell to his knees in the dirt, toppled onto his stomach and lay facedown in the flaming dirt. His legs twitched once, twice. Then his body lay eerily still as the voracious flames consumed what was left of him.

And the entire time Summer stared in horror, she knew it was only a matter of minutes before she suffered that same horrific death.

Something inside her broke, the horror of it too much to process.

Unable to look at Mark's body a moment longer, she covered her eyes with her hands and turned away, sinking to her knees in the dirt. The crackling of the flames and the stench of burning flesh made her sick to her stomach.

She gagged, swallowed the bile back down and huddled there with her arms wrapped around herself, trembling all over, teeth chattering with the force of it.

I can't die like that, she kept thinking frantically. *I can't.* She couldn't bear it.

A sharp popping noise slowly penetrated the layer of numbness encasing her. Then the sound of men's voices inside the building. Urgent. Shouts of alarm.

Her head came up. She blinked to clear her vision, her heart jolting when she saw men scrambling from the front of the building, all grabbing weapons.

Then it hit her. Gunfire. Someone was shooting outside, and the men were alarmed.

Her heart pounded against her ribs as a fragile seed of hope took root deep inside her. Was it a rescue force? Had Adam received and understood her message? She didn't even care who had found them or how, she just wanted out of this cage, to be taken away from this horrific place.

She wanted to *live* and to see Adam again.

Summer stared through the smoky air in the direction those shots were coming from. *Please let me live. Please...*

Just as the bubble of hope began to inflate in her chest, a man rushed through the veil of smoke obscuring the far end of the building. He hurried straight toward her with a focused look on his face that made the blood drain from her face.

She scrambled to her feet and balanced her weight on the balls of her feet to at least give her a chance at dodging what was coming. When he reached her, the man bent down to grab the can of gasoline.

White hot rage suffused her as she realized what was happening. They were in a rush to kill her quickly, before the rescuers could reach them.

Every hair on her body stood up in ferocious denial. *I'm not going to die with help just on the other side of that wall*, she vowed, steeling herself for the fight of her life.

The man raised the can, tried to slosh the contents on her. She dodged the stream, the liquid barely missing her as it puddled on the ground instead. The pungent smell of gasoline surrounded her, burning her nostrils and throat. She coughed, shrank away from the deadly fluid.

Her captor grunted in annoyance and tried again, stepping closer to the bars this time.

And suddenly, she knew. Her only shot at surviving was here and now.

Desperation took over.

Acting without thinking, Summer reached into the jumpsuit pocket for the stone-filled sock at the same time as she lunged forward. Teeth bared, she shot a hand through the bars and grabbed a handful of the man's shirt, locking her fist tight and jerking him hard against the bars.

His eyes widened in surprise for a split second but she was already bringing her right hand up, swinging the rocks toward the side of his head with all her might.

With a cry of rage, she hit him square in the temple, where the bone was thinnest, the force of the impact reverberating up her arm. The man jerked slightly then slumped over and fell against the bars, either stunned or knocked out, she didn't know and didn't care.

The instant he hit the ground she knelt. Grabbed the back of his tunic. Rolled him over until she could reach the gun sticking out from the waistband of his pants. She was panting for breath, her heart racing, stomach rolling and muscles quivering.

But then he stirred, groaning.

Scampering backward out of reach in case he tried to grab her, Summer pulled back the slide on the pistol, curled her finger around the trigger and fired twice in rapid succession between his shoulder blades.

The weapon kicked in her hands, the sound of the shots deafening, so different from when she'd shot on the range with Adam using ear protection. Blood spurted up as the bullets impacted, more of it quickly pooling around the body.

But there were other threats out there that she had yet to face.

Gasping and queasy, she raised her weapon and took aim at the shadows she could see moving through the smoke ahead of her. They'd be coming now. They would have heard the shots and would come to investigate. And the moment they saw their dead comrade, they'd kill her. She had to get out now, had probably mere seconds before someone shot her.

Hurry, hurry...

Her body was frustratingly sluggish, uncooperative in her need for haste. Keeping her weapon up and one eye on what was happening ahead of her, she bent again and reached back through the bars with a shaking hand to search the man for a key, anything she could use to unlock the cage. She cringed as she touched him, but she had to keep looking.

She found nothing but a dirty rag in one of his pockets.

Biting back a cry of despair, she pushed to her feet and backed up a step, aimed the pistol at the lock. She wasn't sure how many shots she had left but she had to risk using at least one more to get out of here.

Taking aim at the lock, she tried to steady her shaking hands. *You can't miss*, she warned sternly. *You have to hit it with the first shot.*

Though her hands and arms were unsteady she focused on her target just as Adam had taught her all those years ago, and squeezed the trigger. Sparks flew and a loud bang sounded as the bullet struck the metal. She cringed, half-expecting the gas on the ground to ignite.

When it didn't, she reared back and lashed out at the lock with a solid kick. The metal gave a little, but held.

Almost.

Spurred on by the raw will to survive, determined to free herself, she kicked again, using all the strength in her lower body, twisting to put her entire hip into it.

The lock bent more, but not enough.

Not enough.

She clenched her jaw, readied to make another kick but movement in her peripheral made her freeze. Her gaze shot to the left just in time to see Hadad materialize through the wall of smoke. A bolt of terror made her heart seize.

He stopped dead when he saw her, and in his dark eyes she saw both a flicker of surprise...

And fear.

Because she was sighting down the barrel of a weapon at him and knew that he was about to die.

Everything shifted into slow motion. Time became elastic, every heartbeat, each individual movement separate and clear.

Summer pivoted to face him, bared her teeth as she adjusted her aim. His right hand reached back for his own weapon, but he wasn't fast enough.

"I hope you burn in hell, asshole," she snarled at him as her finger curled around the trigger.

****

The instant Tarek saw her holding the pistol aimed at him he stopped and stood there immobile, too stunned to move. How had she even managed to get Feisel's weapon in the first place?

Even as he wondered it, a cold blast of panic shot through him. From the way she held it and the determined look on her face, it was clear she knew how to handle a weapon.

Everything happened in an instant.

He reached down for his own pistol, acting on pure survival instinct and the sickening prospect of what would happen if he was killed by a woman.

"I hope you burn in hell, asshole."

Her words had barely registered above the shouts and gunfire coming from behind him when a bullet struck him in the center of his vest, the impact like a hammer-blow to his breastbone. He grunted but the round didn't penetrate the armor.

Bitch! he fumed, biting back a howl of pain.

Before he could bring his pistol up, another round hit him, lower, but still on the vest. He growled, finally jerked the pistol up into firing position but a third slug slammed into his right shoulder.

Fiery pain swept through his arm and he lost his grip on the weapon.

It slipped from his hand. Even as he lunged for it, another tore into his side. He cried out and slapped his free hand over it, falling to his back.

Breathing through gritted teeth, he forced his eyes open and pushed himself upright, managed to get to his knees. His men were still pouring through the doors, engaging the enemy outside. The American woman still held the gun trained on him, was preparing to fire again.

Pure rage infused him. If he was going to die here, it would be in combat against a worthy male opponent.

He would *not* die by the hand of this infidel whore and miss the joys of paradise promised to him by Allah for dying a martyr's death. His love awaited him there; he would not be separated from her for all eternity because of this evil female.

More shouts sounded behind him, growing frantic now as his men rushed to intercept the attacking force.

The enemy was at the gate.

Unease streaked through him but Tarek couldn't tear his gaze off the female as he reached for his fallen weapon. Those cold green eyes bored into his through the bars of the cage and the world seemed to slow even further as her finger moved on the trigger.

He held his breath, braced for another impact...but nothing happened.

Because she was out of ammunition.

Triumph punched through him as he saw the moment she realized her predicament, her face going blank with shock.

With grim determination he reached for his fallen weapon. One of his men was rushing toward him now, rifle aimed at the woman. Tarek snarled for him to leave. This bitch was *his* to deal with and she would die by his hand.

His fingers were stiff as he closed them around the grip but he brought his left arm up, the gun shaking slightly in his grasp. The pain stole his breath, made him light-headed, but he fought through it.

She was frantically checking the chamber now, looking for another bullet that wasn't there.

Summoning his strength Tarek climbed to his feet and rapidly closed the distance between them. She looked up at him, her entire body going still, her eyes locked on his.

"You're a dead woman," he snarled. It infuriated him that this enemy bitch was alive and breathing when Lely was not.

The weight of the pistol was comforting in his hand. He curled his finger around the trigger, itched to raise it and fire right into the middle of that pale face staring back at him.

But that sort of death would be too easy. Too fast, too merciful. No, she had to die the way he'd originally intended. He needed to see her suffer for what she'd done.

A sudden rush of adrenaline muted the pain. He'd kill her and the other hostage, then escape before the enemy could reach him. He transferred the pistol to his other hand, covered a wince as the act of gripping it aggravated the wound in his shoulder.

Ignoring the burning ache of his wounds, he slipped his left hand into his pants' pocket and pulled out a lighter.

Now her eyes widened, fear leaching her face of all remaining color and showing the whites around her irises. It sent a wave of triumph through him.

She shook her head mutely in denial, as if she could ward him off, stop this from happening. But if she was hoping for mercy, she was a fool, for he had none. Not for the likes of her or any other American waging war against his people.

Tarek found himself smiling as he stalked forward, aware of the gunfire growing fiercer outside but unconcerned with it for the moment. Right now all he wanted was *this*. To watch this bitch burn and writhe before his eyes.

She backed away and pressed against the bars, and the rush of euphoria that swept through him nearly made him dizzy. He raised the lighter even higher, an almost sexual arousal flowing through him at the abject terror on her face.

That was better, much better than the determined expression she'd worn just a few moments ago. But it wasn't enough.

He needed to hear her screams, see the flames devour her. Even if only for a few seconds, just long enough to know she was receiving the divine punishment she deserved, that she wouldn't survive. Then he could turn his attention to the coming attack.

More shouts erupted behind him, calls for help, for his guidance. The sounds of his men scrambling to repel whoever was attempting to mount an attack. He would answer in a few moments.

He raised his thumb, flicked the metal wheel so that the sparks struck. A single flame burst free, glowing in the dark, smoky air. It was beautiful, glowing gold and orange with its heat. An insatiable heat that would soon devour her infidel body.

The building was suddenly plunged into total darkness.

Jerked from his trancelike state, Tarek lowered the lighter and half-turned around in confusion. They had a backup generator buried deep in the ground, the power shouldn't have gone out unless—

The far door burst open and multiple explosions went off almost simultaneously.

Brilliant flashes of light blinded him. He staggered back, instinct urging him to move off to one side and bring his weapon up to face the looming threat.

The enemy was here and he would send as many of them to hell as he could before they took him.

Chapter Twenty

Adam's heart pounded as he stood fourth in line along the wall to the left of the door, and waited. The dead guards' bodies lay where they'd fallen and no one else had come out to investigate yet. Colebrook and the sniper team had reported no further threats.

Those bloodcurdling screams from inside had stopped abruptly a few moments ago, but the chilling sound still rang in his ears as he waited for Tuck to give the order to breach the door.

He tried not to think about what the silence meant, but that was impossible when he knew his wife was just on the other side of the wall he waited beside.

The thought that Summer might just have been killed in there while he'd been mere yards away, unable to prevent it...

He blocked the thought as soon as it formed, shoved it into a tamperproof box in his mind and locked it down tight. Because if he dwelled on it for another moment, he'd lose his shit completely and be useless to the team.

He might even become a danger to them, and the entire operation could be blown. None of the hostages would make it out then.

So no. He had to believe Summer was still alive in there, and that he was going to save her.

Just as soon as Tuck pulled the trigger and gave the damn order to breach the building. As soon as he did, one of the snipers would cut power from the generator and put everyone inside in the dark. *Hurry the fuck up.*

Adam's hands remained locked around the grips of his weapon, the butt snug against his right shoulder, muzzle lowered. For now. Every second he waited there, poised to go and kick ass, felt like an hour.

Come on, let's go, he admonished silently, struggling to hold onto the tattered remains of his patience.

"Execute."

Finally!

At Tuck's quiet command they blew the charges on the door. And just like that, everything went into slo-mo.

Tuck went in first, Evers right behind him. Adam surged in behind Cruzie, his heart rate jacked and adrenaline pumping through him. Heavy smoke surrounded him, then he caught the unmistakable smell of burned flesh.

A wave of terror broke over him, punching through the formidable wall of his discipline.

The thick smoke swirling through the air made it impossible for him to clearly see anything at the other end of the building. As Tuck and Evers engaged two targets, Adam took in everything in a single, sweeping glance.

Beyond where Tuck and Evers were clearing the room to his right, what was left of one of the hostages lay smoldering on the ground inside what appeared to be a cage. And for one hideous moment he feared the worst.

Summer!

Was it her? His heart careened in his chest as he

stared at the body and only the stern snap of Vance's voice pulled him out of his head.

"Blackwell, ten o'clock!"

Adam whirled away from the sight of that burned body and turned to his left to face the threat, his training immediately kicking in, and probably the only thing that kept him from losing his mind. An enemy fighter materialized out of the smoke.

Vance fired, taking out the tango Adam hadn't even noticed until now because he'd been too busy staring at the burned body. Reaching down deep to regain his composure and get his head back in the game, Adam scanned the darkness, staring down the barrel of his rifle.

Everything happened so fast, yet time seemed to slow down as well. A tango darted out from behind a corner ahead of him. Adam fired two shots, dropping him in a split second.

To his left he saw two of his other teammates had engaged more fighters. Adam moved forward with Vance to check the far end of the building as the others cleared their own areas, scanning through the darkness with his NVGs.

Another fighter swung out from behind some stacked crates. Adam and Vance fired simultaneously, hitting him center mass. Before he'd even hit the ground, Adam was already searching for a new target. The building was long and the smoke made it hard to see clearly but it was lessening the farther he moved away from the front.

There should have been two more hostages in here but with all the smoke and confusion he couldn't see any sign of them yet. Where the hell were they?

Please let Summer be here and let her be okay.

He shook that thought away too, focused on the darkness up ahead. He funneled out the shouts behind him, the sharp pop of rounds firing, knowing his other teammates had things well in hand.

Then, as the smoke grew thinner, he saw it up ahead.

Another cage. There was someone in it, and they were still moving.

And someone was hurrying away from it.

Adam instantly shifted his focus to the man as the tango whirled, a pistol in hand, a fraction of a second too late. A bullet whizzed past his shoulder, barely missing him while he swung the barrel of his rifle toward the target.

Adam fired a double tap from his M4 at the tango's chest. The man stumbled backward and went to one knee, but didn't drop. And he got off another shot.

The round hit Adam in the lower ribs. He grunted, tensed against the hammer blow to his vest but kept his focus.

Fuck you, asshole. Staring his target down, he squeezed the trigger. Winged him as the guy dodged behind a stack of crates.

Adam followed, determined to kill the motherfucker.

It took every ounce of control to ignore the need to go to Summer, his heart screaming at him to free her and get her the hell out of there. But he couldn't until he'd eliminated this threat.

He crouched and wheeled around the corner of the stacked crates, just as a whooshing sound and a flash of light burned his retinas. He ducked and staggered back a step behind the crates, cursing as he shoved his NVGs up with one hand, momentarily blinded.

He blinked to clear his vision, saw that something on the ground between him and Hadad had ignited.

Hadad appeared through the veil of flickering flames. He was on one knee, raised his weapon as Adam took aim again.

In the light of the fire Adam could see the smug smile that formed on the bastard's face an instant before Adam pulled the trigger.

The round hit Hadad dead center in the forehead, dropping him where he knelt...

Just as a shrill female scream split the air.

Adam's head jerked up, every muscle in his body snapping tight at that sound. He stared in horror through the shimmering flames.

For one brief instant he glimpsed Summer's panicked face as she stood there outlined by the rapidly spreading fire coming toward her. Then Adam lost sight of her behind a wall of smoke and flame.

****

Summer shrieked again as the fire spread toward her and shrank back against the bars of her cage. In the darkness the fire blazed a bright orange and yellow, lighting everything up in front of her.

Even through the thick smoke she could see that Hadad was dead, lying a few yards away, right in the fire's path. It raced over him, sending up more of that godawful stench of burned flesh. The man who'd killed him was somewhere in front of her but she'd lost sight of him a second after the fire had started.

Something must have sparked the gasoline soaked into the ground. It was racing toward her now, moving closer with every millisecond. The heat was already so intense she had to cover her face with her arms. She cowered in the corner of the cell, as far away from the accelerant on the ground as possible, coughing as the smoke rose in a suffocating cloud around her.

Her instinct was to drop to the ground, but she knew she couldn't risk it. Not when more gasoline soaked areas of it.

"Help!" she screamed, hoping to get one of the rescuers to see her, even if she couldn't see anything past the fire. More gunfire cracked in front of her, telling her the good guys were otherwise occupied and couldn't help her.

Oh God, oh God…

With desperate hands she began tearing off her jumpsuit, afraid some of the accelerant had splashed on it without her noticing. Fumes could catch fire and she wanted the hideous thing off her before the flames got close enough to ignite them. Even a few seconds more time might mean the difference between life and death if it provided her rescuers with a long enough window to free her.

She stripped the garment down her legs, wrenched off the remaining sock and the shoes and hurriedly tossed everything through the back bars of the cage. The smoke was slowly choking her. Each time she drew a breath it filled her lungs.

"Someone, help!" she screamed, then choked. "Get me out of here!" She coughed again, covered her mouth and nose with a hand but it didn't help. At this rate the smoke might kill her before the flames reached her if she didn't escape the cage.

Naked except for her bra and underwear, she turned and grimly faced the lock, her frantic gaze automatically measuring the distance between her and the encroaching fire.

Less than ten feet. Only seconds before those hungry flames tore into her shrinking flesh.

A shudder ripped through her and tears burned the back of her throat along with the thickening smoke. She couldn't die with help so close! It was too unfair, too horrible to contemplate.

With her heart thundering against her ribs, she backed up as far as she could into the corner, gathered her nerve and lashed a bare foot at the broken lock with all her might. A roar exploded out of her as she did it, borne of anger and despair.

Pain reverberated from the sole of her foot and up her leg, but she barely felt it, every part of her focused on breaking through that fucking lock and saving herself.

"Summer!"

Her name, that voice, momentarily startled her out of her panic. Hope and recognition swelled inside her ribcage. Adam?

She blinked fast, frantically trying to find him through the smoke and flame, but her eyes were watering too badly. "Adam! Help me!" She doubled over, hacking as her body fought the effects of the smoke.

"I'm coming!"

More male shouts came through the wall of fire trapping her from her would-be-rescuers and the roar and crackle of it grew louder.

She drew a deep breath, coughed twice. "*Adam!*" She screamed it, those two syllables tearing from her throat, forced out by all the terror and horror smothering her as surely as the smoke was.

"Hang on!"

She still couldn't see him. *I can't*, she wanted to cry out, but she was out of breath, the coughing and lack of air weakening her quivering muscles. *I can't!*

The heat was too intense now, scorching her bare skin. She shrank back until the bars dug cruelly into her back, but there was no escape. All she could do was cower there, and shield her face as her flesh crawled with the knowledge that the flames would consume her at any second.

In that moment, everything went eerily silent. The only sound she was aware of was the roaring of blood in her ears. There was nothing but fear and horror and the terrible anticipation of the agony that awaited her.

Then, a miracle.

From out of nowhere a stream of foam sprayed through the bars of her cage. It splashed over her and the ground in wet, cooling rivulets, soaking her, dripping off her hair and skin. Automatically she shielded her face, turned her head to avoid the blast as someone aimed it at her.

"Summer!"

Adam. She couldn't answer him, doubled over in the corner struggling to breathe, coughing and gasping for air. The foam prevented her from opening her eyes. But she heard the hissing sound of it as it sprayed over and around her, felt the heat of the fire recede as it smothered the voracious flames.

And then she caught the sharp squeal of metal on metal as someone finally broke the lock and wrenched the door open.

A second later, strong hands grabbed her upper arms and pulled her away from the bars. Blindly she reached out to grip her savior's wrists as the hands wiped the foam from her face.

"*Summer.*"

Adam's voice, right in front of her. Hoarse and shaken.

God! Her face crumpled as she flung her arms around his neck and buried her face in his throat. She fought back a sob of pure relief and gripped his shoulders tight.

Adam, Adam, Adam, she chanted silently, reeling from everything that had happened, hardly able to believe that he was actually here, actually holding her.

Without a word he hauled her into his arms and lifted her from the ground. The world tipped sideways as he levered her across his wide shoulders and carried her out of the cage that had almost been her slaughter pen. Then he was running through the smoke.

Summer held on tight, kept her head down and her eyes closed. There were no more shots but she could hear men running, urgent commands and voices flowing around her, too fast for her to decipher. She bounced up and down with each of his running strides, hands gripping the back of his uniform.

"Hold up," someone with a Southern accent called out. Tuck maybe? She still couldn't see anyone, it was too dark and smoky.

Adam stopped and she struggled up through the heavy blanket of shock engulfing her, tried to understand what was happening.

"Summer, you okay?" he asked, his voice urgent.

She was alive and Adam was holding her. Nothing else mattered. "Think so," she murmured back, her throat raw from the smoke and the screaming. She was shaking all over, so hard her teeth chattered.

"You're safe now, we've got you. We'll get you out of here in a minute," he reassured her, running a soothing hand up the back of her thigh.

"W-want to go…h-home," she whispered, unable to stop trembling. Every second she could feel herself sliding deeper into shock. She fought it, wanting to stay alert and aware, but it was powerful, and coupled with the exhaustion, she knew it was probably a losing battle. And, as long as Adam was here, she was safe.

"I'll get you home, sweetheart," he promised, that steady hand wrapping around the back of her thigh and squeezing gently. "Just another few minutes and we'll be on a helo back to Amman, then we'll take a look at you and make sure you're okay."

She didn't answer, only clung tighter, savoring the feel of his hard muscles beneath her chest and belly, soaking up his warmth. Two minutes ago she'd been in danger of burning to death and now it felt like she might freeze. Had to be the shock, she reasoned.

Forcing her eyes open, she squinted and lifted a hand to wipe away the residual stinging foam. She was surprised to see they were at the front door now.

What were they waiting for? Adam was poised behind someone even taller and bigger than him and she could make out the silhouettes of other men gathered around them from the thin line of light coming through a crack in the door.

A moment later, she realized why they weren't leaving.

Somewhere outside in the distance she could hear the sound of gunfire. Sporadic, far away. Her stomach clenched as she realized what it meant.

More attackers.

Tuck's Alabama accent came again as he responded to something she couldn't hear. Then, "Ah, hell. The other enemy force spotted the helo. They're moving toward the ridge, between us and the LZ. Sniper team's moving to intercept. We're gonna have to fight our way out of here."

Chapter Twenty-One

God dammit...

*G*od dammit...
If he lived long enough, maybe one day he'd be part of a mission that actually went according to plan. But that day wasn't today.

Bracing for a firefight with another enemy force was yet another shitty complication for them to deal with, on top of the strengthening storm.

Wasting no time, Brody Colebrook organized his sniper team into various positions around the LZ and kept a close eye on the enemy force through his binos.

Visibility sucked ass at the moment and it was only getting worse. The wind howled around him, whipping at his utilities and spraying him and his equipment with sand. Soon it would be bad enough that the helo crews would have a hard time navigating through this.

Those evil fucks inside that building had just burned one of the hostages alive but at least Blackwell's wife and the other hostage were okay. Brody and his team were going to make sure the survivors and assault team got onboard the helos safely.

He got on comms to his team, and Tuck. The first Blackhawk was already here, holding just out of firing range, waiting to attempt a landing on his order. But with the number of enemy fighters he knew about coming out of that valley beneath them, it was too risky.

"Change of plans. We've got company headed our way, so I'm going to request a new LZ, half a klick to the east. I've requested air support as well. Stand by."

As he received replies in the affirmative, Brody got on the radio to the second Blackhawk pilot and motioned for his spotter to get up and follow him. Together they ran in a crouch to a better-concealed position and hunkered down behind a large group of boulders just below the lip of the ridge. From there he had a decent view of the new LZ, and so far, it was clear.

Now he and his team had to keep it that way if Tuck and the others were going to get the remaining hostages out of here in one piece.

"Hey, I got movement at my one o'clock," one of his guys reported from the northeast. "One tango. Appears to be unarmed."

Brody immediately stretched out on his belly to take a look. Sure as hell, off in the distance he made out a man's silhouette skirting around the east edge of the ridge. He was bent forward, one hand raised to shield his face from the blasting wind and sand.

Too far away for Brody to see him clearly through the storm. "You sure he's unarmed?"

"No rifle at least."

Brody peered through the binos. "Civilian?"

"Maybe."

Nah, couldn't be. Not out here, not in this storm.

He clenched his jaw. The rules of engagement for this mission didn't allow them to take out an unarmed target, something their Jordanian hosts had been adamant about. Even if there was a possibility this man might give away their position, if he was unarmed, Brody and his guys couldn't take him out.

But they sure as hell couldn't afford to let him get close enough to spot them, give away their positions to the enemy coming at them from below.

"I'll get him. Everyone else, hold your position and be ready to move. If any of those assholes come within range, take them out. We have to hold them off until the assault team gets the hostages aboard the helos."

Moving fast, he stayed below the lip of the ridge to help conceal his path. Wind gusts pushed and pulled at him as he ran, headed straight for the unsuspecting man. Hunting and stalking were second nature to him—he'd been doing it since he was a kid back home in Virginia, where he'd grown up with a gunny sergeant father and three brothers. The Marine Corps had helped him perfect those useful arts.

Brody paused at twenty yards away from his target. The guy definitely wasn't carrying a rifle. He was headed straight toward Brody, seemed to be headed for a path Brody had seen that would take him down to the valley.

So he could warn the reserve force?

Not fucking happening, pal.

He crept closer, thankful for the flying sand that helped conceal his hiding spot. The man stumbled past, one hand shielding his eyes and the other holding his scarf around his lower face.

Brody pounced.

He dove at the man, caught him around the waist and tackled him to the ground. The guy let out a sharp yelp and tried to twist away, but it was too late. Brody had him facedown, one knee shoved in the small of his back and his hands behind him before he could draw breath to scream.

He jerked the man's pinned hands upward, hard. "Who are you and what are you doing?" he growled, giving a quick visual sweep. His Arabic sucked, but he knew at least that much. The guy was young, had only a pistol sticking out of the back of his waistband. Brody wrenched it from him.

"A-Akram," the man responded, frozen.

Didn't ring a bell. Brody reached into a pocket on his vest and pulled out some plastic flex cuffs, secured the prisoner's hands, then rolled the guy over. He flinched as Brody leaned over him, getting right in his face to cut the wind and get a better look at him.

"Who are you?" he repeated, fisting a handful of dark hair. He didn't fucking have time for this bullshit. Already he could hear two of his guys opening up on targets below, and the crack of AKs returning fire.

The man's brown eyes widened until the whites showed all around. They darted to the U.S. flag on Brody's shoulder, then up to his face. "You American. I help you!"

Nice try. "I don't need your help."

Akram shook his head. Or tried to, wincing when Brody didn't let up on his grip. "No, I help you. I tell your leader about prisoners." He nodded quickly, his expression equal parts sincere and fearful.

Brody reached up one hand and tapped his earpiece, contacting the operations center. "I got a guy here named Akram who says he gave us the location of the hostages. This true?" Whether it was or not, Brody wasn't letting him go.

"Stand by," DeLuca answered.

No problem, Brody thought sardonically. *I'll just hang out here with my new pal, getting my ass sandblasted and waiting for the guys down in the valley to come after us.*

A couple minutes later, DeLuca came back on. "That's affirm, Colebrook. Apparently he's our mystery informant. Bring him back here with the others so we can question him."

Wow. Okay then. "Roger that."

Still not trusting the guy, Brody hauled him to his feet and began half-dragging, half-frog-marching him back to where he'd left his spotter. He kept glancing down into the valley, a tingling at the back of his neck telling him they needed to get the hell out of here, *now*.

His spotter, Napoli, was gawking at them when they reached him.

"Don't ask," Brody muttered, shoving Akram down in front of him and raising his binos to check the valley. "How long do we have?" he asked.

"Couple minutes, maybe," Napoli said. "The guys are picking them off one by one, but we can't get them all."

Ah, shit. *Time's up.* He got on the radio to the Blackhawk pilots again. The first was already moving to the new coordinates. The second was still a few minutes out. Their gunship air support…well, he had no idea how far away that was, or if it was even coming for sure.

"Tango-Romeo, be advised," he said, using Tuck's operating initials, "we've got a situation here." He detailed it as rapidly as possible, then ordered his team to begin moving toward the LZ. "We hold them off until everyone is loaded aboard those birds, understand?"

His guys all responded in the affirmative. Brody turned to Napoli. "Let's go." He hauled Akram to his feet again and scrambled over the lip of the ridge. Dragging the prisoner over it, he straightened and turned to run.

A hot, bright pain sizzled through the outside of his left thigh, stealing his breath.

He went down hard, landing face-first in the dirt. "God *dammit*," he snarled, clapping a hand over the wound as he struggled to get up onto an elbow. Another round plowed into the ground inches in front of him, spraying him with rock and grit.

Napoli started to come back for him, but Brody waved him off. "Take Akram," he shouted, the pain a burning fire in his leg as he brought his rifle around to aim at the men rushing up the hill toward them. He fired at the closest target he could find, watched the man fall.

When he glanced up through the swirling sand he saw the outline of the Blackhawk moving in to attempt a landing at the new LZ and felt a measure of relief. They just might make it out of here after all.

Blood continued to pump out of his thigh, wet and sticky against his palm. His leg wasn't bent at a weird angle. Maybe the femur was still intact.

He fought the wave of fear gathering at the edge of his consciousness. Thoughts of Wyatt flashed through his mind, the IED blast. The endless surgeries that hadn't saved his leg.

I can't lose my leg. He'd seen what it had done to his brother. The way it had transformed him, inside as well as out.

He gave himself a mental shake, pushing the frightening thoughts aside. His leg was still attached and it didn't matter a damn anyway if he got killed out here.

No, he ordered himself sternly. His family had gone through too much already. There was no way he was going to add to their pain by getting killed. He was too exposed though. If he could just make it to one of the helos, maybe he'd make it out alive too.

But to do that he had to clear off some of the enemy rushing toward him.

Fighting through the haze of pain, he rolled to his belly and brought his weapon up, put his eye to the scope and got back to work.

Chapter Twenty-Two

Hunkered down inside the darkened building they'd just cleared, Adam shifted Summer in his lap and made sure his rifle was within easy reach. She was still trembling pretty hard but the worst of the shaking had stopped a couple minutes ago. At least where they were the smoke wasn't too bad.

He glanced up at Tuck, who stood next to the doorway, peering out through the small gap between the edge of the door and the jamb. "What's the ETA on the second helo?" he asked.

"Six minutes," Tuck replied, then put his hand to his ear. "Go ahead," he said to whoever it was on the other end of the comm. Probably Colebrook. "Copy that." He paused to look back at all of them. "Sniper team's gonna give us cover, but it's gonna be tight and the storm's worse." He met Adam's gaze. "You ready?"

Adam nodded once. "Yes." He was so fucking ready to get Summer out of here and onto one of the birds. He took off his scarf and wrapped it around her face to shield it from the stinging sand. Then, lifting her across his shoulders, he clamped one hand on the back of her thigh and gripped his rifle with the other.

"Hostages go first," Tuck said. "We'll cover Blackwell, Vance and Cruzie, then follow. Go." He pulled the door open and stepped outside into the comparatively bright light.

"Keep your head down and your eyes shut," Adam said to Summer. A scarf wasn't going to protect her face completely but it was the best he could do at the moment.

"Okay," she answered in a small voice, her hands clenching around fistfuls of his uniform.

Adam raced out the door and past Tuck. The wind was strong enough that he had to lean into it, and yeah, the visibility was the shits because of all the sand swirling around.

He could just make out the shape of the Blackhawk descending at the new LZ, headed straight for it while gunfire rang out to his right and behind him. He could see the sniper team moving into defensive positions close to the LZ.

And he spotted someone struggling to his feet, then take a lurching step forward before falling.

Adam recognized him instantly, and knew what had happened.

Shit. "Colebrook's hit," he announced to the others. He wasn't stopping though, not until he had Summer safely aboard the helo. Two of Colebrook's guys were already racing toward him as Adam ran for the first Blackhawk.

"I got him." Bauer veered away and pounded toward the injured sniper.

He grabbed Colebrook, tossed him over his shoulders and ran with Adam the rest of the way to the waiting helo. Cruz had the other surviving hostage with him, one hand clamped around the guy's upper arm. Vance carried the third hostage's remains in a body bag.

Cruz and the surviving male hostage got there first. The instant the man was safely inside the helo, Cruzie turned around and leveled the barrel of his weapon at the approaching enemy force. Vance reached it next, climbing inside to unload his burden and then popped back out to add more firepower to Cruzie's efforts.

Adam was breathing hard by the time he got Summer to the Blackhawk's open door. He set a hand on the deck and jumped inside, carrying her as far toward the tail as possible before setting her down and crouching next to her. She'd taken off the scarf. He took her face between his hands, anxiously scanned it. Her skin was smudged with soot and her eyes had that glassy look that told him she was well on her way to going into shock, but he couldn't see any visible injuries.

"You all right?" he asked. "You hurt anywhere?"

She shook her head almost mechanically and wrapped her arms around herself. "No."

Satisfied that she was mostly okay physically, Adam pulled her to his chest and slid his arms around her back to warm her. Outside he could hear the sound of gunfire over the noise of the engines, the pitch telling him it was his teammates.

One of the Jordanian crewmembers handed him a blanket. He wrapped Summer in it and looked back over his shoulder just in time to see Bauer lever Colebrook inside. The sniper's expression was tight with pain, one hand pressed to the outside of his left thigh where blood soaked through his pants.

Bauer looked at Adam. "More of those bastards are closing in," he said grimly. "I need to get back out there. You got him?" he shouted over all the noise.

He nodded. "Got him." Releasing Summer for the moment, he reached across and helped drag Colebrook away from the open door, providing him with at least the protection of the helo's body. Not much, but better than nothing.

"I'm okay," Colebrook insisted, face pale and chalky as he waved Adam off with one hand and pressed a dressing to his wounded leg with the other. "Go clear those assholes off that ridge."

With pleasure. He would do whatever it took to make sure he got Summer out of here safely.

Adam ripped a pouch on his tactical vest open and came up with a fresh pressure dressing for him, then looked back at Summer. Her face was pasty white, her freckles standing out in sharp relief and her eyes were glassy as she stared back at him.

He wanted to stay right here and hold her until this was all over but he couldn't and it made him crazy. But God, he couldn't leave her without giving her some sort of assurance and comfort.

He slid a hand around the back of her neck, leaned in so she'd hear him clearly over the noise. "Everything's gonna be okay, doll, but I've gotta go help the guys secure the LZ. Stay right here and keep warm. I'm gonna get Schroder in here, then I'll be back as soon as I can." He paused, made sure she was focused on him, that she was registering every word. "I love you."

Her eyes widened with a fear that threatened to break his heart in two and she grabbed hold of his wrist, her mouth opening as if she would argue. But he didn't have time because his team needed him and the only way they were getting out of here was if they secured the LZ.

Hating to leave but having no choice, he pulled free and turned for the open door. Weapon to his shoulder, he hopped out of the helo.

Cruzie was on one knee close to the helo's tail and Vance had moved forward a dozen yards or so toward the ridge. Tuck and Evers were both on one knee close to him.

Adam scanned around for Schroder, found the team medic off to the left with Bauer.

Not wanting to distract anyone with chatter over the comms at a time like this, Adam raced for him. His teammates fired controlled bursts at the enemy fighters as the sniper team withdrew and raced up the hill for the LZ.

Adam kept his head down, ran at a crouch over to Schroder and set a hand on the former PJ's shoulder. "Colebrook's on board the helo. You need to look at him and then Summer." He had to keep her and everyone safe, help clear these bastards away until the team was in the air.

Schroder nodded once, his gaze glued to the fighters converging on them from the distant ridge. "Cover me."

Adam released his shoulder and dropped to one knee. "You know it. Go." As soon as Schroder took off, Adam moved into his spot.

"One o'clock," Bauer told him. "Any second now."

Staring through his sight, Adam homed in on that spot and waited. Sure enough, a few seconds later, the first of the reserve enemy force came swarming over the crest of the ridge like ants. Two dozen of them at least, their bodies partially obscured by all the sand and grit flying through the air.

Tuck's voice came through his earpiece, calm and steady. "Maintain suppressive fire and get ready to fall back on my command."

Adam fired at one guy in the lead, hit him in the lower chest. The next he hit in the shoulder, but the guy went down and rolled around on the ground so he focused on the next target.

He could hear rounds whizzing past every so often, but they were high, over his and Bauer's heads. His heart was beating fast but his hands were steady on his weapon as he engaged target after target.

But no matter how many he and the others took out, more just kept on coming. "How many more are there?" he asked over the comms.

"Thirty or so that we know about, but there may be more hidden out of sight," Tuck replied. "Everybody hang tight. Sniper team's moving around to our eight o'clock."

Yeah, but where the hell was the air support, and the other Blackhawk?

The first one couldn't carry all of them out of here. They had to wait for the second to arrive before they could evacuate everyone and they were going to need some serious firepower to allow them to do that. The deteriorating viz was going to make that a challenge for the pilots, but staying here much longer was damn near suicidal.

The enemy was getting closer now. Close enough that Adam could see each individual scarf covering the lower part of their faces.

Someone on the sniper team announced their position, holding off and to the rear left. A bullet hit the ground not five feet in front of him and Bauer, pelted him with bits of rock. Adam squeezed the trigger and fired two consecutive shots, dropping the fighter in the lead.

But more appeared on the horizon.

We need to get the hell out of here.

He thought of Summer huddled under that blanket in the back of the helo, thought of the hell she'd already been through and a protective rage built inside him. He wanted her out of here now, safe from any further threats.

He'd just fired at another fighter when he finally heard it: the faint throb of rotors above and to the right. Sparing a quick glance in that direction, he made out the vague silhouette of another Blackhawk against the rust-brown sky. "Second ride's here," he reported to the others.

"Roger that. Fall back," Tuck ordered.

The sniper team announced that they were headed for the second helo.

Adam got up and ran a few yards toward the first, then dropped to one knee and covered Bauer as he did the same. They leap-frogged their way back toward the waiting Blackhawk while the enemy kept gaining ground.

Sand struck the helo's main and tail rotors, creating a glowing ring of sparks. Vance and Cruzie were directly beside the door now, Tuck and Evers only yards away.

Adam was halfway to them when the lead fighters in the advancing force began firing at the helo. Half a dozen rounds struck the tail, pinging off the metal in bright sparks of light.

Summer was in there.

On a rush of adrenaline Adam whirled and opened up on the enemy. They'd all spread out now, fanned across the open space as they charged toward Adam and the others. He sprayed out his shots while Bauer did the same, trying to mow down as many as possible and buy them time.

But as many as he shot, more took their place.

Bauer shouted at him over the din. "Let's go, move!"

Adam turned and raced headlong for the Blackhawk while the rest of his team covered him and Bauer. He could see the sniper team doing the same at the second helo, saw more sparks fly as enemy bullets pinged off the metal body.

Then a new noise sounded over the chaos. Adam looked up in time to see the unmistakable outline of an Apache gunship burst out from behind the crest of the hill.

Yes!

It rose sharply overhead and immediately opened up its chain gun on the enemy force. He saw the muzzle flashes, heard the buzzing sound but didn't look back.

Only when he was within a few strides of the open door did he look over his shoulder. Black-clad bodies lay strewn everywhere on the horizon, the Apache's harvest.

He leapt aboard with Bauer right on his heels, his gaze immediately moving to the rear of the aircraft. Summer was still wrapped up in the blanket. He saw the flash of pure relief in her eyes when she saw him, and a tidal wave of emotion crashed over him. He climbed over Colebrook and Schroder to get to her.

Hunkering down beside her, he slung his weapon across his back and pulled her into his arms. "You okay?" he shouted over the sudden increase in volume as the Blackhawk's engines powered up.

She nodded, face pressed into the side of his neck, her arms curled against his chest. "Just glad you're safe."

After all this, he should be saying that to her. "We'll be outta here in a minute," he told her, stroking a hand over the tangle of her hair, which was all crusty and smelled of smoke and gasoline.

He buried his nose in it and held her tight as the pilot rocketed the bird into the sky. After a few seconds he looked back, past his teammates and out the open door. As the Blackhawk banked to turn them toward Amman, he got his first clear view of the battlefield below.

There were at least forty bodies scattered over the ground that he could see, and another ten still moving around. All he knew was, he was damn glad to not still be down there.

The pilots leveled them out and cruised back toward Amman. Adam settled back against a bulkhead with Summer curled against him and drew the first deep breath he'd had in a damn long time.

Schroder came over and crouched next to them, putting a hand on Summer's shoulder. "How you doing?" he asked, giving her his patented lady-killer smile, the one he'd used with much success until Taya had come along and changed his world.

"I'm okay," she said, still pressed against Adam. "Just cold."

"Can you humor me and let me take a look anyhow?"

Summer seemed to hesitate. "Let him check you over, doll," Adam told her, easing her away, worried she was in shock and might not be aware of her injuries. At a minimum she'd suffered some smoke inhalation, may have burns inside her throat from breathing in the hot fumes.

Reluctantly she sat up and lowered the blanket around her. She was only wearing her underwear and Schroder moved in closer, angling his body to block her from anyone else's view.

Adam began stripping off his gear, his uniform. He peeled off the T-shirt he'd been wearing under it and tugged it over Summer's head, even though the other guys were all pointedly looking elsewhere, trying to give them as much privacy as possible.

Adam shifted her off his lap so Schroder could get a better look at her. He hid a wince when he saw the reddened area on her hands and arms, where the heat of the fire had singed her. It wasn't blistered but the sight of it still made him want to snatch her up and never let her go because it reminded him of how close she'd come to burning in that fucking cage.

Pushing out a slow breath to calm himself, he watched as Schroder did a thorough examination. He checked her skull, her eyes and didn't seem concerned by anything he found there. The sole of her right foot was bleeding from a few cuts and there were mottled bruises marring her ivory skin.

He wanted to stroke his fingers over each mark, kiss each one of them better. Instead he ran a hand over her hair, just to remind her that he was there and not going anywhere.

Schroder cleaned the cuts on her foot, put ointment on them and her minor burns before bandaging her foot up and tucking the blanket back around her. "There you go," he said to her with a kind smile.

"Thank you," she murmured, and immediately leaned back into Adam.

Something in his chest eased at the gesture, and a sense of peace filled him as he wrapped his arms around her once more.

The aftermath of this was going to be hard, he already knew that. But they'd gone through so much already, he knew they could handle this if they stuck together.

This time, he wasn't going anywhere. He was going to be there for her every step of the way, help her overcome this no matter what it took.

Chapter Twenty-Three

———————∽———————

Back in Amman a flurry of activity awaited them. A security team was waiting for them at the airfield, and whisked them straight to the operations center.

Adam refused to let Summer out of his sight the entire time. He folded his arms across his chest and watched her closely while she answered questions and gave statements.

On the one hand he understood that the director and other intelligence officials needed to talk to her immediately in the off chance that she might give them something that would help them round up other ATB cell members, but on the other hand he wanted to tell them to leave her the hell alone and then carry her out of there. She'd been completely traumatized by what happened and was ready to drop.

The sweats someone had loaned her hung on her small frame, making her look even more fragile and lost. He stayed with her through the two interviews then ran out of patience. She was done, and he couldn't stand watching her suffer through this ordeal another moment.

While the rest of his team went into its usual post-op debriefing he argued his case with DeLuca and the director and finally won his request to take her back to his hotel so she could clean up and rest. By the time he finally got her out of there he was in pure caveman mode, his sole focus on protecting her from everything and taking care of her.

There was a metric shit-ton of paperwork and reports still to be filed but all that was trivial bullshit compared to what Summer was dealing with, and there was still a possibility that he could be pulled away from her again tonight. Director Foster and his people had begun interrogating the guy Colebrook had taken prisoner and Foster was determined that they help the Jordanians destroy whatever was left of this ATB cell *tonight*.

Adam clenched his jaw and fought back the ten arguments that immediately leapt onto his tongue. His wife was teetering on the brink of collapse from exhaustion and he wanted to do whatever he could to see to her comfort right now. It made him insane that he might have to leave her later on.

He drove her to the hotel alone, insisted on carrying her up to his room despite her protests. Two FBI agents were already posted outside the door when he got there.

One of them, a female agent that reminded him a little of Celida, stepped forward to show her ID. "SA Maya Thatcher," she announced, then slid it back onto her belt. "The room's secure."

"Thanks." He stepped around her, paused when he saw Taya waiting in the hall.

"Hi," she said softly, giving Agent Thatcher a brief nod before focusing on Summer. Adam felt Summer tense in his arms but then Taya gave her a disarming, gentle smile. "I'm Taya, Schroder's girlfriend. I just wanted to see if you guys needed anything."

Adam could have kissed her for her thoughtfulness. "If you could send up some food, that'd be awesome."

"Sure. If you think of anything else, just call me."

"I will. Thanks."

Agent Thatcher unlocked the door for him and he carried Summer inside. The instant the door closed behind them, an overwhelming sense of relief hit him. He hadn't realized just how tightly strung he'd been or how much he'd been craving the quiet until now.

He set Summer on his bed, then crouched down to check the bandage on her foot. It was perfect and there was no blood seeping through, but of course he shouldn't have expected anything else, since Schroder was a pro.

He stilled when a gentle hand settled against the side of his face, and looked up.

"I want a shower," she said.

"Yeah, of course."

He pulled her to her feet and followed her to the bathroom. She looked at herself in the mirror and cringed.

"I look like hell," she said.

Adam stepped up behind her, circled his arms around her waist and set his chin on top of her head. Her bright auburn hair was oily and covered with soot and fire retardant. She had dark purplish-blue circles beneath her eyes and her forearms and hands looked like they'd suffered a bad sunburn. "You're still beautiful to me."

She gave him a weary smile. "Thanks."

He reached for the shower nozzle and turned the water on while she stripped. As she stepped beneath the spray she winced, and he realized the heat of it must have stung the burns on her arms and hands. "Too hot?" he asked, immediately reaching for the knob.

"No, it's okay," she murmured.

Adam shucked his own clothes and stepped into the shower with her. Summer stood beneath the water, unmoving, and he could see the exhaustion in every line of her body. He ran his hands gently over her body, cataloguing every scrape and bruise, then worked shampoo into her wet hair and rinsed.

He washed it three times to try and get rid of the acrid smell of the gasoline and smoke. Then he soaped and gently cleaned her body, careful of her sore arms, rinsing away the dirt and grime, but he couldn't wash away the memories or the fear that haunted her.

After they were both clean he shut off the water and bundled her up in a towel. He put toothpaste on his toothbrush and handed it to her as she was finishing toweling off her hair. "Here."

"Thanks." When she was done brushing her teeth she stood up, slipped her arms into one of his clean T-shirts and then put on the hotel robe he'd snagged from the back of the door.

There were so many things he wanted to say and to ask, but he didn't want to push her for conversation right now.

Summer turned to face him, the bright lights over the mirror glinting off her clean hair. "So I'm guessing you got my message in that video, huh?"

"Yes." Running a hand over her hair, he kissed her softly, careful not to abrade her soft skin with his whiskers. "That was so damn brave, and *smart*."

Her lips quirked, her eyes warming with wry humor. "I'm just glad you saw it and figured it out in time."

Needing to kiss her again before his heart split open, he framed her face between his hands and leaned in, but stopped when she set her fingertips on his lips. He blinked at her, surprised.

Her expression was so full of emotion, her light green eyes glistening with tears. "I meant what I said in it," she whispered, her voice rough. "I do love you. More than anything. And I'm so sorry for all the ways I've hurt you and let you down—"

Adam cut her off by covering her mouth with his. God, her words tore him apart, and he hated that's what she'd been thinking about as she awaited what had almost been her execution. They'd both screwed up, were both to blame, but probably him more than her. But he didn't want to talk about that right now, he just wanted to reconnect with his wife.

He held her precious face in his hands and just kissed her, sinking into her, into this moment. She was safe and in his arms and he would never let anything happen to her again. He kissed her deep and slow, a fervent melding of lips and tongues to convey everything she meant to him better than words ever could.

When he eased back he traced his thumbs over her cheekbones, wishing he could take away the shadows both beneath and in her beautiful eyes. "I know, sweetheart. And I love you so damn much. I was so fucking scared that we got to you too late…" His voice caught and he swallowed.

A small shudder rolled through her. "I didn't think I'd ever see you again."

Adam cursed silently and drew her into his arms. She leaned into him, held on tight and just stood there with him for a few minutes, absorbing the feel of each other. "Let's get you into bed," he murmured, bending to slide an arm beneath her knees and lifted her into his arms.

He eased her down onto the bed and walked around it to the other side, about to get in with her when his cell rang.

The sharp, urgent ringtone cut through the room, making them both stiffen. *Fuck, no,* he thought, hesitating at the side of the bed. They couldn't be calling him back in. Not now.

Summer watched him without a word, her eyes full of ghosts he'd do anything to banish.

Adam spun around and went to his phone. DeLuca's number was on the display. "Blackwell," he answered, still hoping his commander might simply be calling to check on him.

"Hey. Listen, I know the timing's shit and you've got other things on your mind, but we need you back in here. The director's got us spearheading a possible op to arrest more of this ATB cell's members. If he pulls the trigger, we'll be sent out within the next couple hours."

God dammit. Adam clenched his jaw as a mix of frustration and disappointment warred inside him. "You need me there right now?" he made himself ask.

"Yeah. I'm sorry, man."

Adam expelled a harsh sigh and rubbed his fingers over his eyes. "All right. I'll be there asap." He hung up and walked back into the bedroom.

Summer was watching him with haunted eyes, her arms wrapped around her upturned knees. "Do you really have to go already?" she whispered.

It made him fucking nuts to leave her right now, but he had no choice. "God, I wish I didn't, but yeah, I do. I'll be back as soon as I can though." Cold comfort to both of them when all he wanted was to climb under the sheets with her and hold her tight against his body. He went over to sit next to her, swore he'd make it up to her somehow once he got back.

"It's okay." She reached up, traced a thumb across his cheek in a gentle caress he felt all the way to his bones. "I'll be fine."

But they both knew she wouldn't be.

Christ. Adam grabbed her again and crushed her in his arms. She hitched in a breath and he squeezed his eyes shut, praying silently.

Please don't cry, he begged her silently. She was more than entitled to a total breakdown but it would slice him to pieces if she did because then there was no way he would be able to leave her.

He could feel himself breaking apart inside as he held her, struggling to hang onto his composure. She needed him to be strong, needed him to keep his shit together. But fuck, he hated to leave her like this.

Summer remained pressed up against him, her arms tight around his shoulders, little hitching breaths telling him how close she was to losing control. But she didn't. Maybe because she was just too emotionally exhausted or maybe because she drew comfort from him, she calmed.

After a few minutes her grip relaxed and she let out a tired sigh. "I'm so tired."

"I know you are, doll. You need to get some sleep." Now he needed to put a positive spin on everything, leave her in the best frame of mind possible.

Taya, he decided. He released Summer and dialed Taya, asked her to come up and stay with Summer while he was gone.

"No," Summer protested in a whisper, shaking her head as he talked. "I just want to be alone."

Much as he understood that, leaving her alone was the last thing he was going to do.

He ended the call, turned to her. "Taya's gonna come up and stay here until I get back. I don't want you to be alone right now."

Summer leaned her head back against the headrest, looking annoyed and tired. "Fine," she muttered.

Adam hugged her one last time and eased back, even though it felt like he was peeling his skin away to do so. "I gotta go now. Taya's awesome, you'll fall in love with her in under five minutes flat, I promise. Have something to eat and then get some sleep. I'll be back before you wake up."

From his pocket he pulled out the vial of prescription pills the doctor had given him at the operations center. "Just in case. And there's no shame in taking them either."

She took the vial, slid her hand around the back of his head and leaned in for another kiss. "Love you."

He pressed his forehead to hers. "Love you too. I'm so damn sorry about this."

"I know."

Rising to his feet, he trailed a finger down the side of her cheek. "See you soon." Then he made himself turn around and leave her, even if it was the last thing on earth he wanted to do.

Chapter Twenty-Four

Summer released a deep breath and ran a stinging palm over her face when Adam left. She'd told him she understood why he had to go, but the truth was she wasn't okay with it. It didn't matter that she knew Adam had no choice in the matter.

She'd almost been set on fire a few short hours ago, pretty much the worst way for a person to die that she could think of, and now the director was insisting Adam leave her here to deal with that and everything else on her own.

The only thing that helped was knowing he'd be back as soon as he could. But without the reassurance of his presence, she felt fragile inside all of a sudden.

Thankfully she didn't have time to dwell on that because a moment later a light rap came at the door and then Taya pushed it open a few inches, peering at her through the small gap. "Is it okay for me to come in?" she asked tentatively.

In truth, Summer would rather be alone at the moment but she was too exhausted to argue and she'd already agreed to this, so... "Sure, come on in." She pulled the robe back on, tied it around her waist.

Taya shut the door and crossed to a chair set in the corner of the room, the straps of a big bag slung on her shoulder and a tray in her hands. "I got you some food."

"Thank you." She took the tray containing fruit and a bowl of soup and put it on the nightstand.

"No worries." Taya's gray eyes were warm. Summer could see the fine webbing of scars that tracked down the side of her neck.

She knew at least some of what had happened to Taya in Afghanistan. Apparently Schroder had gone in to rescue her, and had literally saved her life when a missile had exploded too close to them. Adam had told her about it right after the terrorist attacks at the Qureshi trial, but now Summer was even more curious about her.

Taya waved a hand. "Don't mind me. You go do whatever you need to do and just pretend I'm not here. But if you feel like talking about anything later, I'm a good listener," Taya added.

For some reason the kind offer put her precariously close to tears. Right now all she wanted was Adam, and couldn't have him.

Summer swallowed hard. "Thanks." She was tired and hungry and sore, but she was alive.

In that instant she thought about Mark. She saw him flailing as the flames burned him, heard his chilling, agonized screams. And she thought of Vance carrying what was left of him to the chopper in that body bag. She'd seen it being unloaded back at the airfield, even though Adam had tried to block her view.

Goosebumps prickled across her skin and her stomach twisted.

She pulled the robe tighter around her body, struggled to maintain her composure. Adam's scent rose up from the T-shirt she wore, made her chest ache and tears burn the back of her throat.

Her stomach rumbled. She'd thought she'd want nothing more than to sleep, but dreaded closing her eyes right now, knowing she was probably going to have nightmares for a long while after this.

Summer ate the soup first, then nibbled on the fruit while Taya read in a chair by the window. She hadn't wanted any company but the other woman had an undeniably calm demeanor that Summer found incredibly soothing, and she felt safer not being alone. "Thanks for being here," she murmured when she was done eating.

"You're more than welcome. And don't feel like you need to stay up and chat just because I'm here. If you're ready to sleep, go right ahead. I'll stand watch," she added with a smile that felt like a hug.

She was so sweet. But Summer was afraid that if she did hug Taya, she might burst into tears. And if that happened, she wasn't sure she could stop.

There were a lot of things she wished she could go back and redo, one of them being making an effort to get to know the significant others of the guys on the team. Summer cleared her throat. "You've probably wondered why I never came to any of the team get-togethers."

Taya shook her head. "I'm pretty new on the scene myself and even though I do speaking engagements for a living, I'm not really a social butterfly. I'm still getting to know everyone too. And I figured you had your reasons for staying away."

Summer was pretty sure everyone knew that she and Adam had been having problems, or at least that she'd moved out a while ago. "Well. They don't seem like very good reasons anymore, not even to me." She sighed, shaking her head at herself, regretting having lost all that time with him. "It's true that I tend to work some pretty crazy hours when we've got something important happening at work, but that was only a convenient excuse most of the time.

"With Adam and I…struggling, it just felt too awkward. I couldn't show up and just smile, pretend nothing was wrong. That's not how I'm built. So I thought it best that I stay away." Plus she couldn't stand being judged or talked about behind her back, and she hadn't wanted to open herself up to that kind of thing.

"I understand. I avoided social situations for a long time after I got home from Afghanistan for that same reason. And I'm sorry for what you've gone through. That's another reason I wanted to stay with you right now. When I say I understand what you've been through, I really do mean it. So if you ever want to talk to someone, you can come to me anytime."

The offer was as genuine as Taya seemed and that meant the world to Summer. "Thank you." She lowered her eyes, feeling empty inside. Bereft and grieving and the only thing that could make her feel better was Adam. "I'm pretty tired now. I think I'll try to sleep for a bit."

"Of course, go ahead. If you need anything, I'm here."

Summer smiled at her. Adam was right; after only a few minutes with Taya she already adored her. "Once I get home and take some time to process all this, I'm going to make sure I spend some time with you and the others." It was way past due and she'd felt really bad about that.

Taya held up a hand, shook her head. "Whenever you're ready, there's no rush. I know the others would love that though. They're a pretty special group of ladies. Each of us has been through our own trials and tribulations, and God knows it's not always easy dealing with everything that comes with loving our guys. Their job is dangerous. It's nice to know we all have each other's backs."

Summer loved the sound of that. With her family living so far away she'd felt isolated and without a support network. She'd denied herself the sense of community and sisterhood Taya had just talked about because she'd been too buried in her own pain.

After sliding between the sheets she eyed the prescription bottle on the nightstand. Tired as she was, she preferred the idea of oblivion rather than a restless sleep or risking waking up with nightmares. Mind made up, she took two of the sleeping pills and burrowed under the covers.

At first, vivid memories tormented her.

Summer squeezed her eyes shut, fought to banish them. Even with her eyes shut she knew Taya was right there, and that nothing would happen to her. After a while the exhaustion took hold and a sort of numbness invaded her and wiped her mind clean, whether from sheer fatigue or the pills, she didn't know.

Sometime later she woke with a scream in her throat. She jerked up onto an elbow and opened her eyes, only to find herself in complete darkness.

A hand settled on her shoulder. She wrenched away from it, her heart careening in her chest until she caught the low, soothing rumble and the spicy, clean scent that could only be Adam.

"It's okay, doll, I'm here."

Adam. He's back.

Summer swallowed a whimper, tried to slow her galloping heart. She was covered in a film of sweat, the image of Mark twisting in the flames fresh in her mind.

She shivered and took a deep breath. The instinct to pull away was strong. Pull away and climb out of bed, retreat into the bathroom where she could be alone and fight to get a grip on herself. It's what she'd done in the weeks following the stillbirth. What she'd conditioned herself to do in response to an emotional crisis.

But now she realized that by pulling away from Adam before, she'd made them both miserable. She refused to make that same mistake again.

Though it went against her ingrained instinct to withdraw and curl into herself, she rolled over to face him and moved straight into his waiting arms.

And the instant they closed around her, she felt safe again.

****

Adam bit back a groan of sheer relief and gratitude when Summer reached for him rather than pull away. That single gesture hit him right in the heart and meant more to him than she'd ever know, because he'd been bracing for her to push him away again.

He wrapped his arms around her and pulled her in close, one hand cradling the back of her head as she tucked her face into his chest, her fingers digging into his skin. It felt so good to feel her arms around him, to know that she needed and trusted him.

He squeezed his eyes shut, sighed deeply. That must have been one hell of a nightmare if it had woken her from a dead sleep, and he could imagine all too well what it had been about.

"I got you," he murmured against her hair, holding her tight. God, he wished he could make this all go away for her.

He hated that she'd been through all this, that she'd been scared and cold and fearing for her life, wondering if she'd ever get out alive. There was still a faint tinge of gasoline beneath the scent of her shampoo, reminding him of how close she'd come to dying. It made him want to crush her to him and never let her go.

He'd fucking *loathed* leaving her earlier, had rushed back here as soon as he could. Thank God they hadn't been called out for the op. That was the only reason he'd been allowed to leave.

In response she pulled in a deep, shuddering breath, and let it out slowly. Her body remained tense against his, but at least he didn't think it was because she couldn't bear his touch. She'd come to him willingly, needing comfort. He'd give her all that and more, whatever she needed.

To his relief she burrowed in closer yet, hooking one leg over his, as though she couldn't get close enough. The unspoken trust and need for comfort turned his heart over and brought all his protectiveness to the surface.

"It's okay now," he whispered, smoothing his hand over her hair. He'd never forget the sight of her in that fucking cage, or the look of pure terror on her face when that fire had started right in front of her.

Her fingers flexed against his chest, restless, edgy. "When did you get back?" she asked, her voice rough and groggy with sleep.

"About an hour ago." He'd left the operations center as soon as he could, after finishing up the most critical reports and meetings. The other guys were still there but DeLuca had let him go early so he could get back to Summer. It was already one in the morning now.

"Didn't even hear you come in," she murmured.

Taya had told him Summer had taken the sleeping pills, so he wasn't surprised she sounded so groggy. "You were fast asleep when I got here." He'd slid in beside her, careful not to wake her, and just stared at her in the faint light seeping in from around the edges of the blackout blinds covering the windows. She'd slept peacefully until now.

She sighed and relaxed, her body melting against his. God, it felt so damn good to hold her this way. The only thing better would be to peel his shirt off her so she was naked. He was already hard against her abdomen, but sex had to be the last thing on her mind at the moment so maybe it was better this way.

He was just thankful that the feel of his erection against her stomach didn't make her pull away. Whenever they did have sex again, he didn't want it to be because she was looking to escape the fear and trauma. He wanted it to be because she couldn't bear to be without him a moment longer, the way he wanted her.

"Glad you're here," she mumbled, her heart still racing against his.

"Me too." He stroked her hair again, savoring the feel of her, wanting to calm her, make her feel secure again.

During the meetings he'd heard details from her boss about what happened during their captivity that would give him plenty of sleepless nights for the next while. Apparently Summer had somehow managed to disarm one of the captors and then killed him with his own weapon before turning it on Hadad. If not for the vest he'd been wearing, she would have killed him before Adam and his team had burst in.

Dammit, he wished he could have protected her from all that.

He was worried as hell about her mental and emotional state, considering what she'd already been through. But then he thought about that video message she'd put together and he was amazed by her resilience all over again.

Did she realize how strong she truly was? How brave and incredible she was, to come up with all that under that sort of stress? He wasn't going to bring all that up now though. Not when he knew she needed sleep, and time to deal with everything.

"Think you can go back to sleep now?" he whispered instead.

She nodded against him, stifled a yawn, and settled into a more comfortable position. "I want to go home," she murmured a moment later against his chest.

"I know. I'll get you out of here as soon as I can tomorrow." Just as soon as he could get clearance to leave and find them a flight, they were out of here.

She shook her head. "No, with you. And I mean I want to go to *our* home," she stressed, tilting her head back to look up at him in the dimness.

A sweet, sharp pain pierced him at her words. He'd been waiting, hoping for this for so long now, waiting for her to be ready to move back home so they could live like a married couple again. A wiser, more dedicated married couple.

"Yeah, sweetheart," he whispered, his own voice rough and his eyes stinging. "I'll take you home."

She snuggled back against his chest, pressed a kiss to his sternum. "Love you."

God. Throat tight with emotion, he wrapped her up tight in his embrace and kissed the top of her head. "I love you too." More than life itself. "Go ahead and sleep now, doll. I'm going to be right here holding you the rest of the night."

A sigh of relief escaped her. "Good," she murmured.

He lay awake beside her while her breathing turned slow and deep, all her muscles relaxing as she drifted off to sleep, and just held her, overcome with joy and hope for the future they'd come too close to losing forever.

Tomorrow, come hell or high water, he was taking her *home*. They'd pick up the pieces and finally start their lives again.

Together.

Chapter Twenty-Five

Virginia, two days later

Just outside their kitchen door, Summer paused and stood there watching Adam finish putting away the last of the groceries he'd laid out on the center island while she was out. He reached up into a cupboard beside the stove, the muscles in his arm bunching with the movement, the ones across his back and shoulders flexing beneath his shirt.

Heat and arousal stirred her blood. It felt like she was waking from a deep sleep after the chaos of the past few days.

After spending over two hours in her therapist's office, venting about everything that had happened in Jordan, she felt stronger now, more like her old self again. The initial horror and exhaustion and numbness had faded, allowing her to see what was most important in her life.

He was standing right in front of her. She was never letting him go again.

Adam could have given up and moved on when things had fallen apart for them. A lot of men in his position would have. Instead he'd stepped up and joined the fight to save their marriage. Then, just three days ago, he'd risked his life to rescue her, had literally carried her to safety.

A deep and abiding love for him filled her heart, making it swell so much it hurt. She swallowed hard.

In some ways it felt like she was seeing him through new eyes. This strong, brave and sexy man was all hers. Had been hers all along, even though she'd sometimes failed to recognize that for the gift it was.

A lump formed in her throat as she thought of how close she'd come to succeeding in pushing him away for good. That she'd nearly lost him forever.

But not anymore. She refused to hold back with him anymore, and she was done with holding onto the past. He'd made an effort after screwing up and she would too. After all this time they were finally on the same page. Starting here and now, she was reclaiming her man.

He looked over his shoulder when she stepped into the kitchen. A smile curved his delicious mouth amidst those dark whiskers as he turned toward her. She knew he was worried about her though, she could see it in his eyes. "Hey. How'd it go?"

"Good. I feel way better." The Bureau had set up everything for her while she was still in Jordan. She'd insisted on going to her first counseling session alone, even though he'd wanted to go with her.

It was important to her that she get everything out first without Adam there, so she could relay the events and all the chaotic emotions without making things harder on him. But she'd been careful to make sure he knew she wasn't shutting him out, that she'd just needed this time to process everything. She wanted him to go with her to as many of the remaining appointments as he could, if his schedule permitted it.

Gratitude and excitement fizzed inside her as she closed the space between them. She set her purse on the counter then wrapped her arms around his waist, leaning into his solid frame.

He returned the embrace, and just the feel of all that warm, hard strength enveloping her made her go tingly all over. And he smelled delicious, all clean and male. They'd arrived home late yesterday morning but with all the meetings keeping them busy, they hadn't had much time together. And when they'd finally both crawled into bed last night, they'd been too exhausted to do anything but sleep and had passed out in a matter of minutes. She sensed that he wanted more but had been worried about her, that he'd been tentative about touching her intimately.

But she wasn't tired now, and there was something she needed far more than food or rest. She needed her husband.

Taking his face in her hands, she leaned up to press her lips to his, knowing how lucky she was. He was her rock. Her hero, and the love of her life. She'd missed being intimate with him, ached to feel his hands and mouth on her naked body again.

The make-out session during their date at the drive-in had been pure torture, and she'd been impatiently waiting to make love ever since. After facing her own mortality a few short days ago, more than ever she wanted to lose herself in pure pleasure and wasn't waiting a second longer.

"I want you," she whispered against his mouth.

Heat and surprise flashed in his eyes but he didn't question her, didn't say anything at all as he plunged his hands into her hair and kissed her back. Long and deep, sliding his tongue into her mouth to stroke hers.

Summer pressed her body flush against his, relishing the feel of that steely strength. God, she'd missed him. Missed touching and kissing and having him inside her, the sense of connection, the pleasure she knew he could give.

Hungry for it, she moaned, rubbed her breasts over his chest as her tongue explored, her nipples already hard and aching and a restless ache building between her thighs. It had literally been months since they'd last had sex. At least four.

He growled low in his throat and picked her up, his hands holding her ass. She wrapped her legs around his waist and her arms around his neck, pressing the hot ache between her thighs against the rigid length of his erection she could feel through his jeans.

"Upstairs," she whispered, frantic to get them both naked. "In our bed."

Had to be in their bed, this first time since she'd moved back home. As a symbol of a new beginning for them.

Adam murmured his agreement and carried her up the stairs, his lips never leaving hers. The blinds were open on the windows over their bed, letting light stream in. With one hand he pulled the covers back and laid her down against the flannel sheets. The way he stared at her then, the raw hunger and need on his face, made her desperate.

She reached for him, dragged him down on top of her and grasped the hem of his shirt, impatiently peeling it up and over his head. Adam's fingers went to the buttons holding the front of her dress together, his mouth fused to hers.

Together they stripped each other's clothes off, tossing them aside onto the bed and floor in their haste to get each other naked. By the time she was bared to him, Summer was half-frantic with need, her heart racing.

Adam stilled her when she reached for him this time, splaying a big hand in the center of her chest and pushing her back onto the sheets instead and sitting back on his heels next to her. "Don't move. Let me look at you," he rasped out, his eyes like blue flame as they raked over the length of her naked body.

Summer did as he said, the sight of him poised there beside her with the light gilding his muscles making her toes curl in anticipation. She drank in the sight of his naked body, the breadth of his shoulders and the defined muscles, his hard erection jutting outward, swollen with need. He shook his head once, as if he couldn't speak, his expression so full of hunger it was all she could do not to pull him back into her arms.

"God, you're beautiful," he whispered in a reverent voice as he ran that warm palm down the center of her body and back up again.

She felt beautiful, every nerve ending alive, little zings of pleasure swirling outward at every place he touched. When he reached her breasts he cupped them, thumbs teasing her aching nipples as he leaned in to take her mouth once more.

Summer opened to the demanding pressure of his tongue, got lost in him. The kiss left her panting, aching for so much more. She wound her hands in his hair, tipped her head back and closed her eyes while his mouth blazed a scorching path down the side of her neck, lower to take a hard nipple between his lips.

Her back bowed, her legs coming up to lock around his hips. She'd wanted this for so long, the rightness and sense of connection between them.

"Adam," she whimpered, wanted to pull him up and slide onto the hard length of his cock she could feel against her thigh.

"No," he insisted, his hands moving down to lock around her hips. "Lie still for me."

That firm yet gentle show of authority turned her on even more. This is what it had been like between them before everything had begun to go wrong. It got her so hot when he took control in bed.

She let herself float in the warm current of arousal carrying her, getting lost in the caress of his hands and lips as he worshipped her body. She was so damn wet already, dying for him to ease the empty ache inside her. It had been so damn long since she'd felt this, let him take her on the dizzying climb to release.

When at last he knelt between her legs and pushed her thighs apart, she gripped his hard shoulders, breathing fast, her heart knocking against her ribs. He gave a low growl in the back of his throat, his expression absorbed, intense as his gaze locked on her slick folds, the anticipation so high she could hardly stand it.

She bit her lip, couldn't hold back a soft cry of need when he bent forward and pressed his mouth to her aching core, then the tender, hot stroke of his tongue. The low, bass rumble of enjoyment he gave nearly undid her. Just that one caress and she was on edge.

His hands closed around her hips once more, holding her down in a silent command to stay still while his tongue licked and caressed her most sensitive flesh. Sparks of pleasure raced through her body, the sweet ache building inside her with every flick of his talented tongue. God, how had she lived without this for so long?

Never again. She couldn't live without this, without him again. He meant everything to her and she was so damn grateful that they had a second chance.

"Adam," she gasped, squeezing her eyes shut when he slid his tongue into her, the raw intimacy of it stealing her breath. Her hips rocked against his tongue, demanding more. He withdrew his tongue to swirl it slowly around her swollen clit, then paused to suck softly, his eyes locked on her face.

God! Impatient, desperate and already starting the climb to orgasm, she sank her fingers into his hair, tugged him upward. "Now, *now*," she pleaded breathlessly, her entire body trembling with the force of the desire and emotions swamping her.

He made a sound of protest and kept on licking her, clearly wanting to make her insane. But she was already there and needed him inside her when she came this first time. She'd gone too long without him and didn't want to wait another second.

She tugged again, and when he wouldn't budge, sat up to grab hold of his shoulders and pulled. With a deep chuckle he lifted his head to nip at her abdomen, then worked his way up her body. "You want me in you." His tone was pure seduction, knowing it would make her even hotter.

"*Yes*." Greedy now, she reached down and curled her hand around the hard length of his erection. He groaned at her touch, bowed his head and shuddered with eyes closed, his expression tortured.

Her heart turned over. *I know, baby.*

She stroked him from root to tip, adding a swirl with her fist over the head. His breath was hot as it gusted against the side of her neck, his muscles twitching as she worked him. Needing her so badly he was practically shaking. It had been so damn long, she thought with a pang, too long for them both and she wanted to make this as good for him as it was for her.

Wrapping her free arm around his back, she kissed his temple, his cheek, the edge of his jaw, working her way to those full lips. Adam turned his head and crushed his mouth to hers, one big hand coming up to lock around the back of her head. He devoured her, nipping and licking and caressing until she was dizzy.

Then, finally, when she was gasping and trembling all over, he pulled free of her grip to settle over her and rested his weight on his elbows, both his hands holding her head.

She sucked in a breath as the hot, hard length of him rubbed against her wet folds with every slow motion of his hips, the tiny, maddening caresses teasing her throbbing clit. He stared down into her eyes, features taut with arousal, eyes blazing with need.

"My Summer," he said in a possessive tone that shot a thrill through her as he eased back to lodge the head of his cock against her opening.

Summer couldn't answer, could barely breathe. She nodded to acknowledge that she was his and his alone and wound her legs tighter around him, rocking her hips up to meet his.

Holding her gaze, his hands fisted in her hair, Adam pushed into her, burying himself to the hilt inside her.

Summer moaned and closed her eyes to better absorb the sensation of him filling her. Stretching her with all that hot, delicious thickness. "God, Adam... I've missed this so much," she choked out, a knot of emotion lodged in her throat.

"Me too," he groaned. They clung to each other for a long moment, savoring the connection they'd both missed so much.

"Want to feel you come around me," he rasped out, slipping a hand between their bodies and began to gently circle her clit with his thumb.

The flame he'd kindled inside her suddenly burst into a raging fire.

Digging her fingers into his shoulders, she sought his mouth with her own and rolled her hips against his, the motion making pleasure burst deep inside her. Her throat tightened and she held him tighter. "Oh, Adam, more. *More...*"

He groaned and plunged his tongue into her mouth, cutting off her pleading cries as his hips moved in a smooth but languid rhythm that drove her crazy. He knew her body so well. Knew exactly how to move, the angle and pressure she needed. The pleasure swelled higher and higher with each stroke, until she was ready to explode.

She loved him so much. Summer squeezed her inner muscles around him, flung her head back as that sweet ache exploded into pure rapture. She dimly heard her cries of release ringing through the room, clutched him tight to her while he drove deeper, harder, his movements growing rough and urgent.

He buried his face tight in her neck and plunged deep, a low, ragged shout of raw need and pleasure tearing from his throat. His big body shuddered, his muscles bunching tight beneath her greedy hands as he came.

At last he let out a deep, satisfied sigh and lowered his full weight onto her. She absorbed it gladly, arms and legs still wrapped around him, and smoothed her hands over the damp expanse of his back and shoulders. Holding him close, never wanting to let him go again.

The moment was so perfect, words would only spoil it. So she held him to her, savoring the feel of his heart beating strong and steady against her.

After a while he gently withdrew and rolled to his side, taking her with him. He slid one hand into her hair, his other arm wrapping around her back to hold her close as he kissed her, long and soft and tender. She melted into it, felt the sudden prick of tears at the backs of her eyes and let her fingers stroke over the back of his neck.

He sighed as he pulled back to smooth the hair away from the side of her face. "I've missed you so damn much these past few months."

"I know. I've missed you too." She swallowed and stared deep into his eyes, making herself completely vulnerable to him in a way she hadn't allowed in forever.

"I took you for granted. I didn't mean to, but I did. And I'm so sorry it happened at all."

"We both did that, both made mistakes," he corrected with a shake of his head. "But I promise that going forward, I won't let that happen again."

She gave him a soft smile. "Me neither."

His fingers combed through her hair in a gentle, lulling caress that had her eyelids dropping with a delicious sense of fatigue. "You talk to your family today about coming to visit?"

"Yes, on the way to the appointment this morning. They sounded like they were going to get on the first plane down here but I asked them to hold off until I'm ready."

Her mom and sister hadn't been happy about it, but they'd grudgingly agreed to give her some time. "I want at least a week or two alone with you before they come to visit. I know they mean well, but right now all I want is you."

A low, possessive rumble of approval vibrated in his chest. "Good. Because I've got the next week off and I don't plan to let you out of my sight."

Her smile widened and she gave a mock shiver. "You know I love it when you get all possessive like that."

His expression turned wry. "I seem to recall getting a verbal smackdown from you about it once upon a time, early on in our relationship."

She lifted a shoulder in a careless shrug. "I just didn't want you thinking you could control me or call the shots in this relationship."

He laughed softly. "Trust me, those two thoughts have *never* crossed my mind in relation to you."

She leaned in for another kiss. "Good. Means I got you trained early on."

He pinched her butt lightly. "I just let you think that."

Snickering, she snuggled down until her cheek lay against his chest, stroked his ribs. "I love you so much," she murmured. "Thank you for not giving up on me, and for fighting for us."

He squeezed her tight, whispered against her hair. "I'd never give up on you. Not if I thought there was even the slightest chance you still loved me."

She shook her head, adamant. "I never stopped loving you. Not even once." She was quiet a moment, collecting her thoughts, then leaned back to look up at him. She wanted—needed—to let go of the past and move forward. "Can we just start over again? As of right here and now?"

Adam's eyes darkened and rolled her beneath him once more. "Doll, we can do anything if we do it together," he murmured, and sealed that promise with a hungry kiss.

Chapter Twenty-Six

Twelve weeks later

"Don't be nervous. They're all great, seriously. You're gonna love them."

Sitting in the passenger seat, Summer flashed a smile at Taya and smoothed the folds of her dress down. "It just feels weird, showing up at a baby shower when I don't even know any of them."

But she'd meant it when she'd told Taya she planned to make an effort to get to know the team's significant others. This was her chance to start building a relationship with the other women. Something that was long past overdue.

Of course, that wasn't the only reason she was feeling anxious about coming to the shower. Not that she was going to tell Taya the rest.

Taya waved her concern away with one hand and slowed at the stop sign at the next corner. "Don't be silly, you're one of us. After twenty minutes you won't be nervous anymore. And the guys will be over for the barbecue in a couple hours anyhow, so you'll have Adam there soon."

"You're right."

"Of course I am," Taya said with a grin. She pulled up in front of a high-end condo building and parked along the curb. Summer grabbed the flowers and the presents while Taya took a tray of cupcakes from the trunk.

"So, it sounds like a pretty big deal that Bauer and Zoe are having a girl," she said on the way up in the elevator.

Taya let out a short laugh. "Oh yeah. It's awesome, big, gruff guy like him being a daddy to a little girl."

Yeah, that did sound pretty awesome. But from the little she knew of Bauer, she'd bet he would turn into a pile of mush the second that baby was born. Summer predicted that baby would have him firmly wrapped around her little finger within a matter of days after she was born.

She stood back a few steps as Taya rang the doorbell. Muted feminine voices came from inside the condo and a few seconds later the door opened, giving Summer her first sight of Zoe. She caught a glimpse of long, dark hair with a section of shocking pink in the front.

The mother-to-be's face lit up when she saw Taya standing there. "Hey!" she squealed, reaching out to drag Taya into a hug.

"I love the new hair color," Taya told her.

"Thanks. I thought I should match the baby girl theme Celida's got going on in here."

Those vivid gold eyes, made even more intense by the heavy black eyeliner and shadow, moved to Summer. Zoe gave her a friendly smile that showed off her perfect white teeth, a little diamond stud twinkling at the side of her nose. "And you must be Summer."

"Yes, hi," she began, and stepped forward to offer her hand.

Zoe looked at it in disbelief, then up at her. With a scoffing noise she reached out to grab Summer by the shoulders and pull her in for a hug.

Summer hid her surprise and put one hand on Zoe's back, trying not to put pressure on the sizeable baby bump pressing against her stomach.

"Taya and I are the huggers in this group," Zoe informed her. "You'll get used to us."

Summer smiled, completely disarmed and relieved by the warm welcome. Both Adam and Taya had told her not to worry about meeting the other wives/girlfriends and now Summer understood why.

Zoe released her and eased back, but kept hold of Summer's shoulders, smiling at her. "It's so good to finally meet you. And I love the outfit. You look like springtime itself."

"Thanks." She'd worn one of her favorite 50s-style dresses that she'd rarely gotten to wear the past couple of years. The strapless dress was made of pale yellow chiffon with pink roses on it. It had a pink satin sash around the waist, the skirt flaring out and ending at her knees. April in Virginia was still on the cool side so she'd worn her favorite bubblegum-pink cardigan with three-quarter length sleeves over top.

"Well come on in and meet everybody," Zoe said, stepping back to urge them inside.

The spacious condo was full of pink streamers and balloons and bouquets of pink flowers, interspersed with touches of black. A stack of presents sat on one table and an array of food was laid out on another. As they walked toward it Summer immediately noticed that most of the dishes were black. One of the platters was in the shape of a coffin and a tray was shaped like a large bat.

My first Goth baby shower, she thought with a grin, taking it all in.

"I know, it's pretty awesome, right?" Zoe said, coming up beside her. She hooked an arm around Summer's waist. "Celida's my best friend for a reason. She knows me so well."

Zoe walked her out onto the huge patio balcony where the other women were and introduced her to everyone. Summer could feel the curious stares coming her way and knew the others must be wondering about what had happened to her in Jordan, or maybe why she'd stayed away from events like this in the past, but everyone was so warm and friendly that her initial nerves didn't last long.

She sat next to Taya for the first little while but after a few of the women made a point of coming over and talking with her one-on-one to say hello, she felt completely at ease.

Part of her felt like she owed them an explanation as to why she hadn't come to team functions before now, but a baby shower was no place to ruin the mood by telling them about her stillbirth and resulting marital problems. Not that she would ever tell them until after she became friends with them.

She was so thankful that dark period was behind them now, and that Adam and her were better than ever. These last few months had flown by and things were still going great. Their communication lines were better than ever and Adam had been home a lot, so that all helped.

Celida, the FBI agent married to Tuck, came outside with another platter of food. Little tea sandwiches cut into coffin and bat shapes, and a tiered stand of the cupcakes Taya had brought, decorated with black icing and pink sprinkles.

Summer grabbed herself a glass of non-alcoholic punch and returned to her seat just as Zoe began unwrapping the gifts. Baby Bauer got a zombie bear from someone and all the other necessary things for taking care of a baby, but the best gift was one Zoe opened near the end.

Her eyes went wide and she laughed as she held up a little black onesie with a frog skeleton on the front and the words *My Dad Can Kick Your Dad's Ass* beneath it.

Zoe squealed and hugged it to her chest. "Oh my God, where did you find this?" she asked Carmela, Vance's fiancée and also Cruz's sister.

Carmela shrugged, laughter in her golden brown eyes. "I have my ways."

"Yeah, it's called Google," Marisol, Cruzie's better half, said dryly between sips of wine.

"It's so perfect," Rachel, Evers's girlfriend agreed. "Bauer's gonna love it."

Zoe set the onesie aside when her cell rang. She spoke for a few moments, then hung up. "That was the man himself. The guys are all down in the clubhouse getting everything ready. Y'all ready for more food?"

Taking their drinks and the desserts with them, they all headed down to the bottom floor as a group. When the elevator doors opened and they all poured out into the clubhouse foyer, the scent of grilling burgers made Summer's mouth water. Which was a nice change of pace, since she hadn't been all that hungry recently.

She trailed behind while the others walked out of the open French doors and onto the patio where some of the guys were assembled. At the door she paused, shading her eyes with one hand as she scanned the grassy lawn. She spotted Adam immediately, helping Vance set up lounge chairs over to one side of the yard.

Her heart turned over and her belly fluttered. A big, sappy smile spread across her face as she stood there watching him, admiring the flex and play of his back and shoulder muscles beneath his collared shirt. Even after all these years together, the sight of him still turned her inside out.

As though he sensed her stare, he paused and turned his head to look her way, an easy smile curving his mouth when he saw her.

Stepping up beside her, Taya nudged her hip gently. "I wish I had my phone out to take a picture of your face just now," she said, sipping at her white wine. "That was a look of total adoration you were giving him."

Summer shrugged, feeling suddenly emotional. "I'm just so happy."

Taya slid an arm around her waist, gave her a friendly squeeze. "Well you deserve to be. And it looks good on you, by the way."

"Thank you." She was still smiling as Taya walked away.

Glancing over at Zoe, she found the mom-to-be over by the grill standing next to her man. Bauer was grinning at whatever she'd just said, both his big hands framing the swollen mound of her belly.

Summer smiled to herself, her heart beating a little faster at the sight.

She sat with Adam while they ate, talking with Taya and Schroder and then Vance and Carmella. Everyone was so friendly, she was glad she came.

"How are you, anyway?" Schroder asked her before he took a big bite of his second burger. Just like Adam, these guys could *eat*.

"I'm doing pretty well, I think," Summer said, then looked to Adam for confirmation. She'd been keeping a regular schedule of two appointments a week with her therapist. Adam came with her when he could, and the sessions were definitely helping her deal with what had happened back in Amman. Though she'd never completely get over watching Mark die the way he had. "Yes?" she asked him.

"You're doing great," he said, one hand curling around her waist.

"You totally are," Taya confirmed. She cocked her head, narrowed her eyes slightly. "You look different, too," she murmured. "I dunno. Content." She nudged Schroder.

"She does," he agreed absently, polishing off his burger loaded with an obscene amount of bacon as Summer smothered a laugh.

She glanced at Adam, shared a secret smile that the others didn't seem to notice. Which was perfect because neither one of them was ready to share their news.

They spent the rest of the evening visiting with the other couples and by the time things began to wind down, Summer felt like she was part of the family.

After talking to the other girls for a while she went in search of her husband, found him talking with Tuck and DeLuca. When they got up and excused themselves she sat in Adam's lap and looped an arm around her husband's neck, then leaned down to rest her forehead against his. "Adam?"

"Hmm?" he murmured, hands resting protectively atop her still-flat abdomen and his lips nuzzling the side of her neck.

She was more than ready to go home and have him all to herself for the rest of the night. To get the message across, she leaned in and pressed her breasts against his chest. "Take me home."

He gave a low chuckle and gathered her close for a slow, thorough kiss that left her breathless. "Anything you want, doll." He got up, gripped her hands and helped her to her feet.

Hand in hand, she stole another glance at him as they walked up the lawn toward the patio, shared another smile with him. She knew exactly how lucky she was to have him at her side, to have him walk with her through the rest of this life.

They'd gone through hell but their marriage had survived it all and she'd been given the unexpected gift of a second chance with her husband.

And in doing so, she'd wound up falling in love with him all over again.

Epilogue

Seven months later

Okay, this hurt every bit as much as she remembered. No, *more*.

Summer whimpered and squeezed her eyes shut as another contraction hit. They were coming so fast now, one right on top of the other with no break.

Panic and fear kept threatening to overtake her, her mind whispering that something might be wrong, that something might *go* wrong. The labor had started unexpectedly last night around ten, two weeks before her due date.

Stop it. It's not like last time. She wasn't alone and the baby was fine. He or she had just decided to come a little early, that was all.

The pain just built and built with no letup, her uterus cramping like a vise. She gritted her teeth, gripped the backs of her knees and bore down, pushing with all her might. It felt like she was trying to move a concrete bowling ball out of her body, rather than a baby.

The pregnancy had come as a total shock. A month after returning from Jordan they'd started talking about the possibility of looking into the adoption process again, had decided they might start the paperwork later this year. Neither of them had even thought of using any protection since the doctors had told them years ago they would never get pregnant without intervention.

And yet here she was, against all odds, having a baby they'd conceived on their own.

And it freaking *hurt*.

"Adam," she cried when she could breathe again. God, she didn't know if she could do this, it hurt so bad. She was so glad he was here with her. He'd been a rock through everything, hadn't left her side since they'd arrived at the hospital.

He shifted position, leaning closer to tighten his arm around her shoulders and released her left thigh to cup the side of her face in his hand. His pale blue eyes were full of sympathy. "I know, doll, this part sucks. But it's almost over. You're doing great and I'm so damn proud of you," he finished, his voice slightly rough as he grabbed a damp washcloth and gently wiped her face with it, the coolness giving her the only shred of relief she'd felt over the past six hours.

She shook her head as another contraction began to build, but it didn't stave off the inevitable. Things had progressed so fast, the medical staff hadn't been able to give her an epidural and though they'd tried five times to get an IV into her, her veins had kept jumping all over the place. So once again, unfortunately she was doing this cold turkey.

"Don't let go," she panted. Two hours of pushing had all but exhausted her. She barely had the strength to lift her head.

"I won't," he vowed. "I'm not going anywhere." His

strong, solid arm gripped her tighter, his other hand sliding down to hook under her left thigh, pulling it back for her so that she didn't have to waste precious strength.

Everything funneled out except the pain as her body twisted from the inside out. The terrible pressure was indescribable.

It was terrifying but there was nothing to do but get through this now and she just wanted it over as soon as possible. She could hear the steady blip of the baby's heartbeat from the monitor they'd set up beside the bed, knew that at least it was still alive and well.

She gasped and panted, struggling to escape the pain and pressure. It felt like she was on fire down there, like she would be torn apart at the seams at any moment.

And then, with one final push, she felt something pop through. A high-pitched scream tore out of her as she felt her flesh tear.

"The head's out!" the doctor told her. "Just one more good push, Summer, and the baby will be out."

Come on, baby, she told it, bearing down for one last push. They didn't know the sex, had wanted it to be a surprise at the end of all this. After everything they'd been through, they just wanted a healthy baby.

She dimly heard Adam's low voice in her ear murmuring words of comfort and encouragement, clung to them and his strength while she bore down for the final time.

Her entire body shook, her teeth bared and eyes squeezed shut. A roar of agony and desperation exploded from her throat.

She felt the baby slip free.

The pain stopped instantly. Summer opened her eyes and scrambled up onto her elbows, heart pounding as she stared between her legs. There was no crying. Why wasn't the baby crying?

"It's a boy," the doctor announced with a smile.

He was *smiling*. A smile must mean everything was okay, right?

Summer heard his words but was too busy worrying about why he wasn't crying yet. Then the doctor suctioned the baby's little mouth and an outraged cry filled the room, his little legs and arms flailing.

The doctor looked up at Adam with a smile and Summer felt the relief flood through her. "You want to cut the cord, dad?"

Adam was at the foot of the bed in an instant, and cut the umbilical cord. By the time it was done Summer already had her arms out, reaching for her son. She took the baby from the doctor and automatically cradled him to her chest.

She stared down at him, fought away the images from last time that filtered into her brain and drank in the sight of her son. His skin was pink, not red, and he was much bigger than A.J. had been. His little eyes opened a tiny bit. He seemed to be trying to focus on her face.

A wave of pure love washed over her, so powerful it took her breath away. She blinked to hold back the sheen of tears that flooded her eyes. "Hi, Sam," she whispered to him. He was a tiny miracle, entrusted to her and Adam.

A nurse injected something into her thigh but she barely felt the sting, all of her attention focused on her precious newborn son.

Adam moved in behind her and bolstered her so that her back was to his chest. She leaned back into his embrace and looked up at him, exhausted but thrilled, and found him gazing down at her with tears in his eyes. "You did it," he whispered. "And he's perfect."

****

Adam couldn't take his eyes off his son as a nurse took him to be weighed and checked over. He followed them, watched everything with an eagle eye. He'd thought he was prepared for the birth and what to expect, but the truth was, nothing could prepare you for something like that.

Seeing Summer suffer that way had been damn hard, especially since there was jack he could do to help her. Now he understood what she must have gone through the first time, alone, knowing that even when she did give birth there would be no happy ending. But she'd done amazingly well and now little Sam was here and he could hardly believe it.

His wife was so damn brave and amazing.

He smiled when the weight appeared on the digital scale, snapped a picture. "Seven pounds, three ounces," he called out to Summer. She didn't answer, occupied with the doctor, delivering the placenta.

When the nurse was finished checking Sam over and wrapped him in a blanket, she handed him to Adam. For a moment he was terrified of dropping or hurting him, which was stupid because he'd held Libby—Liberty Raven Bauer—Bauer and Zoe's daughter, plenty of times over the past few months.

But this was *his* child, and it was completely different.

A huge lump formed in his chest when she placed the little bundle in his arms. Jesus, he was tiny. "Hey, little dude," Adam whispered roughly, all choked up as he stood there cradling his little son. It felt surreal, the enormity of his responsibility as a parent hitting him hard. "Happy birthday."

Summer was sitting up again, a soft smile on her face when he crossed back to her. He sat one hip on the edge of the bed and eased the baby into her arms.

She cradled him to her chest so naturally, her expression so full of maternal love and pride she was practically glowing. One of the nurses took pictures of them with Adam's phone but he barely noticed her, too caught up in the moment with his little family.

"He really is perfect," Summer breathed, stroking a fingertip down the side of his little cheek.

Adam wrapped his arm around her and pressed a kiss to her sweaty temple. "You were amazing." But God, he was just so glad everything had turned out okay and that she wasn't hurting anymore.

She let out a dry laugh. "I've never been in that much pain in my life, but it was worth it." She bent to place a gentle kiss on Sam's forehead. "You were so worth it, little man."

The doctor finished tending to Summer and then a nurse encouraged her to try and feed Sam. After that, they told her she could have a shower. Adam steadied her as she gingerly eased her way over to the edge of the bed. "Want me to help you?"

She grimaced as she shifted and handed the baby to him. "No, I'll be okay. Can you take him out to show my family? I know they're dying out there."

"You don't want to do it?" he asked in surprise. He'd called his family when Summer had gone into labor and would call again soon to tell them the news. As soon as he did, his parents would undoubtedly be on the next flight up here.

"I don't want to make them wait and I really want to clean up before I see anyone."

"All right." Cradling his son to his chest, Adam stepped out into the hallway. Summer's parents and sister all jumped out of their seats, identical expressions of wonder and joy on their faces. "It's a boy," he told them. "This is Sam."

Summer's mom and sister were both crying as Adam placed the baby in his grandmother's arms. He took pictures of them and posed for others, enjoying the obvious love everyone had for little Sam. *You are one lucky little dude*, he told his son silently as Summer's dad handed him back.

"You look pretty natural, holding that baby, son," he told Adam.

"I've had some practice," he said. "One of the guys on the team just became a father a few months ago."

"We met one of your teammates a little while ago," Summer's dad said. "I went into the waiting room to grab a coffee and I saw him in there. Brad Tucker."

Adam blinked in surprise. "Tuck was here?"

"Still here," Summer's dad corrected. "He said he wanted to wait in there to give us all some privacy."

Adam was touched that Tuck would come here. The team had been out on a late night training mission and would only have finished up in the last hour or so. He nodded toward the end of the hallway. "I'll just say a quick hello and then come back. Summer said you guys can come into the room once she's all cleaned up."

He carried Sam to the end of the hall and pushed the door open. And stopped dead at the sight before him.

Tuck was there, all right. Along with their five other teammates and DeLuca. All of them were still dressed in their fatigues, clearly having come straight here from the training.

All the guys stood up, big smiles on their faces when they saw Adam holding the baby. "Hey, congrats, Dad," Bauer told him, the first to break away from the group and approach him.

"Thanks. This is Sam," he told everyone.

A chorus of cheers and congratulations went up. Sam jerked in Adam's arms at the sudden noise, his little arms flailing for a moment, but then he went right back to sleep.

To Adam's surprise, Bauer reached for the baby. Adam handed him over, the sight of Sam held in Bauer's huge arms making his chest go tight. These guys weren't his blood, but they might as well be. They'd had his back from day one, and his teammates being here right now meant the world to him.

"God, I've forgotten how tiny they are when they're first born," Bauer murmured, a big grin on his hard face as he stared down at Sam. He looked up at Adam, let out a soft chuckle. "You look like you've been through a war, man. How you doing? Pretty surreal, right?"

He still felt a little dazed by it all. "Yeah. It's hard to believe he's finally here."

"Well, all I can say is it's a good thing you're no stranger to handling sleep deprivation. The first few months are fun times."

"I'm up for the challenge."

"How's Summer doing?"

"Good. Great, actually, all things considered. I thought I knew what to expect through the birth, but…" He blew out a breath, shook his head. Watching her suffer like that had ripped his guts out.

Bauer nodded. "I know. It's intense and scary as hell, watching your wife go through that. I almost fucking fainted when Zoe—" He winced, looked down at Sam in apology. "Sorry, buddy. You're not even an hour old yet and you've already heard your first curse word."

"Pretty sure it won't be his last," Schroder remarked dryly, and Adam couldn't help but grin.

Bauer grunted and looked back at Adam. "Anyway, I remember how it was when Libby was being born." He gave a mock shudder. "Never seen anything like that and not sure I want to again."

Intense didn't even cover it, but he knew his teammate perfectly. "Yeah. Me neither."

Bauer glanced over at the others. "Anybody else wanna turn holding this good-looking little dude?" When nobody moved he started to hold the baby out to Schroder.

The medic held up his hands and backed up a step, shaking his head, clearly terrified to touch the baby. "Uh, no, I'm good. Thanks." Cruzie, Vance and Evers all backed up with him, looking slightly worried, like Sam was a live grenade or something.

Bauer snorted and tucked the baby back against his chest, glowering at them. "Pussies."

"I'll take a turn," DeLuca said, and all eyes turned to him in surprise. He and Briar had just gotten married a couple months before, eloping on a day off. "What?" he asked with a scowl. "I'm planning to be a dad someday, so I might as well start getting the hang of it now." His expression melted into a smile when he took Sam from Bauer. "He's a handsome little guy, all right," he said to Adam. "Must take after his mama."

Everyone laughed but Adam nodded. "I can't argue with that." Next Tuck took a turn holding the baby before carefully handing him over to Adam.

Adam held Sam close, already feeling more comfortable, already in love with and feeling insanely protective of his son. This was by far the best day of his life, bar none.

Looking around at his teammates, he cleared his throat. "I appreciate you guys all coming down here." They were no doubt all beat up and tired, probably dreaming of a hot shower and their beds, yet here they were, on their own time, to support him and Summer. "It means a lot."

"Hey, we wouldn't miss it," Tuck said, slapping him on the back once. "We're really happy for you guys."

Adam nodded. "Thanks." It had been a long, hard road for him and Summer to get here, but that only made him more appreciative for what he had. A loving wife and a beautiful newborn son. "Well. Guess I'd better get this little guy back to his mama."

"Give Summer our best," DeLuca told him. "We'll see you back at work in a few days."

"You know it."

Heading back down the hall to Summer's room with their son in his arms, Adam gazed down at little Sam and couldn't help but smile.

Yeah. Best day of his life by a long shot.

—The End—

Thank you for reading RECLAIMED. I really hope you enjoyed it and that you'll consider leaving a review at one of your favorite online retailers. It's a great way to help other readers discover new books.

If you liked RECLAIMED and would like to read more, turn the page for a list of my other books. And if you don't want to miss any future releases, please feel free to join my newsletter: http://kayleacross.com/v2/newsletter/

Complete Booklist

Romantic Suspense
Hostage Rescue Team Series
Marked
Targeted
Hunted
Disavowed
Avenged
Exposed
Seized
Wanted
Betrayed
Reclaimed

Titanium Security Series
Ignited
Singed
Burned
Extinguished
Rekindled

Bagram Special Ops Series
Deadly Descent
Tactical Strike
Lethal Pursuit
Danger Close
Collateral Damage

Suspense Series
Out of Her League
Cover of Darkness
No Turning Back
Relentless

Absolution

Paranormal Romance
Empowered Series
Darkest Caress

Historical Romance
The Vacant Chair

Erotic Romance (writing as *Callie Croix*)
Deacon's Touch
Dillon's Claim
No Holds Barred
Touch Me
Let Me In
Covert Seduction

Acknowledgements

Many thanks to my team for helping me with this story! This is a bittersweet moment for me, ending this series when I've become so attached to this cast of characters.

About the Author

NY Times and USA Today Bestselling author Kaylea Cross writes edge-of-your-seat military romantic suspense. Her work has won many awards and has been nominated for both the Daphne du Maurier and the National Readers' Choice Awards. A Registered Massage Therapist by trade, Kaylea is also an avid gardener, artist, Civil War buff, Special Ops aficionado, belly dance enthusiast and former nationally-carded softball pitcher. She lives in Vancouver, BC with her husband and family.

You can visit Kaylea at www.kayleacross.com. If you would like to be notified of future releases, please join her newsletter: http://kayleacross.com/v2/contact/

Printed in Great Britain
by Amazon